### 'When I kissed you, you kissed back,' Burke taunted.

Candace's face flushed. 'You're making far too much of a trivial incident that never should have happened.'

'But it did happen, didn't it? You could like me a lot and you know it.'

Anger simmered within her. 'A man and a woman can have three relationships—friendship, an affair or marriage. You eliminated friendship by kissing me. I doubt very much if marriage is on your mind. Do you actually have the brass to presume that I'm going to have an affair with you while you're in Montana?'

'I wouldn't rule out any of those three options if I were you,' he said, pressing her body to his.

He was so close, his macho maleness on full throttle. And what Candace had been fearing so much was happening: he was making her want him!

Dear Reader,

Whether or not it's back to school—for you or the kids—Special Edition™ this month is the place to come for romance!

We're pleased to announce that September brings *Waiting for Nick* by award-winning author Nora Roberts. This heart-warming story features Freddie finally getting her man...the man she's been waiting for all her life. Revisit the Stanislaskis in this wonderful addition to Nora Roberts' bestselling series, THOSE WILD UKRANIANS!

If handsome rogues quicken your pulse, then don't miss this month's THAT SPECIAL WOMAN! title *Ashley's Rebel* from Sherryl Woods—the second instalment of her new series, THE BRIDAL PATH. And three little matchmakers scheme to bring their unsuspecting parents back together again in *Daddy of the House*, the first of Diana Whitney's themed novels on PARENTHOOD.

*Marry Me in Amarillo* is a charming story from veteran author Celeste Hamilton, and there's also Kaitlyn Gorton's deeply emotional tale, *Separated Sisters*, portraying the joy of lasting love. Finally, Jackie Merritt's MADE IN MONTANA continues with *Montana Lovers*. The last novel in that series will be a December Desire™, *Montana Christmas*.

Happy reading!

The Editors

# Montana Lovers

# JACKIE MERRITT

SILHOUETTE

SPECIAL EDITION

*Silhouette, Silhouette Special Edition and Colophon are
registered trademarks of Harlequin Books S.A., used under licence.*

*First published in Great Britain 1997
Silhouette Books, Eton House, 18-24 Paradise Road,
Richmond, Surrey TW9 1SR*

© C.J. Books, Inc. 1996

ISBN 0 373 24065 1

*23-9709*

*Printed and bound in Great Britain
by Mackays of Chatham PLC, Chatham*

# JACKIE MERRITT

and her husband live just outside of Las Vegas, Nevada. An accountant for many years, Jackie has happily traded numbers for words. Next to family, books are her greatest joy. She started writing in 1987 and her efforts paid off in 1988 with the publication of her first novel. When she's not writing or enjoying a good book, Jackie dabbles in watercolour painting and likes playing the piano in her spare time.

## Other novels by Jackie Merritt

*Silhouette Desire®*

Big Sky Country
Heartbreak Hotel
Babe in the Woods
Maggie's Man
Ramblin' Man
Maverick Heart
Sweet On Jessie
Mustang Valley
The Lady and the Lumberjack
Boss Lady
Shipwrecked!
Black Creek Ranch
A Man Like Michael
Tennessee Waltz
Montana Sky
Imitation Love
†Wrangler's Lady
†Mystery Lady
†Persistent Lady
Nevada Drifter
Accidental Bride
Hesitant Husband
Rebel Love
Assignment: Marriage
*Montana Fever

*Silhouette Special Edition®*

A Man and a Million
*Montana Passion

*Silhouette Summer
   Sizzlers 1995*
'Stranded'

*Made in Montana
†Saxon Brothers series

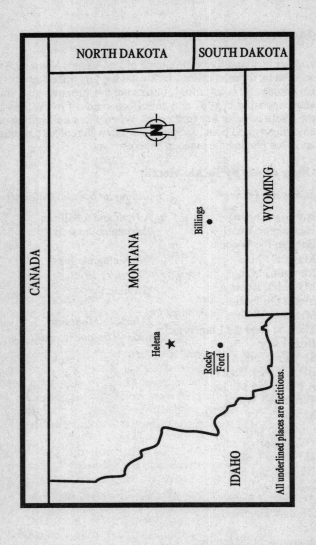

# Prologue

The room was large and cluttered with desks, chairs, computers, file cabinets and odd pieces of furniture. In front of the bank of windows on the west wall was a scarred and somewhat battered conference table. To the six men and three women seated around the table, the chaotic appearance of the room was deceiving and in direct opposition to the team's efficiency. Each person had his own space, his own desk and computer, his own working area. Normally the air would be buzzing with conversations, an occasional joke and laughter, ringing telephones and the clicking of computer keys.

This afternoon, however, Hal Morrison, the man who headed the governor's task force in the seemingly unending battle against drugs in the state of Montana, had called a meeting to hear progress reports on the cases assigned to the agents. It happened about once a week, and whichever agents were in Helena at the time would bring their case files and find a chair at the old table. Telephone calls were routed through police dispatch to elude interruption. Hal, a solemn, serious and sometimes gruff man of fifty years, sat at the head of the table and asked questions. The agents answered.

After about thirty minutes of relatively low-key discussion, Hal brought up a case that had been dragging on for months. "What about Benny Slocum? Any changes there?"

Burke Mallory exchanged meaningful glances with several of his co-workers. No one was eager to impart the latest news on Benny, who was a slick, clever lowlife and from what they had uncovered so far, one of the biggest drug dealers in the entire state. They were on the verge of an arrest, impatiently waiting for just a little more evidence to put Benny away for good.

"Well?" Hal growled, glowering from beneath his bushy eyebrows at the best law-enforcement people in the state. The task force had been handpicked and recruited from every sheriff's and police department around the state. These were tough, intelligent, courageous men and women, the cream of the crop, people who despised street drugs and the scum who sold them, people who had dedicated themselves to cleaning up Montana.

But somehow Benny had become invisible; no one knew where he was. Yesterday they did, but today they didn't.

Burke cleared his throat. Hal's gray eyes moved to him. "Mallory?"

"Well, it's like this, Hal. Benny's gone."

"Gone? What do you mean, he's gone?"

"He vanished in the night."

"And no one noticed," Hal said with heavy sarcasm. "Where in hell were the agents assigned to watch him?"

The faces of two men got beet red. "We were on the job, Hal," Kelly Graves said. "We can't figure out how Benny did it. He went into his apartment house at ten-fifteen last night and never came out. We all know he was aware we were watching him, so when he didn't show we had the manager check his apartment." Kelly looked away with an embarrassed expression. "He wasn't there and neither were his personal possessions."

"You mean he carried suitcases out of that apartment building right under your noses?" Hal said with a derisive snort.

"No, he did not. How he got his things out is a mystery. Hell, how he got out himself without us spotting him is a mystery. Hal, we were there, watching both doors to that building. I have a descriptive list here of everyone who went into and came out of the building all night."

"Let me see it." Hal held out his hand.

A sheet of paper was passed down the table and given to Hal. He studied it with a scowl on his ruddy face. "Lots of traffic." He looked up. "More than usual, wasn't it?"

"A lot more. The tenants in apartment 212 were giving a party. It went on most of the night."

Tossing the paper to the table, Hal sat back in his chair. "That's your answer. Somehow Benny walked out as one of the guests."

"I swear he didn't," Kelly said. His partner nodded vehemently. But then they looked at each other. There was no other explanation, was there?

At the same time, Burke said quietly, "He was probably wearing a disguise."

Cursing under his breath, Kelly grabbed the list and studied it. "What about his things? No one was carrying suitcases last night," he declared hotly.

"He could have been moving his possessions for weeks, one or two things at a time," Burke answered.

Hal tugged at his ear. Every person at the table bore a frustrated, angry expression. They had put months in on Benny's case, and now he'd given them the slip.

"He's probably out of the country by now," Hal said disgustedly. "Or well on his way."

A pall of silence ensued. No one even shuffled papers or doodled on the pads in front of them. Losing Benny Slocum was a major setback, and each agent felt it in his or her gut.

Finally someone asked, "Do we put out an APB, or what?"

"I don't know right now," Hal said. "Let me think about it."

"Maybe he's still in Helena," Burke suggested. "It's not impossible that he merely went into hiding at a different address."

Hal stared at him for a long time, finally agreeing, "No, it's not impossible. Just not very damned feasible."

"Unless his business wasn't quite concluded and our close surveillance was putting a damper on his activities," Burke said.

"Could be something to that, all right," Hal concurred. "Okay, everyone keep their eyes open and their ears to the ground. Word gets around. Talk to your snitches and contacts. Maybe someone knows something and will be willing to talk about it." He got to his feet. "That's enough for today. You can all go back to work."

The agents got up and headed for their desks, talking among themselves. Burke caught Hal before he reached the door.

"Listen, I have this gut feeling about Benny," Burke said. "I don't think he went very far. There's too much evidence of a big drug deal coming down. You know it's what we've been waiting for, Hal, and I think it's still going to happen. Benny's too greedy to turn his back on several million dollars."

The phones were ringing again; obviously someone had notified dispatch to put the calls through. The one on Burke's desk began jangling. He sent it an irritated glance, because he wasn't through getting his point across to Hal.

"Can we talk again later?" Burke asked his superior.

"You know where to find me," Hal growled. He wasn't very happy with this turn of events and wasn't the type of man to pretend otherwise.

Burke bounded over to his desk and picked up the phone. "Hello."

In the background he could hear the others speculating on where Benny might have gone and what disguise had carried him out of that building in plain sight of two agents.

"Maybe he was the pregnant woman," one guy wise-cracked, which made the others laugh, even though it was entirely possible.

A whispery, unfamiliar voice in Burke's ear said, "Are you interested in where Benny Slocum went?"

Burke sat up straighter. This could be a crank call or the real thing. "I'm interested. Have you and I met?"

"No questions. I'll say only what I want to say, get it?"

"I got it. Go ahead." Burke honestly couldn't tell if he was speaking to a man or a woman.

"Benny is in a little town in the lower portion of the state. It's called Rocky Ford. I know this to be fact and if you don't believe it, you're a damned fool. Goodbye."

"Wait!" Burke's plea was in vain. The connection had been broken. Slowly he put down his phone. He appeared calm though his pulse was racing. Instinct told him he'd just heard the truth. Options bombarded his brain. Benny could have left the state. He could have left the country. Instead, he went to a little town called Rocky Ford. Why?

Burke's pulse moved even faster as the answer came to him: the big drug deal they'd all been waiting for was going to take place in Rocky Ford.

"Then he'll leave the country," Burke muttered under his breath while getting to his feet. He all but ran from the room to find Hal. He had his reasons for volunteering to go to Rocky Ford, some of them personal, but first he had to convince Hal that the call was legitimate.

## Chapter One

Burke pulled his four-wheeler to the curb across the street from an establishment called Charlie's Place and turned off the ignition.

He had arrived in Rocky Ford with a solid plan and had been implementing it for five days now. His first order of business had been to familiarize himself with Rocky Ford's layout, which he'd accomplished by driving every street and byway. It was a small, pleasant-looking town, with some well-tended residential areas and lots of old trees. As it was October, most of the deciduous trees were denuded of leaves. The grass in people's yards had turned tan, some of the shrubs were wrapped in burlap and the rosebushes were cut back and banked in anticipation of winter weather. The nights were frosty and the days crisp. It was revitalizing weather, with mostly sunny, clear skies and a nipping temperature. That would soon change. Helena, Burke knew, had already seen snow. Rocky Ford was just that much farther south to have a milder fall.

Burke wasn't thinking of the weather, however. Benny Slocum was somewhere in this little town, and Burke fully intended to find him. He was playing a long shot, to be true, hoping to spot him all on his own. No one in town knew his game, not even the local police. Burke had checked into the Sundowner Motel under the guise of tourist and then, after memorizing the town's layout, began a methodical exploration of every tavern, restaurant, grocery store and business that might draw Benny's interest. In truth, there weren't that many.

He had also put on his friendliest face and chatted with anyone who would talk to him, always steering the conversation to one particular subject. *I really like Rocky Ford. Does the town draw many strangers?* It seemed that once he mentioned an affection for the town, people opened up. And no, he'd heard many times, the town didn't attract many strangers, especially at this time of year. Thus far, he'd learned nothing that might lead him to Benny.

But he wasn't at all discouraged. His blue eyes sparkled with energy and determination. His long, sinewy frame was inwardly tense and ready for anything, while his handsome face appeared relaxed and curious in a friendly, laid-back manner. He had thick dark hair and today was dressed in jeans, a red flannel shirt, cowboy boots and a tan suede vest with sheepskin lining.

His gaze was on the sprawling old house across the street. This morning's agenda called for a visit to a coffeehouse called Charlie's Place, and he hadn't expected it to be in someone's home. Foxworth Street, he had discovered, bore an eclectic mixture of residences and businesses. Charlie's Place looked small-town homey and totally innocent. A few people were going in and coming out, but it was apparent that he wasn't going to run into a crowd inside. It wasn't likely to be a hangout that would appeal to the likes of Benny Slocum.

Still, he couldn't overlook any possibility. He reached for the door handle, then sat there holding it. A young blond woman and a child in the toddler stage had just come around from the back of the house and were getting into a yellow car. Burke couldn't make out her facial features very well, but she was a small woman and admirably attentive to the child. A boy, Burke thought, although he couldn't be sure from this distance. Both the woman and child were clad in jackets and jeans, and the child had a knit hat on his head. There was something about the woman that grabbed at Burke's awareness. He grinned slightly. Strange women didn't normally affect him so physically. That lady must have a powerful sexual aura.

But odds were that she was married, he thought with resignation while turning the handle to open the door. Besides, he wasn't in Rocky Ford for romance—casual or otherwise. Thinking of what he'd left behind in Helena, his lips twitched with the hint of another grin. At least he had temporarily escaped his mother's determination to marry him off to a woman with what Meredith Mallory considered the proper credentials and background.

He was thirty-one years old, happy—most of the time— with a career that Meredith thought was vastly beneath a Mallory, and further garnering her disapproval by eluding a personal liaison in which he had no interest. Diane Prescott was from an old banking family, well educated and a nice person; it wasn't her fault. Meredith was a force to reckon with, regardless that he was a grown man and contented with his chosen way of life. The problem was that the Mallory family had been wealthy since the old mining days in Montana, when copper had been king and the state had been ruled by the copper barons. Burke didn't fit the mold of his predecessors; he really couldn't care less about increasing the family fortune, which drove Meredith up the wall. Burke knew that his mother hoped marriage to the right woman would bring him in line, but he knew differently. It was an impasse with polite debates and arguments. They never raised their voices or became truly angry with each other. They were, after all, the last of the Mallory line and they loved each other.

But damn, it felt good to be away from it all. Bounding across the street, Burke breathed in the snapping fresh air with an exhilarating sense of freedom. Finding Benny was his primary goal and ranked up there with the most-important assignments of his career, but was there anything wrong with enjoying himself in the process?

When he opened the door of Charlie's Place, a little bell jingled. It took only one glance around for Burke to catalog everyone present. An older man and woman were sitting at a table reading newspapers and drinking coffee. The woman peered at him over the top of her glasses. Another table was occupied by two men and a woman, who also displayed some mild curiosity. Three men sat at the counter. That was it, eight customers in all, none of whom was under fifty and most were over sixty. Again Burke thought that he wasn't apt to run into Benny in here, but he would bet anything that these people knew almost everyone in town. They were old-timers, people who'd probably lived in Rocky Ford most of their lives.

Burke's smile took in everyone present, and he received several smiles in return. He closed the door. A delicious aroma of rich coffee assailed his nostrils. The radio behind the counter was tuned to a country-music station. Its volume was at the perfect pitch, audible but not obtrusive. As he'd expected, the place was homey and comfortable. He walked to an empty stool at the counter and sat down. The man behind the counter gave him a friendly grin.

"Yes, sir, what can I get for you?" he asked.

"A cup of that coffee that smells so good," Burke replied. In two seconds he had absorbed the man's appearance: medium height and build, thinning light brown hair, about fifty-two to fifty-five years of age and the warmest, kindest eyes he'd ever seen on anyone.

Charlie filled a large cup from the pot on the back counter and placed it in front of Burke. "Got some mighty fine doughnuts, if you'd like one. The lady that makes 'em uses only the finest ingredients." Charlie's eyes twinkled merrily. "She guarantees they don't contain any calories or cholesterol."

Burke laughed. "In that case, how could I refuse?" When Charlie brought the doughnut on a plate, he offered his hand. "I'm Burke Mallory."

Charlie shook his hand. "Charlie Fanon. New to town, aren't you?"

Burke took a sip of his coffee, and it was as delicious as it smelled. But he was more thrilled with Charlie's curiosity than with his coffee. If Benny had shown his face in this part of town, Charlie knew about it.

"Five days new, Charlie. Just nosing around doing something I've wanted to do for years—explore Montana."

"Then you're not a native? Could've fooled me," Charlie said.

The men on the other stools decided to get into the conversation. "Have you been to Custer's Battlefield?"

"Seen Yellowstone yet?"

"How about Virginia City?"

Burke nodded at them. "I've been to all the usual tourist sites, but thanks for the suggestions. Right now I'm more interested in seeing Montana's back roads. Stumbled into Rocky Ford without even knowing it was here. Great little town, just great. I just might hang around for a while."

Everyone looked pleased, as though each felt responsible for his hometown being "great." Burke thought of the photo of Benny that he carried in the back pocket of his jeans. If he flashed it among this group, would someone say, *Oh, sure, I've seen him?*

But just how gossipy were these people? Word could get back to Benny. *A guy by the name of Burke Mallory has a picture of you and is asking questions.* No, he couldn't risk it. If Benny got wind of someone being this close on his trail, he would undoubtedly bolt and run.

A man came in, picked up several newspapers, bought coffee and sweet rolls to go, and while Charlie was waiting on him, the men on the stools next to Burke responded to his remark of "This is really great weather" by telling him it might not last, that it had gotten down to twenty-eight degrees last night, that there were years in the past when snow had piled up before the end of September and, yes, this was really great weather. Hope it holds.

Burke felt good with these people, more relaxed than he'd felt in years. He would bet anything that the weather conversation repeated itself every time they got together. That was nice, he thought. Everyone knowing everyone, even to anticipating their friends' next remarks.

He especially liked Charlie, though why the man stood out from his neighbors wasn't quite clear. But he seemed to be the focal point around which the others revolved. Charlie joked and laughed while he sold newspapers, magazines, coffee and sweets. Those people seated at the tables got up and left with comments about seeing Charlie tomorrow. Steady customers.

Charlie refilled Burke's cup. The men on the stools finally left. A man Charlie called Virgil came in, bought one of every newspaper Charlie carried and left. Everyone had gone, Burke realized. He and Charlie were alone now. Charlie walked behind the counter with a tongue-in-cheek grin. "The rush hour's over," he said, causing Burke to chuckle.

Charlie poured himself a cup of coffee and sat on a stool behind the counter, appearing to settle down for a nice long chat. "So, where do you hail from, Burke?"

Burke didn't want to lie to Charlie, but what else could he do? "Born and raised in Seattle."

"Big city. Pretty, though. I was in Seattle about...let me see...must be twelve, fifteen years ago. Always wanted to see Puget Sound. Like you always wanting to see Montana, eh?"

"Something like that," Burke agreed.

Charlie brought his cup to his lips. "Guess you're not disappointed."

"Not at all. Montana's a beautiful state. I'm particularly taken with this area, though."

"Hmm. Well, never can tell what will appeal to a person. Rocky Ford's a quiet little town. Oh, we have our moments, don't think we don't. My niece was robbed by a guy with a knife in her own store a while back. The police were really on the ball, though, and caught the guy within hours."

"Good police department, huh?"

"I'd say so. Good volunteer fire department, too. For a small town, we're pretty well organized."

"Sounds like it. I noticed that someone's putting in an airstrip."

Charlie nodded. "Community effort, that was. It's a private company putting it in. Should be ready for use pretty soon. I think the landing strip is completed, but they're still working on the terminal."

"That's what it looked like to me. I was driving around the other day and stopped out there to see what was going on."

"Well, it won't accommodate jumbo jets, but a lot of folks think we need air service. I've heard that a couple of commuter companies have already leased terminal space."

"Don't you think the town needs air service, Charlie?"

"I go both ways on that, Burke. Air service probably is needed, but by the same token I like the town the way it is." Charlie grinned. "Gettin' old, I guess. Change is getting harder to deal with."

"You don't want the town to turn into a city."

Charlie nodded. "That's it, I suppose." After a swallow of coffee, he asked, "Does your family live in Seattle, too?"

Burke prepared himself for another lie, which wouldn't quite come out of his mouth as planned. "There's only my mother, Charlie. How about your family?" he quickly added in an effort to avoid further questions about his background.

Charlie smiled. "I'm blessed with a wonderful family, Burke, and they all live around here. My daughter, Serena, is a lawyer and married to Travis Holden. Maybe you've seen one of his car lots. He's got 'em all over the state. Then there's Lola, my niece, who's married to a rancher, Duke Sheridan. Finally I've got Candace, and little Ron, my grandson. They live right here with me."

"And Candace is another daughter?"

"Daughter-in-law." Charlie looked down at his cup. "My son, Ron, was killed in the military."

"I'm sorry, Charlie," Burke said gently, feeling a sudden, sharp pain of sympathy for this man. His own personal tragedies were few and far between. The death of his father was twelve years old and only a faded memory. Two unmarried uncles had passed away since then. There was just his mother left, which was probably the reason he couldn't openly defy or hurt her in any way.

"Yes, well, we all have our crosses to bear," Charlie murmured. His countenance brightened. "But my grandson is a crackerjack, Burke. Smart as a whip. And his mother, Candace, is the sweetest little woman God ever created."

"And she lives with you." She had to have been the woman he'd seen getting into that yellow car, and she was a widow. Even though guilt struck him, he couldn't banish the elation he felt about her marital status. He wanted to meet her, and there had to be a way. "Does she work, Charlie?"

"Works right here in the house," Charlie said proudly. "You've never met a better homemaker, Burke. Takes care of her son, does the cooking and housecleaning and loves every minute of it. Candy doesn't want a career. She says her career is to raise her son to be the best man possible. Isn't that remarkable in this day and age?"

"Yes, remarkable," Burke agreed. He honestly didn't know any women who were totally dedicated to home and family.

But he would like to. Candace Fanon. Yes, indeed, he sure would like to meet her.

"So," said Charlie, "what line of work are you in?"

Damn! He hated lying to Charlie Fanon. This wasn't something he had anticipated while preparing for this job. Undercover work required lies, and lying on the job had never bothered him before. But Charlie was different. He was probably the most guileless man Burke had ever met. The most friendly, open and honest man he'd ever met. It wasn't right to lie to and deliberately deceive a man like Charlie.

"I'm a teacher," Burke mumbled. He had enough college credits to teach if he ever wanted to; thus, he had decided to use that persona. "On a yearlong sabbatical," he added.

Charlie smiled and nodded. "And using it to see Montana. Teaching is a fine career. Do you teach high school?"

"Uh, college level. Sociology."

"Oh." Charlie sounded disappointed. "Well, a college is one thing Rocky Ford lacks. Maybe we do need to progress a little more."

Burke's eyes narrowed slightly. The disappointment in Charlie's voice had been distinct and impossible to miss. But why was he disappointed? Surely he hadn't been thinking of doing a little matchmaking, had he? He obviously loved having Candace and little Ron living with him. Would he deliberately attempt to find his daughter-in-law another husband?

What incredible unselfishness. Charlie Fanon was indeed a special man, putting his daughter-in-law's happiness before his own.

Burke suddenly couldn't tell this man one more lie today. He reached into his pocket for some money. Getting to his feet, he laid down a five-dollar bill. "That should cover it. Keep the change, Charlie."

Charlie got up, too. "Your tab is only two dollars, Burke. I can't accept a three-dollar tip."

"Do it for me. It was great talking to you." Burke walked to the door, then knowing that he had to come back here however much lying pinched his conscience, he stopped and turned. "I'll be back tomorrow morning."

"Glad to hear it. See you then. Look, if you haven't already read the morning papers, take what you want."

Burke glanced at the newspaper stand, then walked over and picked up two. "Thanks."

"See you tomorrow, Burke," Charlie called as Burke left his establishment.

Burke jogged across the street and got into his vehicle. Something unique had just happened to him; he had met an instant friend. The kind of rapport he felt with Charlie Fanon didn't come along every day, and Burke valued it highly.

The rest of the day would be bland and dull after this, he thought while starting the engine and driving away.

In truth, he could hardly wait for tomorrow morning.

Candace put on a blue skirt and matching blouse for dinner. She always set a nice table and didn't like sitting down to it in the jeans she'd worn all day. Tonight's dinner was beef stew and buttermilk biscuits, one of Charlie's favorite meals. Ronnie was in his high chair, Charlie at the head of the table and Candace to his right.

Charlie said grace, then surveyed the serving bowls. "This looks great, Candace. If I keep eating your good cooking, I'm gonna get fat." He moved the bowl of stew closer to Candace's plate.

Candace smiled and began dishing up. "You'll never be fat, Charlie."

"Gettin' a paunch, honey."

"Barely noticeable. You're a fine-looking man."

Charlie grinned and reached for one of those mouth-watering biscuits. "You always say the right thing."

Recently Ronnie had decided to feed himself rather than eat from his mother's hand. Candace mashed vegetables and slivered a tiny piece of beef into his bowl. The first thing Ronnie did, bringing a smile to his mother's and grandfather's lips, was to mix everything together with his child-sized spoon. Charlie fondly suspected he liked the mixing more than the eating, though the little boy had a good appetite and usually ate whatever was put in front of him.

Dinner was when Charlie and Candace caught up on each other's day. "So, you went shopping today. How'd it go?"

"Just fine. Ronnie's growing so fast he can only wear his clothes a short time before they're too small. I bought him some new pants and shirts today. Some winter boots, too. They're lined with sheepskin, Charlie. Really nice boots."

"They'll keep his feet warm and toasty. He likes playing outside and has to have the right gear." Charlie sent her a glance. "Buy anything for yourself?"

"A sweater. It was expensive but I couldn't resist it."

"And why should you? A pretty woman like yourself should have pretty clothes."

Candace's smile became shy. Compliments always made her feel shy. "Thank you."

Charlie changed the subject. "Had an interesting customer today."

"Oh?"

"Fellow by the name of Burke Mallory. He's a college professor in Seattle. Well, I don't know if he's a full professor, but he teaches college. Sociology. Nice-looking young man and friendly as can be. He's on sabbatical leave and exploring Montana. Says he's quite taken with this area and might hang around for a while."

"It's a nice area," Candace said. Ronnie had started beating a tattoo with his spoon against the tray of his high chair. Candace touched his hand and said quietly, "No, son. Eat your dinner."

"Anyway, I was thinking about something. Burke said he'd be back for coffee tomorrow morning, and since he's going to be around for a while, I was wondering if you'd mind if I invited him to dinner one evening. I think you'd enjoy meeting him."

Candace became quite still. She never minded guests for dinner, and Charlie knew it. Asking her permission and suggesting she would enjoy meeting Mr. Mallory cast a peculiar shadow on the event. Surely he wasn't thinking she would like Mr. Mallory or that it was time she started dating, was he?

And yet Charlie bore a completely normal expression. She shouldn't second-guess his kindly nature. Apparently he liked Mr. Mallory and simply wanted to expand their friendship by having him come to dinner.

She spoke softly. "I don't mind at all, Charlie. Invite whomever you wish, whenever you wish."

Looking pleased, Charlie nodded. "I knew I could count on you."

Candace sent him a slightly perplexed look. Of course he could count on her. That was another thing he knew as fact. There was definitely something different in the air this evening. Caused by this Burke Mallory person, apparently.

Well, Charlie was no fool, and if he liked Mr. Mallory, there must be something to the man. She would serve a good dinner and do her part to make him feel welcome. Imagining that Charlie would try his hand at matchmaking was a bit farfetched. After all, who knew better than him that she still mourned the loss of her husband?

That night, lying in bed in the silent house, Candace thought of how the members of the Fanon family had opened their hearts to her. She and Ron had been living in Germany when he was killed. Charlie had immediately flown overseas and to her side. It was his strength that had gotten her through the terrible ordeal of funeral and travel arrangements, then he had insisted she and the baby return to Montana to live with him. Having no family of her own, she'd been grateful to have a place to go.

But her gratitude had turned to love for this wonderful family, especially for Charlie. She was positive there was not a kinder, gentler man on the face of the earth. Maybe more important than anything else, he adored little Ron, just as the little boy adored his "Gampy." And Charlie made it clear every day that he wanted her and Ronnie in his home and life. Why would she ever leave? She was happier here than she could ever be living alone in some strange place. And Charlie also respected and admired her preference for living quietly, for caring for the house and her son and for not possessing even the slightest desire to seek a career. He accepted her exactly as she was, without ever suggesting she do this or do that to fit other people's ideas of what a young woman should be doing in today's world.

By the same token, he also respected and admired his daughter's and niece's careers. Obviously Charlie's credo was that everyone should do what made them happy. Candace liked that as much as she liked Charlie himself.

She couldn't consider herself a lucky woman, not after losing her husband at such a young age, but for her circumstances she was doing as well as one could hope for.

Of course Charlie could invite Burke Mallory to dinner. What on earth difference would a stranger at the table for one evening make in the scheme of things?

She might even wear her new sweater.

## Chapter Two

That evening Burke phoned Hal at his home in Helena, which Hal had told him to do. Hal was good about calls. If you needed to talk to him, when and where wasn't a problem. Of course he, too, was busy, and sometimes finding him wasn't a simple exercise. Tonight, however, Burke got him right away.

"Hello, Hal. Just checking in as promised. I really don't have anything earthshaking or even particularly promising to report."

"No sign of Slocum?"

"Not yet."

"Well, I'm still not completely convinced that whoever called you with that information was on the up-and-up, Burke. You could be on a wild-goose chase."

"It's possible," Burke had to agree. "But I really felt that caller was shooting straight, Hal."

"Instinct isn't always reliable. In fact, what some people call instinct is nothing more than hope."

Burke didn't want to get into a debate about instinct with Hal. His own was usually reliable, and he still believed that Benny was somewhere in the area. The only thing that bothered him was time. If Benny was here for one final deal before leaving Montana for good, then timing was everything. Hal knew it, too, so there was no fooling around on that aspect of this investigation.

"You've stuck to your plan to operate alone?" Hal asked.

"Right. I haven't told anyone what I'm really doing here. There is a chance of that, though. I was talking to someone today who spoke highly of the local police, so if something doesn't break soon, I'll probably pay the police department a visit. I still feel that I've got a better chance of stumbling across Benny if no one knows I'm looking for him, so that's the way I'd like to keep it for a while longer. Bringing in the local law could botch the whole thing. People talk a lot around here, Hal. Rocky Ford's your typical small town. Nice little place, though," he added as an afterthought.

"Have you asked yourself why Slocum would pick a 'nice little place' for his final deal?" Hal asked dryly.

"Many times. I know there's a reason—probably a darned good one. I just haven't figured out what it is yet."

"Okay, it's your ball game. Keep me informed. Still staying at the same motel?"

"Nothing's changed. I'll let you know if anything does."

After signing off, Burke sat there thinking. He *was* on the right track, wasn't he? Frowning, he got up and paced his room. The possibility that Benny had been behind that call, using it to throw the task force off his true trail, crept into his mind every so often. And it was a possibility, make no mistake. Slocum was damned wily. How else would he have walked around a free man for so long when everyone knew he was involved up to his eyeballs in drugs? Proving his criminal acts in a court of law was a far cry from street knowledge, however.

But did they have any other leads than that call and Rocky Ford? Anywhere else to look for Benny?

Determination and belief returned abruptly. Permitting doubts to fester would only undermine the trust he had in his investigation. After all, trust was all he had to go on; he couldn't get discouraged so soon.

After a shower and shave, Burke left the motel and dropped into two taverns, nursing one glass of beer in each place so he could get a look at the customers and employees. He struck up conversations with anyone who was willing to talk and finally returned to the Sundowner Motel around midnight with no more information than he'd had earlier.

He went to bed and fell asleep almost instantly.

Around 4:00 a.m. Burke sat up in a jerky, disoriented movement. After a moment he had his bearings and he lay down again. But his eyes were wide open, and he felt as though he'd slept ten hours instead of four.

Maybe there was a reason for his unusual early-morning alertness, he thought with a tightening of his gut while throwing back the covers and getting out of bed. Maybe there was something out there he should be seeing. Criminal investigations sometimes took the strangest twists. Important facts were often discovered by chance, stumbled across by accident. And he wasn't entirely dubious about omens and premonitions, either.

He got dressed and quietly closed the motel door behind him. The black night was cold; his breath fogged in front of his face. He headed for his vehicle, climbed in and started the engine, then let it idle for a few minutes so the defroster could clear the windshield. Pulling out of the Sundowner's parking lot, he turned right without rhyme or reason.

The streets were all but deserted. Night-lights burned in various buildings and in some yards. The town was still sleeping. Why wasn't he? His stomach was churning, as though he was suddenly going to spot something of great import.

It didn't happen. After a while his stomach settled down and the expectation faded from his system. Slowly he drove

up one street and down another. Then he realized that he
was on Foxworth Street, and he kept going until he saw
Charlie's Place. He pulled to the curb directly in front of the
big house and ducked his head to peer at it through the pas-
senger window. A few lights were on in the business part of
the structure. Night-lights, obviously. Everything looked
quiet and peaceful.

Sitting there with the engine idling, he thought about
Charlie and the kind of man he seemed to be—a solid, law-
abiding citizen. Then he thought about Candace and won-
dered how he could meet her. Dare he come right out and
ask Charlie if he could meet his daughter-in-law? Forward,
yes, but would Charlie think so? Burke had gotten the im-
pression that Charlie had been disappointed over there be-
ing no chance of him moving to Rocky Ford, since there was
no college for him to continue his teaching career. He'd also
received the impression that Charlie's attitude had had
something to do with Candace.

For a moment Burke chewed on his bottom lip. He could
be imagining things as far as Charlie's attitude went. After
all, how much time had they spent together? Had Charlie
instantly liked and trusted him as he had Charlie? Strange
how some people's personalities blended immediately.

Slowly steering back onto the street, Burke decided to re-
turn to the motel. Out of sheer habit, he noticed that there
were a few other cars parked on the roadside rather than in
driveways. He was two blocks away when something hit him
right between the eyes. One of the cars, the one parked di-
rectly across the street from Charlie's Place, didn't have
frosted-over windows as the others did. Had someone been
sitting in it and running the heater and defroster? His own
late-night prowling had an ulterior motive. Wouldn't an-
other insomniac have a motive for sitting in his car at this
unholy hour, as well?

Cursing under his breath, he made a U-turn. Only, his
four-wheeler didn't make U-turns without a lot of space,
and Foxworth was a narrow street. What color was that car?
he thought frantically as he backed up to straighten his

wheels. What make? What year? Was he getting feeble-minded, or what?

Before he got turned around, he saw the car speeding away. It made a right turn at the first cross street. Finally heading in the same direction, Burke took up the chase. It startled him when he turned the same corner that the car had and the street loomed empty as far as he could see.

Slowing down at every cross street, he searched for that car with his pulse racing. Blue, he thought then. It was a blue sedan. But where in hell had it gone?

"Damn," he muttered, slapping the steering wheel in frustration. How could he have been so negligent? It wasn't that he thought there was a connection between this peculiar event and Benny Slocum, but why in hell would anyone be parked on the street with the engine running at five in the morning?

There was just no finding that blue car, he thought after another half hour of driving around. It could have pulled into a driveway or even a garage.

Disgruntled, painfully curious and blaming himself for inexcusable inefficiency, he drove to the motel.

*Andrea's heart was pounding so fast and furiously, she marveled that it didn't burst through her rib cage. Who was that man in that dark vehicle? And why had he chased after her? Oh, God, she thought as fright nearly ate her alive.*

*She couldn't stop thinking about it. That person—that man—had deliberately stopped in front of the Fanon home and looked at it for at least five minutes. She'd been so startled that she had frozen for a few moments, but then her wits had returned and she had ducked down, just in case he should glance across the street.*

*She was now safe in the driveway of her rented house, concealed from the street by the numerous trees and shrubs between the house and road, and still her heart wouldn't slow down. What a frightening experience, and so unexpected. Often when she couldn't sleep, she drove to Foxworth Street and parked near Charlie Fanon's home and*

*business. She had also made a habit of driving past it dur-
ing the day. It drew her as a magnet did iron filings. Charlie
was the reason she was even in Rocky Ford, Montana, after
all, and it was a rare moment when he wasn't uppermost in
her mind.*

*She inhaled a long breath as her system began to calm
down. Someday she was going to walk into the Fanon house.
Someday she was going to . . .*

*A shiver went up her spine. When she had come here, she
was going to do it immediately. Where was her nerve? Her
courage? It had to be done. Sooner or later it had to be
done! She would never rest until it was, and she was be-
coming vexed with sleepless nights and a nervous knot in her
stomach.*

*Realizing that her hands were still trembling, she turned
off the ignition, got out of the car and went into the house.
Recently she had also been battling loneliness. Leery of
giving herself away, she had avoided making friends, an at-
titude that was beginning to pinch. Finally, only last week,
she had deliberately gone outside and to the fence when she
saw her neighbor, an older man, raking leaves. His name
was Lucas Wilde, and he had been elated that she had come
out to meet him. He was friendly and chatty, and in ten
minutes she had learned his personal history. He was a wid-
ower with a grown son. A doctor, Lucas said with a pride-
ful gleam in his eyes.*

*"What kind of doctor?" Andrea had inquired, simply to
further the conversation since it felt so good to be talking to
someone.*

*"A plastic surgeon in southern California. He's married
to a very pretty young woman. No children, though," he'd
added with a regretful sigh.*

*Anyway, Andrea had felt much better afterward. She was
teaching herself to cook and planned to ask Mr. Wilde over
for dinner one of these days. Mr. Wilde hadn't seemed par-
ticularly curious about her, which she liked, as she didn't
want to start telling lies to the very pleasant gentleman.
Maybe she had made a friend.*

*Inside the house she breathed a relieved sigh. It was only a small rental house, but it was homey and comfortable. More important, she felt safe there. Until tonight she'd had no real reason not to feel safe. No one in Rocky Ford knew her background or why she was in town, so what was there to fear?*

*But now there was something very peculiar going on. And that man had tried to follow her car! Why had he been so interested in Charlie's house? Was he a burglar, casing the place? Should she go to the police and tell them what she'd seen?*

*No, she couldn't do that, not without giving her own self away.*

*And what would that man have done if he'd caught up to her?*

*Trembling again from all of the frightening possibilities racing through her mind, she put on the kettle for a cup of tea. She had a great deal to think about, but first she must attain a calmer state of mind. A cup of hot tea would help.*

Candace sat at the breakfast table with a second cup of coffee while Ronnie played on the floor nearby with his favorite toy truck. Even without makeup she was a lovely woman, with flawless skin, light blond hair and hazel eyes heavily fringed with dark lashes. Candace was a small woman, barely five feet two, with a delicate bone structure and a perfectly proportioned figure. Her fragile appearance was deceptive, however; she was strong enough to clean the entire house in one day, tend her son throughout and cook a delicious dinner at the same time.

But this morning her thoughts weren't on cleaning. Rather, they had gone in a direction that was really quite exciting. She would have to discuss it with Charlie, of course. This was his house, after all, but wouldn't it be fun to redecorate it? She would tell Charlie that she would pay for the whole thing. She had received a great deal of money from the death of her husband—certainly nothing in which to rejoice even if it did make her financially secure—but she was living here with Charlie and her only contribution to the cost of running the household was the ingredients necessary to prepare the good meals she so enjoyed cooking. Charlie had refused, adamantly, her offer to pay rent or to at least pay the utility bills.

But redecorating this old house wouldn't be inexpensive, and Charlie would surely permit her to foot the cost. If he agreed to the transformation at all, that is. One thing she knew for certain: if he hesitated at the idea, or seemed even slightly reluctant, she would immediately drop the subject. He had lived in this old-fashioned house for many years and seemed completely content with it. She would not interfere with that contentment for anything. Loving Charlie had come easily and naturally. There was not a kinder person on the face of the earth, and she felt a deep, abiding affection for and from him that she would not risk just because she thought the house would greatly benefit from an overhaul.

Besides, wasn't the project really for *her* benefit? Hadn't she finally reached the stage where she needed something more than cooking and cleaning? After Ron's death she had wondered if she would ever again be the enthusiastic, happy woman she had been before the awful event.

Gradually it was happening. She didn't cry herself to sleep anymore and hadn't for quite some time. She was finding happiness in small things again, and she was able to smile and laugh like everyone else. Yes, she was definitely returning to normal. She would never forget Ron, of course, but life did go on.

Looking at her adorable little son making motor noises as he rolled his toy truck along the floor, she smiled. He was her blessing.

But so was the Fanon family. Especially Charlie.

Getting up from the table, Candace brought her cup to the sink. She would talk to Charlie about the house renovations sometime today. If he agreed with any enthusiasm at all, she wanted to get started on it right away.

* * *

Burke and Charlie were drinking coffee together at the counter, Burke on one side of it, Charlie on the other. The scene was the same as yesterday morning. Customers had come and gone, some lingering for a cup of Charlie's special coffee, some merely dropping in for their favorite reading material. At the moment no one else was in the place. Apparently the morning "rush hour" was over, as Charlie had quipped yesterday.

Burke liked that Charlie could joke about his low-key business operation. Obviously he was running the coffeehouse because he enjoyed doing it, not because he was taking in a fortune.

"What did you do before opening this place?" he asked Charlie.

"I worked as a lineman for the telephone company. After retirement and about a year of twiddling my thumbs, I came up with this idea. Foxworth Street had been rezoned for some years, and businesses and apartment houses were gradually springing up among the houses—sometimes just filling in a vacant lot—so I didn't have to contend with zoning restrictions or variance hassles.

"Mind you, I didn't want something that would keep me hopping every minute of every day," Charlie added with a grin. "My ambition went only so far." He glanced around his shop. "This turned out just the way I wanted it. Brings in a few extra bucks and gives me something to do. Besides, I get to see a lot of my friends."

Burke set his cup down. This morning's strange incident hadn't stopped eating at him, and Charlie mentioning friends was a good opening to ask some questions.

"Do your friends and customers live in this neighborhood?"

"Most of them." Charlie got up to refill their cups.

"But strangers wander in now and then, right?"

"Oh, sure." Charlie grinned again. "You did, didn't you?"

Burke nodded. He'd wandered in with a purpose, and it bothered him to pretend with Charlie. But what else could he do until he got a handle on Benny's whereabouts?

Charlie resumed his seat. "Are you sure you don't want a doughnut or sweet roll?"

"Thanks, but I had breakfast before I got here, Charlie." He patted his washboard stomach. "Gotta watch the old waistline, you know."

"But you came in for coffee, anyway. That's exactly what I meant about friends dropping in. I like people, Burke, and what in heck would I be doing every day without this place?"

Burke smiled teasingly. "I'm probably the only stranger you've seen in months."

Charlie thought a moment, then shook his head. "Nope, you're not."

Burke's inner antenna went up, but he casually took a swallow of coffee before expanding the subject. "So how many strangers have wandered in during . . . say the last two weeks?"

Charlie had to laugh. "Not many. Actually I think it's only been one before you. He's still coming in, by the way. Every so often in the morning when I first open up. Unfriendly cuss, though. Buys every newspaper I carry and a large coffee to go. Never says much."

The photo of Benny in Burke's back pocket was suddenly burning the seat of his jeans. Dare he show it to Charlie and ask if the man in the photo was the "unfriendly" stranger? The urge to do so was so strong that Burke could hardly contain it. But this morning's incident with that blue car meant something, and he had better play it close to the chest until he knew Charlie a little better.

"Since he shows up every so often, he must have moved to Rocky Ford," Burke said in a purely conversational tone. "Do you think he lives around here?"

"I think he must," Charlie replied. "I've never seen him get out of or into a car. Probably lives in one of those apartment buildings down the street."

*Or parks his car far enough away that you can't see it.* Burke's system was buzzing. This could be the break he'd been hoping for. That early-morning customer could be Benny.

But what about that blue car? Who had been driving it, and why had it been parked across the street from Charlie's house at five in the morning? It didn't seem like an innocent incident. A person without an ulterior motive would not have sped away when Burke turned his vehicle around to get a better look.

On the other hand, the whole damned thing could have merely appeared suspect. Maybe the person had been warming up his car to defrost the windows and had driven away without even noticing Burke turning around.

Getting off the stool, Burke took his coffee and meandered over to the front windows. Directly across the street was a house of about the same vintage as Charlie's, although it was much smaller. The person driving that blue car could live there, even though there was a white pickup truck parked in the driveway. Burke frowned as ambiguities stacked up in his mind.

"Seems like a real quiet neighborhood," he remarked while looking in both directions as far as he could see. Even with the smattering of businesses on Foxworth, traffic was light. Of course, the residents of Rocky Ford had probably never endured a traffic jam in any sector of the town.

"Gampy!"

Burke turned to see a little towheaded boy running into the room and heading behind the counter. Laughing, Charlie got off his stool and caught the child in his arms. "Hi there, big guy," he said affectionately.

More interesting to Burke was the young woman following the child. Up close, Candace Fanon was the prettiest little woman he'd ever seen. He was suddenly as excited as a schoolboy.

Smiling slightly, he walked back to the counter. Charlie was looking at his grandson. "Say hello to Mr. Mallory, Ronnie."

"H'wo," the boy said.

"Hello, Ronnie." Burke held his right hand across the counter. "Shake?"

The boy put his hand in Burke's. He was an adorable little fellow, with big brown eyes and an infectious smile. Charlie's feelings for the child were all over his face, and small wonder, Burke thought. Who wouldn't love a grandchild like Ronnie?

He turned his gaze to Candace again and felt something sigh within himself. The mother was as adorable as the son, with the added attraction of feminine maturity.

Charlie did the honors. "Candace, I'd like you to meet my friend, Burke Mallory. Burke, this is my daughter-in-law, Candace Fanon."

"Hello, Mr. Mallory," Candace said, not quite looking him in the eye. She felt embarrassed. Never could she have imagined the man Charlie wanted to invite to dinner to look like this. Tall and handsome, young and vital. And she felt his admiration clear to the center of her bones.

"Hello, Mrs. Fanon," Burke said quietly.

"Here, now," Charlie admonished. "What's all this formality about?"

Candace's cheeks got pink, and Burke rushed to dispel her discomfort. "I'll call her whatever she prefers," he said to Charlie.

"'Candace' will do," she said softly, only because Charlie seemed to like Mr. Mallory so much. If it was left to her, she would keep things strictly formal with Burke Mallory. He disturbed her on a very personal level, which was so unexpected she felt discombobulated by it. She was not, after all, looking for a male friend, especially one who had seemed to be instantly attracted to her.

"I'll take Ronnie and leave you two be," she said to Charlie. "He just ran in without any warning, and I was sure you had a customer. Which is why I followed," she added, explaining something that was completely obvious and proving how addled she felt.

Charlie merely hugged his grandson closer. "He can come in to see me any time he wants, honey. And you're just as welcome in here as he is."

"Yes, but . . ." Candace's voice trailed off. She was making too much of something that happened on a regular basis. Ronnie was forever running to find Gampy, and unless Charlie was exceptionally busy, she rarely interfered. Actually many of Charlie's customers loved seeing Ronnie when they came in for their coffee and newspapers.

Candace knew that her unusual conduct this morning was because of Burke Mallory watching her with that completely male light in his incredible blue eyes. In truth, she didn't know where to put herself. She wanted to leave and yet didn't want to appear rude. Charlie had seemed so pleased to introduce her to Burke and, in fact, was still beaming.

"Your son is a handsome child," Burke said to her, which was only the truth even though he knew he would have said anything just to talk to her. He felt a pang because she seemed so reluctant to talk or even to look at him.

"Thank you," she murmured, still not meeting his eyes.

"Burke," Charlie said. "Do you have plans for dinner tonight?" Candace's heart sank clear to her toes as she thought *Oh, no!* but she said and did nothing to give her inner feelings away. She hoped she was succeeding, anyway.

"No plans, Charlie. Why?"

"'Cause Candace and I would like you to have dinner with us. Isn't that right, honey?"

Candace produced a feeble smile. "Yes, Charlie."

These two people couldn't be further apart as far as he and dinner were concerned, Burke realized. But Candace hadn't given him a chance. She had acknowledged the introduction and turned off on him. He wasn't going to pass up this opportunity for her to get to know him, however uneasy she was with the prospect.

"I accept," he said with a smile. "What time?"

Charlie looked to Candace for that answer. "You name it, honey."

She heaved a silent, resigned sigh. "Six." Then she took her son from Charlie's arms. "See you later, Charlie." She started for the door.

"Nice meeting you, Candace," Burke called.

Stopping, she turned slightly. "Nice meeting you, too, Burke. See you tonight."

He stared after her. My Lord, she was beautiful. Somehow he had to break through her wall of reserve—he *had* to.

## Chapter Three

It was midafternoon before Candace caught Charlie alone.

"I've been thinking about something, Charlie. Do you have a few minutes to talk?"

"I've always got time for you, honey. What's on your mind?"

They sat at the kitchen table. Candace was suddenly self-conscious. Who was she to tell Charlie his house could use a face-lift?

She took a breath. "You know I love this old house, don't you?"

"I thought you might, but we've never talked about it. Why, honey?"

"Well, I appreciate living here, Charlie, very much, and I hope you don't get the wrong idea. What I mean to say is that there's nothing wrong with the house as it is." She paused for another breath. "It's just that I've been needing something more to do lately, and I would really love to redecorate the house."

Charlie's eyes squinted slightly as he glanced around the old-fashioned kitchen and at the same time thought of the rest of the house. When had he last painted any of the rooms? Or revarnished the paneling adorning the walls in some of them? Years, he thought then, sighing quietly. Years. Time flew by much too quickly. Where did a person's life go? One day your kids were toddlers, and the next they were all grown-up with kids of their own.

He smiled at his daughter-in-law with a rather nostalgic expression. Candace looked nervous and uneasy, as though she was worried that she'd gone way over the line with this conversation. He must dispel that worry immediately. This was her home, too, and he wanted her to believe that with all her heart and soul.

"You do anything you want to the house, Candy," he said firmly.

"Do you really mean that?" Excitement began dancing in her eyes.

"I certainly do mean it. What've you got in mind?"

"I'm really not sure. I'd like to do a good job, so I don't want to start willy-nilly without a plan. And, of course, I won't change everything. I mean, some of your furniture is very good. Naturally I'll work those pieces into the overall design."

Charlie nodded. "Well, tell you what. I'll set up a charge account at the hardware store. You can get the paint and—"

Candace touched his hand. "No, Charlie. I want to pay for this. I won't do it if I can't."

He frowned. "Honey, you shouldn't be spending your money on paint and such for the house."

"What should I be spending it on? Charlie, you know I've already set aside the money for Ronnie's education. Please let me do this." She wasn't just thinking of a little paint and wallpaper. The living room needed new drapes, and some of the furniture definitely had to go. Ideas ran rampant in her mind, although she'd told Charlie the truth about not being certain of anything. Planning the decor would be as much fun as the actual work, and when it was completed, she wanted to be proud of the result. Even more important, she wanted Charlie to be proud. To like what she'd done.

He tugged at his left ear while mulling it over. He could tell she was thinking of redoing the whole house, and that meant a lot more than a new coat of paint for the walls. But she had apparently reached the point of needing more to occupy her time than housework and cooking, which pleased him no end. She was young and shouldn't be totally dedicated to her son and father-in-law, admirable as her tender, loving care was, to the exclusion of everything else. The house was only a house; Candace's emotional health was a hundred times more important.

He made up his mind. If it made her happy, she could do anything she wanted. Much to Candace's delight, he nodded. "All right, young lady, it's your baby." Then he grinned. "I ask only one thing."

"Anything, Charlie," she agreed with a smile.

"I never liked that ultramodern stuff. You know, chrome and fluorescent colors?"

Candace laughed. "Neither have I, Charlie. Don't worry. You won't see a speck of chrome or fluorescent color anywhere in the house. I swear it."

Candace had decided that she was not going to change her planned dinner menu just because Burke Mallory would be eating with them. But after talking with Charlie, she felt so good that she made a Waldorf salad and an apple cobbler to accompany the baked chicken and rice pilaf.

At five she set the table with Charlie's best dishes, then took Ronnie to play in her bedroom while she changed clothes and refreshed her makeup. Looking nice for dinner was a habit she enjoyed and had nothing to do with Burke Mallory's presence this evening. After all, he meant no more to her than any of the other people that Charlie occasionally had over for dinner.

And yet she couldn't completely categorize Burke as just another dinner guest. He was not one of Charlie's old friends. In fact, Charlie had just met the man. Wasn't it a little soon to be asking him to dinner?

On the other hand, didn't Charlie make friends faster than anyone she'd ever known? Charlie seemed to like everyone. Had she ever heard him say a truly unkind word about anyone? Even about those people who didn't deserve respect? And there were some of that ilk in Rocky Ford, make no mistake.

Sometimes when the whole family got together, his niece, Lola, and his daughter, Serena, would pass on a story—gossip, really—and get a good laugh over it. Charlie would smile, but he never added anything to the gossip. In fact, if he said anything at all about it, it was usually some comment in defense of the person's behavior.

Candace didn't put on her new sweater. It was really too heavy to be worn indoors, especially when she would be dealing with a hot oven. Instead, she donned a simply styled print dress that hugged her waist and flared from there almost to her ankles. It had a collar at her throat and sleeves to her elbows, a nice dress that was appropriate for dinner and yet would send no personal messages to Mr. Mallory.

She already thought he was attracted to her just from the expression in his eyes during this morning's introduction; she was not planning to encourage that attraction in any way, which he would discover this evening. She would be polite but distant, she thought while brushing her hair. If he had any intelligence at all, he would get the picture. And of course he was intelligent; he was a professor of sociology, after all. He wouldn't present a problem, and she shouldn't be looking for one.

But if all of that was true, why did she have a giddy little flutter in her stomach? Surely *she* felt no attraction for him!

Appalled at the idea, she dropped the hairbrush on the dresser and turned to her son. "Come, sweetheart. Mama's finished. We'll go to the kitchen now."

* * *

Burke arrived promptly and was greeted at the door by Charlie.

"Come in, come in," Charlie said with a jovial smile of welcome. "Let me have your jacket."

Burke stepped into the house, took off his jacket and handed it to Charlie, noticing in the process that the back door opened directly onto a large country kitchen. Candace was at the counter and she turned to say hello, but only for a moment. Little Ron was standing near his grandfather, looking at Burke with big eyes.

"Hello," Burke said to Candace, then bent down to speak to the little boy. "Hello, Ronnie."

"H'wo," the boy said.

Burke straightened up. "Smells mighty good in here." He was looking at Candace again, who was so pretty in that dress he wished he could just stand there and stare at her. He wished for more than that, to be honest. If she would turn around again, look directly into his eyes and give him a genuine smile, he would be one very happy man.

She did turn, but it was to look at Charlie, who was hanging Burke's jacket in a small closet. "Dinner will be on the table in about fifteen minutes. Why don't you take Burke to the living room until then?"

"Come on, Burke," Charlie said with a small chuckle. "Women don't like men underfoot when they're cooking. Learned that a long time ago." He sent Candace a grin so she would know he was teasing. Then he spoke to Ronnie. "Come on, big guy. You come to the living room with us." The boy gladly followed.

Candace breathed a sigh of relief when Burke was no longer gaping at her. Indeed, she had not imagined his admiration this morning. She had felt it again, very strongly, the second he'd walked through the door.

What really bothered her was that she couldn't deny noticing *his* good looks. Not that there was anything wrong with a woman privately acknowledging a man's looks. If that's all there was to it, that is. But she had a feeling that

Burke was going to try something with her, like maybe asking her for a date. The last thing she wanted was a date with any man. Since he was Charlie's friend, she would have to be tactful in her refusal. But would Burke be tactful in accepting a refusal?

Sighing, she tossed her head and told herself to stop putting the cart before the horse. So he admired her. It probably didn't mean a thing. Maybe he was one of those men who admired every woman he met.

She really shouldn't be dreaming up discomfiting scenarios, she thought while carrying food to the table. For one thing, it wasn't like her to fantasize about men. In fact, the only time she could remember of ever doing so was when she had met Ron Fanon.

For a moment she stood still and went into the past. She had been smitten by Ron at their first meeting. It was only after they had dated for a few weeks that he'd told her the same thing had happened to him. How handsome he'd been, both in his military uniforms and in ordinary clothes. She'd been so much in love that she'd had stars in her eyes. So had Ron. One didn't easily forget a love like that.

Heaving a long sigh, she returned to the present. She could think of Ron now without crying, but she was far from ready to even consider dating another man. If Burke did ask her out, that was what she would tell him. Tactfully, of course.

Everything was on the table. Candace looked it over and gave it her stamp of approval. Then she went to the living-room doorway. "Dinner's ready, Charlie." She held out her hand. "Come, son."

The child ran over to take her hand, and together they led the way to the oversize kitchen table.

It was easy for Burke to pick out his place. Charlie would sit at the head of the table, and a high chair was near the place on his right. Burke would be sitting on Charlie's left.

Candace lifted her son into his high chair. She glanced up and noticed the men hovering. "Please, sit down," she told them.

Charlie pulled out his chair. "Go ahead and sit, Burke. We like Ronnie to take his meals with us, and Candy will join us as soon as she gets him settled."

*Candy?* A nickname, obviously. Burke wasn't sure he liked it. "Candace" was a lovely name, befitting a lovely, mature woman. "Candy" sounded like a bubble-gummer, or worse, a bubblehead, and disliking that picture didn't require any debate at all. The nickname didn't suit this quiet, beautiful little woman in the least. He would never call her "Candy," never.

Charlie bowed his head and Burke followed suit, though it was rare when he sat at a table where grace was said. Charlie's words of thanks were simple and brief, but spoken with feeling.

Then he grinned at Burke. "Dive in, my friend. I guarantee you'll never eat better cooking."

Candace's cheeks got pink. "Please, Charlie."

Charlie chuckled. "Don't be embarrassed, honey. You're the best little cook in the whole darned West, and I can't help saying so."

Candace turned her head to place Ronnie's dish on his high-chair tray. It was a child's dish, with divided compartments already containing various foods. Candace put a child's spoon in Ronnie's little hand. "There you are, son," she said softly.

Warmth for this gentle, soft-spoken woman swelled within Burke. He had dated women with children in the past, but he had never witnessed the kind of love that Candace showed her son. It touched him in a way nothing else ever had, and he felt a little choked up for a few moments.

Getting a grip on his emotions while filling his plate, he wondered just how hard he was falling for Candace Fanon. He realized that he wasn't questioning the "falling," but just how far the plunge would take him.

And she wouldn't even look directly into his eyes. What was he doing, deliberately looking for heartache?

He took a swallow from his glass of water to dampen his suddenly parched throat. He wasn't in Rocky Ford to fall in love, especially with a woman who couldn't care less. He'd best remember that and concentrate on finding Benny Slocum.

Dinner went smoothly. Charlie kept the conversational ball rolling, and Burke held up his end just fine. Candace made a comment now and then, but she never once asked Burke a question or addressed a remark directly to him.

So be it, he thought with a grim sort of finality. His finding her breathtakingly attractive didn't mean a damned thing. It was his problem, not hers, and he'd get over it.

Hopefully.

He offered to help with the dishes, but Charlie told him to relax and he and Candace had the kitchen in order in ten minutes. Then Charlie took him back to the living room.

"Sit down, Burke. Candace will join us after she puts Ronnie to bed."

Burke chuckled. "He's one great kid, Charlie. I thought I'd bust a gut when he rubbed that handful of mashed carrots in his hair."

Charlie laughed. "Me, too. It was all I could do to keep a straight face."

Burke was still grinning over the incident. While he and Charlie had sat there nearly bursting from holding back their laughter, Candace had calmly wiped Ronnie's hair and hands with a napkin. Then she'd put the spoon back in his hand, with neither a harsh word nor expression.

"Candace is a wonderful mother, isn't she?" Burke said.

"The best, Burke, the very best."

"She has a Southern accent. Where's she from?"

"South Carolina. A small town on the coast. Ron was stationed nearby, and that's where they met."

"Does she miss the ocean?"

"Probably does." Charlie paused. "But she's never said so. I think she really likes Montana. Besides, she doesn't have any family back there. The Fanons are her family now. That probably makes a difference, wouldn't you say?"

"She has no family at all? Was she an orphan?"

"More or less. She was raised by an elderly aunt who passed away when she was just out of high school. She doesn't talk about her parents and I don't pry, but I honestly believe that she doesn't remember them."

Burke nodded. "I understand."

Candace walked in. "Excuse me, Charlie. Ronnie is asking for you."

Charlie heaved himself up and out of his chair. With an air of pride, he told Burke, "I always spend a few minutes with Ronnie at bedtime. I won't be long. Candace will keep you company, won't you, honey?"

"Of course," Candace murmured. She'd known this would happen when she came in and, in fact, had worried about it while getting Ronnie ready for bed. She had nothing to say to Burke Mallory and was leery of what he might say to her. But there was no polite way of avoiding these few minutes. Thank goodness it would *be* only a few minutes, she thought while uneasily perching on a sofa cushion.

Burke was thrilled to find himself alone with Candace. However, it wasn't something he had expected. Having sensed her disinterest so acutely from the moment he'd entered the Fanon house, he could only play this encounter by ear.

"I'd like to compliment you on dinner," he said quietly. "Charlie wasn't wrong about your cooking."

"Thank you. I enjoy cooking."

She still wasn't looking at him. Oh, her gaze fluttered his way, but that was about it. Was she afraid to look directly at him? She looked at Charlie when she spoke to him, so it wasn't her natural tendency to look past people when talking to them.

He, of course, had no such compunction. Looking at Candace was a pleasure he wouldn't even attempt to deny himself. Her hair gleamed like sunlight, lovely, soft-looking hair that swung with her head movements. Did she know how truly beautiful she was?

Candace frantically sought a neutral subject. "Have you always lived in Seattle?" came out of her mouth, followed immediately by a wish that she hadn't asked him a question about himself.

Burke hesitated. He didn't want to start lying to Candace, and if they talked about him, he would have to.

"Not always," he replied, then remembered telling Charlie that he'd been born and raised in Seattle. If they compared notes for some reason... Damn, he thought, quickly changing the subject. "Charlie tells me you're from South Carolina. That's a beautiful part of the country."

"Yes, it is, but so is Montana." So, he and Charlie had been talking about her. What else had been said? Knowing Charlie, it was nothing derogatory, but she still wasn't comfortable with the picture of them discussing her. It wasn't Charlie's doing, she would bet. She felt even less friendly toward Burke now.

Burke nodded. "I agree."

"Oh, that's right," Candace said, simply because she couldn't think of anything else to say. "You've been exploring Montana."

"Have you seen much of the state?"

She gave her head a small shake. "Just this area. It's a very large state, and I have a son to look after."

"He's a great kid, Candace."

For the first time she looked directly into his eyes. What felt like a lightning bolt rocketed through Burke. Eye contact could be dynamite, and he prayed she wouldn't break it right away.

"Yes, he is," she said in a near-whisper, shaken by the deluge of emotion she felt just from looking into Burke Mallory's piercing blue eyes. It was a mesmerizing few moments, and she had to force herself to look away. Instantly she was angry with herself.

Rising, she went to the door. "I wonder what's keeping Charlie. I'm sure you would rather be talking to him."

Burke got to his feet. "Not true, Candace. I can't think of anyone I would rather be talking to than you."

She swung around. "Why?"

"Why?" he echoed. "That's a funny question."

She walked back into the room and stood near a table. "It's not a funny question. Why would you rather talk to me than to anyone else?"

So, there was plenty of fire behind that sweet Southern drawl, Burke thought as sexual excitement exploded in his system. Unwittingly she had just made herself more desirable to him.

Okay, she'd asked for honesty, and he'd give it to her. "Because I think you're one very special lady."

"And what makes me so special?" Why was she doing this? Inwardly she groaned. She was vexed with herself more than with him, and it was coming out in a very peculiar manner. She sounded, in fact, as though she was trying to pick a fight.

"A lot of things," Burke said calmly, though his pulse was racing. "You're beautiful, intelligent and interesting. I've never been around a better, more loving mother, and—"

Candace broke in. "Thank you, that's quite enough. At the risk of being rude, I'm going to set you straight, Mr. Mallory. I am not flattered by your interest, nor do I intend to encourage it. You're Charlie's friend, and I will treat you as I do all of his friends. But there will be no personal conversations between us. Have I made myself clear?"

Burke was thunderstruck by her candor. To be honest, he felt as though he'd just been slapped in the face. Or kicked in the gut.

"I'm sorry if I offended you," he said. "It won't happen again."

"Thank you."

Charlie walked in smiling. "He's already asleep, Candy. Let's all sit down and—"

"You'll have to excuse me, Charlie," Candace said. "There's something I must do. Good night."

Both men watched her hurrying from the room. Charlie's gaze swung to Burke. "Is she upset about something?"

Burke sucked in a breath. "It's my fault, Charlie. I told her I thought she was a very special lady, and apparently she didn't like it." He gave a dry little laugh. "She put me in my place in no uncertain terms."

"She did?" Clearly Charlie was perplexed. But then he sighed. "Have a seat, Burke. How about you and I having a little nip of brandy?"

"I could use one, thanks." Burke sank into a chair. He'd never before been chastised as Candace had just done. And without raising her voice even one decibel, in the bargain. There was a trembling in his system that was brand-new and disturbing. Candace wanted nothing to do with him, and he wanted her more than he had before the dressing-down. Why was this happening to him?

In her bedroom Candace was shaking like a twig in a windstorm. Never had she spoken to a man the way she'd just done with Burke. Her vow to be tactful, should Burke say something personal to her, was so much dust. Instead of tact, she had resorted to outright rudeness. She hated what she'd done, and regret actually brought tears to her eyes.

If only he would leave Rocky Ford, she thought passionately. Go to another area of Montana and do his exploring. Why on earth was he hanging around Rocky Ford? There was only so much to see, and surely he'd seen it all in a few days.

And why didn't he seem like an educator? Certainly he wasn't like any teacher *she'd* ever known.

With tears dribbling down her cheeks, she undressed, put on a nightgown and crawled into bed.

There had been major upheavals in her life, to be sure, but none that she'd caused herself.

Darn it, how would she ever face him again?

# Chapter Four

That blue car being parked across the street from Charlie's house at five in the morning wouldn't leave Burke be. For his own peace of mind, he had to know if it belonged in the Foxworth Street neighborhood, and he got out of bed at 4:00 a.m. to find out.

It wasn't there this morning, which tightened the knot of suspicion in his gut. The theory that a neighbor of Charlie's had been defrosting the windows before going somewhere—perhaps to an early-morning job—didn't seem feasible now. Driving slowly down Foxworth Street, Burke checked every driveway and parking area he could see. As Charlie had told him and he'd already scrutinized for himself, there were several apartment buildings not far from the Fanon home. They weren't large complexes, and the occupants' vehicles were parked beneath carports.

There were a couple of blue sedans, Burke noted, which didn't make him happy. Blue was a common color for cars, and he couldn't start suspecting every blue car he ran across. He'd been remiss yesterday morning about picking up on the make and year of the car, and negligence always returned to haunt an investigator.

Driving past Charlie's house again, Burke's lips thinned in self-rebuke. Instead of paying attention to duty and details yesterday morning, he'd been thinking of Candace Fanon. Well, he sure knew where he stood with Candace now, didn't he? She'd pulled no punches. *I'm not flattered by your interest.* How much plainer could a woman speak?

So it was forget-Candace time. He'd live. Her disinterest wasn't the end of the world.

Still, he'd never struck out so fast with a woman before, and he didn't think the emotional wrenching he felt was merely a wounded ego. It went deeper than that, clear to the heart of him. He'd never met a woman who had impressed him more, and if Candace had reciprocated, no telling where it might have gone.

Guess it just wasn't in the cards, he thought about a second before noticing a police patrol car coming up behind him. No red lights flashed on, but he drove with one eye on the rearview mirror. It followed him to the Sundowner Motel, then stopped and waited while he got out and went into his unit. He would bet anything they had run his license number, which was clean as a whistle and would give them very little information. But they wouldn't forget his vehicle; he was going to have to be a little more cautious about driving around at odd hours of the night if he wanted to remain anonymous.

Stretching out on the bed with his hands locked behind his head, he stared at the dark ceiling. He was either going to have to accomplish something very soon or let the local police know who he was and why he was in town.

His only lead on Benny—slim as it was—was Charlie's comments about a stranger dropping in now and then to buy coffee and newspapers.

He trusted Charlie, and maybe it was time to impose on that trust. Burke's eyes narrowed speculatively. Yes, that's probably what he should do. The stranger might or might not be Benny, but he couldn't hang around Charlie's Place every day to find out on his own, not without drawing attention. He had no choice but to tell Charlie the truth and show him that photo of Benny.

He would do it later this morning, when Charlie's rush hour was over and they were alone in the coffee shop.

With that decision final, Burke turned over and closed his eyes. He might as well catch another few hours of sleep.


After breakfast and a few chores around the house, Candace started taking inventory of the good pieces of furniture in the house, those items that she would weave into the redecorating project. Ronnie followed her around, talking his sweet baby talk, and when she sat down in the living room, he began playing with the little truck he'd been carrying with him.

Candace was thinking of the house as a whole. Unquestionably it was a rancher, and she couldn't turn it into a Cape Cod, for example. She wondered why Charlie had bought such a large house when he came to Montana—six bedrooms and four baths was a very large home in her book, especially when every room was spacious. Besides, before he had remodeled to accommodate his business, the house had also contained a second living room.

She laid her notebook on the table next to her chair and put her head back. The idea of redecorating was still exciting, but she couldn't seem to get past last night's troubling incident with Burke Mallory to concentrate on it.

And something else had started bothering her, as well: how would Serena and Lola feel about her changing Charlie's house? After all, she was a virtual newcomer to the family. Would they think her presumptuous to even conceive such an idea?

There was nothing she could do about her rudeness with Burke, but she certainly could find out Serena's and Lola's opinions of this redecorating project before getting too involved in it.

Rising, she went to the kitchen phone and dialed Serena's office number. Karen Breen, Serena's secretary, answered. "Law office."

"Hello, Karen. This is Candace. Is Serena busy?"

"Hi, Candace. Serena's at her desk, but I'm sure she has time to talk to you. Hold on."

In a few moments Serena's voice was in her ear. "Hi, Candy. What's up?"

Candace sat in the chair next to the phone. "I need to talk to you about something, and I'd like you to be brutally honest about it."

Serena laughed. "Brutally?"

"Well, honest, okay?"

"Sure. Go ahead."

"Thanks. I have Charlie's permission to redecorate the house, but then it occurred to me that you might want the house you grew up in to remain exactly as it is."

There was a silence on Serena's end, and Candace bit her lip through it. Then it was over and Serena said cheerfully, "Listen, Candace, and I really mean this. If Dad said it's okay to redecorate, you also have my blessing. Go to it, kiddo."

"You're sure?"

"I'm positive. You know, I'm going to be facing some decorating myself very soon. The construction of our house is coming along on schedule. It should be completely finished by the first of the year."

"Oh, Serena, that's wonderful. I'm so happy for you."

"Yes, well, I'm happy for myself. Trav is...well, what can I say? He's just the greatest guy ever." Serena laughed then. "I'm sure every woman in love thinks that about her man."

"I'm sure she does," Candace agreed, recalling her own happiness with Ron.

"Oh, Candace, I'm sorry," Serena said in a chagrined voice. "I shouldn't be going on like that when you—"

Candace broke in. "Serena, you must never hide your happiness because of me. It would bother me terribly if I thought you were watching your words around me, about any subject. We all loved Ron, and certainly none of us will ever forget him. You, especially, his only sister. But I'm recovering, Serena. I'm returning to normal, and I'm very happy for you and Trav. For Lola and Duke, as well.''

''I can see why Ron loved you so much,'' Serena said gently.

''Yes, he did. I cherish the memories, Serena. So many lovely memories.'' Candace sighed softly.

''But a woman your age can't live on memories for the rest of her life. Someday you're going to meet someone else, Candace, and when you do...'' Serena's voice trailed off, as though she had suddenly gotten the feeling that she was going too far.

''Maybe someday,'' Candace said. ''Not for a while yet, though. Getting back to the house, I'm really quite excited about redoing it.''

''Are you planning to do the entire house?''

''Right now, yes.''

''That's an ambitious project, Candy. You're not intending to do everything yourself, are you? I'm talking about painting now. Girl, if you painted every wall in that big house, you'd be wielding a paintbrush for three years.''

''Once I get a solid plan in mind, I might hire someone to help. I'm not certain of anything yet. Except that I want to do a good job.''

''I'm sure you will.''

''Thanks, Serena. I won't keep you any longer. I'm going to call Lola and get her input, too.''

''Tell her hello for me. I haven't talked to her in several days. Both Trav and I have been very busy, what with our work and the new house. Say hi to Dad for me, too, okay?''

''Will do. And you give Trav my best. Bye, Serena.''

''Goodbye, Candy. Call anytime.''

Candace's call to Lola was virtually the same conversation, except that Lola added, ''We have to get the family together one of these days, Candy. I'm going to work on it. Everyone's been so busy lately, but we can't let other things keep the family apart.''

"I couldn't agree more, Lola. Thanks for the chat. Oh, before I hang up, how are you feeling?" Lola's pregnancy had prompted the question.

"I feel so good I can't believe it. Apparently I'm one of those fortunate women who sail through pregnancy without even one bout of morning sickness."

"That is fortunate, all right. Have you had any bites on the store?" Candace asked. Lola owned a men's-clothing store and had put it up for sale after her marriage.

"A few. Nothing substantial, though. I'm not discouraged. Someone will come along and want to buy it."

"I'm sure they will."

"Candy, if you decide to hire help for your project, I know some reliable people."

"Wonderful. I might be calling you for their names. Bye for now, Lola. Say hello to Duke."

Candace put down the phone, feeling lucky to be a member of the Fanon family. They were always concerned about each other and supportive of any idea one of them might have. She'd already known that, but she was glad she had called Serena and Lola about the house project, anyway. Now there would be no surprised faces when they dropped in and found her knee-deep in paint and wallpaper.

Returning to the living room, she picked up her notebook. Now for that inventory.

Burke walked into Charlie's Place around nine-thirty that morning. As always, Charlie seemed glad to see him. But he was busy with other customers, so Burke took a cup of coffee and a newspaper to a far table and sat down to wait out the rush hour.

He read the paper from the headlines to the last page. Gradually the coffee shop cleared out. It was close to eleven before he and Charlie were alone.

Charlie refilled Burke's cup and brought one for himself to the table. "Busy morning," he said, pulling out a chair and sitting.

"Busy is best in the retail business. More sales, more income."

"Yeah, well, money never was my goal here."

"Charlie, you're the most contented, unruffled man I know. Don't you ever feel stressed out?"

Charlie sipped his coffee. "I used to. A long time ago." He grinned at Burke. "Didn't do a damned bit of good, so I gave it up. Cold turkey."

Burke laughed. "How old are you, Charlie?"

"Fifty-six. Your next question is how come I retired from the phone company before the usual retirement age, right?"

"It does come to mind."

"Well, the bigwigs at the phone company were making some major changes at the time. To cut back on personnel, they offered a bonus, a lifetime of medical insurance and a good retirement income to employees with so much time under their belts. I was tired of climbing poles and took the offer." Charlie's eyes twinkled merrily. "How'd I know it wouldn't be two months before I was climbing the walls."

"Instead of poles," Burke said with a laugh. Charlie laughed, too. Burke felt such a warm camaraderie with Charlie that he knew his decision to speak candidly was right.

His expression sobered. "Charlie, I need to talk to you about something."

"Is it about Candace?"

Burke blinked in surprise. He *would* like to talk about Candace, but what would he say? *Charlie, I fell pretty hard at first sight of her, and she won't give me the time of day. Got any suggestions?* No, he wasn't going to get into that with Candace's father-in-law. Whatever did or did not happen between him and Candace was not Charlie's responsibility.

"No, it's another matter entirely." Charlie was looking at him curiously. Burke cleared his throat. "I'm going to tell you something that will probably surprise the hell out of you."

"You've already got me sitting on the edge of my chair. What's going on?"

"This can't be passed on to anyone else, all right?"

Charlie frowned. "Fine."

"Charlie, I mean not one other person. Not even anyone in your family."

"Whatever you say." Charlie was looking deadly serious about now.

"Okay, here it is. I'm not a teacher and I don't live in Seattle. I'm a member of the governor's task force against drugs in Montana. The reason I'm in Rocky Ford is to locate a man named Benny Slocum. He slipped through our fingers in Helena, and we have reason to believe he came here."

Charlie looked stunned. "You're really not a professor?"

"Never was, Charlie. I've always worked in law enforcement."

"And you're looking for this Slocum fellow. Hell, Burke, why would he come to Rocky Ford?"

"That's what I intend to find out, but first I have to find him. Remember when you mentioned a stranger coming in every so often for coffee and newspapers?"

Charlie sat back. "So that's the reason you've been coming in every day."

"Not the only reason, Charlie," Burke said quietly, realizing that Charlie's feelings were a little hurt. "I look at you as a friend, and I value friendship."

"So do I, Burke, so do I." Charlie fell silent for a few moments, obviously digesting all he'd heard. "Okay, what about this guy? Are you thinking that stranger is Slocum?"

"I'm hoping, Charlie." Burke got up to pull the photo of Benny from his back pocket. He sat down again and pushed the photo across the table. "This is a picture of Slocum. Take a look at it and tell me what you think."

Charlie picked up the photo. He studied it for so long that Burke's hope began fading.

Then Charlie looked up. "Would Slocum dye his hair?"

"I think he'd do anything to keep from being recognized. Why, Charlie?"

"The man who comes in has black hair and mustache, and now that I think of it, he always wears dark glasses, even if the sun's not out, so I've never really seen his eyes. The guy in this picture is blond and clean shaven. Looks younger. I'm not sure, Burke. It could be him, but if it is, he sure did change his appearance."

"But there is a chance he's the man in the photo." Burke's spirits were reviving.

"There's a chance," Charlie concurred. He suddenly looked excited. "What do you want me to do the next time he comes in?"

"I *don't* want you getting hurt," Burke said quickly. "Slocum's a dangerous man, Charlie. If he comes in again, treat him exactly as you did before. Anything else might arouse his suspicion, and I don't want him getting the idea that someone's asking questions about him. Besides, you've got to remember that this guy might *not* be Slocum. Just play it cool."

Charlie rubbed his jaw thoughtfully. "I wish there were a way you could be here all the time. You're the one who should be seeing this guy."

"That's true, but I've been here quite a few mornings and he hasn't appeared. I can't move in, Charlie."

Charlie looked at him for a long time, then his face lit up. "Why not? Burke, that's the answer. Move in with me. There's plenty of room. We could tell people you decided to stay in Rocky Ford a while longer and wanted to get out of that motel. We could tell 'em you're renting one of my bedrooms. Hell, I've got six of them. My regulars wouldn't think a thing about it, and you'd be here around the clock. It's a great idea."

Burke could tell that Charlie was really getting into this. He'd run into the same thing before, where an ordinary citizen got all caught up in being a part of "catching the bad guy." There was nothing wrong with it, although a lot of people thought police work was glamorous and fast-paced, as it was portrayed on television, which couldn't be further from the truth.

But he couldn't deny that Charlie's idea had merit. Even though Charlie couldn't absolutely connect that stranger to Slocum's photo, he had said they might be the same man. Burke couldn't ignore the opportunity to find out for sure, and getting out of the Sundowner was also a good idea. It would certainly throw the local police off his scent.

But Charlie wasn't the only player here. "How would Candace feel about my moving in?" he asked.

"Why would she care?" Charlie frowned then. "On the other hand, she's planning to redecorate the house and might find a guest a problem." Charlie paused to think again. "I think we can get around any objections Candace might have. I'll talk to her."

"Not about the truth, Charlie. I don't want her involved."

"Heck, no, not about the truth. I'll think of something that makes sense, don't worry." He grinned then. "This is really something, Burke. Imagine me helping out on a case like this. Slocum must be a drug dealer, eh?"

"One of the biggest, Charlie. We've been trying to bring him down for a long time now."

"Well, you can count on me. Give me a chance to talk to Candace—a few hours should do it—and then bring your things over."

Burke got to his feet and returned the photo to his back pocket. "Maybe I should call first and make sure you've come to an understanding with Candace."

"Not necessary." Charlie got up, looking like a child in a candy store. "This is really something. I can hardly believe it. Here I've been thinking of you as a professor, and all the time you've been a cop. You know, you're a pretty darned good actor."

Burke laughed. "See you in a few hours, Charlie. But listen, I'll be at the Sundowner—room 128—and if Candace should object to my moving in, call me."

Charlie walked him to the door. "Don't worry, everything will be just fine. See you later."

Candace was making sandwiches for lunch when Charlie walked into the kitchen. Little Ron was in his high chair, munching on soda crackers.

"Hi, big guy," Charlie said to his grandson, pausing to give him a kiss on his rosy, plump cheek. Then, smiling at Candace, he pulled out a chair at the table and sat down. "Those sandwiches look good."

"Everything must be quiet out front," Candace said with a pleased expression. When the coffee shop was busy at noon, she brought lunch to him, but she enjoyed her own lunch more when Charlie ate with her. They always had something to talk about, never anything earthshaking, but Charlie was good company.

"Quiet as a church," Charlie confirmed.

Candace set the plate of sandwiches on the table, along with napkins, place settings, pickles and celery, and poured two glasses of lemonade. Then she took her seat. Before anything else, she cut one of the sandwiches into small pieces and gave them to her son with the comment "He loves tuna, don't you, sweetheart?"

Charlie reached for a sandwich. "So does his grandpa. Oops, almost forgot. Let's say a word of thanks."

They bowed their heads and Charlie said grace, then he looked at Candace and smiled. "I have some news."

"Oh?" Candace took a sip of her lemonade.

"Burke was in. He's going to stay in town for a few more weeks, but he's tired of that motel. He was going to look for something to rent."

An unnerving premonition invaded Candace's system. "Something, as in what? An apartment? A house? He's going to have a problem finding a rental for only a few weeks, Charlie."

"That's exactly what I told him. Guess things are different in Seattle, but around here rentals are at a premium and owners don't have to monkey around with short-term renters. Anyway, I told him he could rent one of our extra bedrooms."

Candace slowly lowered her sandwich. Her body was suddenly rigid with tension. Burke would be living here, in the house with them? No, no, *no!*

But however she felt internally, she couldn't voice her strenuous objections to Charlie. This was his house, Burke was his friend and he was obviously tickled pink over Burke moving in.

"I told him you were planning to redecorate the house, honey, and he said that he'd be sure to stay out of your way."

Candace's heart was in her throat. Envisioning Burke eating with them, using a bedroom, *living* with them, was so disturbing she could barely breathe. In fact, the only thing she could think of to say that wouldn't hurt Charlie's feelings had to do with the redecorating project.

"Once I get started, there'll probably be some mess to contend with," she said in a thin little voice.

"It won't bother Burke, honey. And you're not to worry that it might. You just go right ahead with your plans."

How could she? Nothing would be normal with Burke in the house. Her appetite had vanished just from this conversation. How would she react when he was actually underfoot twenty-four hours a day, looking at her with those electric blue eyes, smiling at her and trying only heaven knew what? She didn't want to know Burke better. He made her edgy and uncomfortable. He made her behave rudely. He caused unwanted feelings within her, even to altering her personality.

But she could say none of that to Charlie. Her disruptive feelings toward Burke were her problem, not Charlie's. The elated expression on his face told the tale; he was actually beaming from ear to ear over Burke moving in for a few weeks.

Sighing inwardly, Candace forced herself to pick up her sandwich and take a small bite. Regardless of how uneasy and troubled she felt about this turn of events, she had to behave as normally as possible.

Pray God Burke's residency would only be for a few weeks.

## Chapter Five

Burke prowled his motel room, thinking of what he was about to do. Candace wouldn't like him moving in, but would she speak plainly enough to make Charlie understand how she felt? Burke really didn't want to put her on the spot like that, and neither did he want to give her a tangible reason for disliking him. But he had to do his job wherever it might lead him. Right now living on Foxworth Street made sense. Instinct told him he was on the right track; years of experience told him that the track could turn in another direction tomorrow. He might be staying with Charlie one night or a dozen.

Tugging at an ear, he shoved the worry over Candace's reaction into the back of his mind. All he could do was be as unobtrusive to Fanon family life—and stay out of Candace's way—as much as possible.

Sitting on the edge of the bed, he picked up the phone and dialed Hal's office number in Helena. It took a few minutes, but Hal finally came on the line. "Morrison."

"It's Burke, Hal."

"Any breaks?"

"Possibly. Nothing you can hang your hat on yet, but I do have one slim lead. The reason I called was to let you know I'm moving into a private home. The phone number is 555-6623. I might not always be able to talk, but if you need me, you can call and I'll call you back from a pay phone."

"A private home? How come?"

"Because I trust the man who lives there and confided in him. His name is Charlie Fanon, and he has a little coffee shop in the front of his house. Charlie said a stranger's been coming in on an irregular basis. I showed him Slocum's photo, and he said there's a chance the guy is Benny. He couldn't positively ID him from the photo, as the man coming in has black hair and mustache. But you and I both know that Benny is damned good with disguises.

"Anyway, Charlie suggested I use his extra bedroom so I can see this guy for myself. I called to bring you up to speed."

"Fine, glad you did." Hal cleared his throat. "Burke, your mother's been phoning and demanding to know where you are. I think you'd better give *her* a call."

Burke let out a groan. He had told Meredith that he would be working on a case and away from Helena for an unpredictable length of time; apparently she thought he'd been out of touch long enough.

"I'll call her," he told Hal. Meredith knew all the right people—in her estimation—in Helena, including the governor, and if she bowed her neck and really decided to find her son, she would do it. The last thing he needed was his strong-willed mother calling every day to tout Diane Prescott's good points. "I'll do it right now," he added.

"Good. Anything else?" Hal asked.

"That's it for now. Talk to you soon."

They hung up. With a grim expression, Burke picked up the phone again and dialed his mother's number. A maid answered, which he'd known would be the case, and he waited impatiently for Meredith to come on the line.

He finally heard her mellow voice. "Hello, Burke."

"Hello, Mother. How are you?"

"Very well, thank you. I hope you're calling from your condo in Helena."

"No, Mother, I'm not."

There was a heavy sigh in his ear. "Burke, I insist you give me a number where I can reach you. There are times when I really must talk to you."

"Even if it means endangering my life?"

"Are you telling me you're working on *that* kind of case?" There was shock in Meredith's voice.

Damn, Burke thought. He never should have said that. "There's no immediate danger, Mother, but I do need complete anonymity."

"I will never understand how you can bear being cut off from your roots this way. Do you go so far as to work under another name?"

"In some cases, yes. This time, no. Mother, I'm sorry my job distresses you. We've talked about it many times, and—"

"It more than distresses me, Burke. You put yourself in danger unnecessarily. You run all over the state doing work you don't have to do. Your true responsibility lies here, in Helena, taking care of the Mallory assets. You should be married and giving me grandchildren. Diane won't wait around forever, you know."

She had finally said it, *Diane*.

Burke never raised his voice or let his vexation show. "We'll talk when I return to Helena, Mother."

"And when will that be?"

"Right now I have no idea. I'm sorry, but that's the only answer I can give you."

"A very unsatisfactory answer, Burke." The disapproval in Meredith's voice was similar to the growling of a volcano on the verge of eruption. Not that Burke had ever seen his mother lose her temper. But shrieking in anger was not Meredith's way. She dealt with problems and hurdles in a ladylike, lethally effective manner.

All Burke could do was break up this conversation, which in his opinion was going nowhere. Besides, they'd had it before, too many times to count.

"I have to hang up now. I have an appointment. Goodbye, Mother. I'll call again when I can."

With a sigh of relief, Burke put down the phone. What made Meredith think Diane Prescott wanted to marry *him?* Diane had never once given him the impression that she wanted to be more than his friend. In fact, she was even blasé about friendship. She was a pleasant, attractive woman with a life of her own. Burke suspected that the marriage idea was strictly his mother's. She had met Diane, decided she would be the perfect wife for her son and that was that. Her mind was made up, and one didn't easily change Meredith Mallory's mind on any subject. Burke could only hope that she wasn't badgering Diane—subtly, of course—about marrying him.

"Damnation," he muttered while getting to his feet. His bags were packed, and he grabbed them up and carried them out to his vehicle. From there he went to the motel office to settle his bill.

Charlie showed Burke to a bedroom, then closed the door. Burke set his suitcases on the floor and looked at the older man, who seemed to be jumping out of his skin.

"Burke," Charlie said in an excited whisper. "He was here. He came in right after you left." Burke was floored. He should have been here. Damn! "Burke, I'm almost positive he's the guy in the photo."

"You treated him as always?" Burke's pulse was racing.

"Sure did, just like you told me. But listen, this time I paid closer attention when he left. He walked east, Burke, and east is where those apartment houses are situated. Bet you anything he's staying in one of 'em."

"Could be, but he also might be parking his car down the block so no one in your shop gets a look at it. Slocum's a clever, slippery man, Charlie. He has a high IQ and he pays attention to details."

Charlie scoffed. "He can't be very smart if he's dealing drugs."

"He's smart, believe it," Burke rebutted. "There's big money to be made in drugs, Charlie, and even smart people get involved. If all criminals were stupid or dense, police work would be a lot easier." Burke could tell that the concept of intelligence in criminals went against Charlie's grain. Being a completely honest, law-abiding person himself, he couldn't grasp anyone with half a brain dealing drugs for a living. But many ordinary citizens felt that way.

What went against Burke's grain was that he'd missed seeing the guy by only a few minutes today. That wasn't the only thing bothering him, however.

"Candace's car is in the driveway, but I didn't see her when I came in. Do you know where she is? I'd like to say hello." *She's probably hiding in her bedroom so she doesn't have to say hello.*

"She's here somewhere," Charlie replied.

"How did she react to the idea of my moving in?"

"She didn't mind one little bit, Burke. Listen, I have to get back to the business. Got two tables of pinochle players to serve. Feel free to look around. You'll run into Candace in one room or another." He paused for a second, then added, "I want you to feel at home here. This bedroom has a private bath, through that door over there. Anyhow, make yourself comfortable. Use the laundry facilities, watch TV, eat a snack, or anything else you might want to do."

"Thanks, Charlie. I really appreciate what you're doing."

Charlie looked proud again. And thrilled. "Glad to help out, Burke. See ya later."

Burke glanced at his suitcases after Charlie left, but before he unpacked or did one other thing, he had to talk to Candace. So, she didn't mind him moving in one little bit? Yeah, right. He'd believe that when hell froze over. Or if she told him so herself, which wasn't apt to happen. Regardless, he had to find out how she really felt. He hoped he wasn't merely seeking another tongue-lashing for some strange reason, or harboring an unlikely wish that she had changed her mind about him.

Maybe what he really wanted to accomplish was to let her know that just because they would be living under the same roof didn't mean that he intended becoming a threat to her peace of mind. He would not be making passes or hinting at anything personal between them with either subtle or blatant innuendo, and she should know that.

Leaving his room, he walked down the hall of the bedroom wing. The large country kitchen was empty, and he passed through it on his way to the living room.

He stopped stock-still in the doorway. Candace was on a stepladder. The drapes on all the windows had been drawn wide open. She held a tape measure and was reaching up, stretching to measure the top width of one of the windows.

Burke's heart was suddenly in his throat. Just seeing her made his blood run faster. She was wearing jeans and a white shirt. The jeans were old, faded and soft looking, and they hugged her hips and thighs. Her blond hair gleamed from light coming through the window. She was the loveliest woman he'd ever known, and he could tell himself a thousand times to ignore her, to keep cool around her, but he just wasn't able to control his feelings. He wanted her as a man wanted a woman, and he knew, sadly, that it would never happen. Why didn't she like him? What was there about him that put her off?

He suddenly tensed. The stepladder was old and rickety. Candace was moving up from the fourth step to the fifth to better reach the top of the window. Everything happened so fast. The ladder gave way, Candace began falling with a surprised yelp and Burke ran to the rescue.

With a clatter, the ladder struck a table and lamp. How Burke moved so fast he would never know, but he caught Candace in his arms before she hit the floor. Even though her weight was slight, the impact brought him to his knees.

Her eyes were big with shock, and she looked at her benefactor as though he had materialized out of thin air.

Holding her, even under these conditions, felt incredible to Burke. He dampened his dry lips with the tip of his tongue. "Are you all right?"

"You . . . you caught me." She seemed dazed, as though not quite grasping what had happened. "How . . . ?"

"I was just coming in to say hello and saw the ladder teetering." It thrilled Burke that she was at long last looking straight into his eyes. Her own eyes contained remnants of the fear she must have felt when she realized a fall was imminent.

"Lucky for me," she said in a husky voice. Lying across Burke's lap, in his arms, should not feel so good. He had saved her from a nasty fall, but she was perfectly all right and knew she should get up and away from him. But his eyes were so blue, and she felt herself drowning in them. She had not felt so soft and womanly, so safe and protected, in such a long time, and she couldn't seem to force herself to ignore or destroy those remarkable feelings.

Burke's system was rife with emotions that weren't all that familiar to him. He would sit here and hold Candace all day if she permitted it, but that wasn't all that was going on behind his warm and tender expression. This lady was special, and what magic did she possess that made her stand out so acutely from the other women he knew?

He realized the air around them seemed to be charged with electricity. He was becoming more aroused with every breath, and all of his thoughts compacted into one: he wanted to kiss her, more than he'd ever wanted anything.

She was still looking into his eyes, and he saw no denial, no remoteness, none of the guardedness she had thus far shown him. Slowly he brought his head down; gently he pressed his lips to hers.

Her warm breath mingled with his. My Lord, she was kissing him back! Had he died and gone to heaven?

"Mommy?"

Ronnie was standing in the doorway in his underwear, dragging a small blue blanket, his little face flushed from sleep.

"Oh, Lord," Candace mumbled while scrambling to her feet. Her own face was as flushed as her son's, and she certainly hadn't been sleeping. She spoke to her son. "Did you wake up from your nap, sweetheart?"

"Waked up," Ronnie said.

Burke slowly got up. "Hi, big guy."

"H'wo," Ronnie replied. "Me thirsty, Mommy."

"I'll get your juice, darling." Without even the briefest glance at Burke, Candace scooped up her son, blanket and all, and hurried from the room.

Burke stood there. Without the baby's interruption, how far would Candace have let him go? More kisses? Deeper, sexier kisses? He gritted his teeth as the desire racking his body gained in intensity. He had to stop thinking about it.

Walking over to the ladder, he moved it from away from the table and lamp. It was an ancient old thing, and Candace should not have been using it, except for maybe the first few steps. But she'd been on the fourth step and climbing to the fifth, extremely dangerous business. Burke would bet anything that Charlie didn't know his daughter-in-law had been using the rickety old thing.

Picking it up, he carried it to the kitchen, where Candace was tending to her son's thirst. "Is this the best ladder you have?"

She flicked him a quick glance. "It's the *only* ladder we have."

Burke heard the resentment in her voice. She was back to not liking him, or acting as though she didn't. Obviously she regretted that kiss, and her regret was his pain.

He spoke tonelessly, concealing the ache in his chest. "It's not safe. You're not to use it again."

Her eyes widened. "I beg your pardon. Who are you to be telling me what I can or cannot do?"

"Like it or not, you won't be using it again," he said flatly. Carrying the ladder outside, he stomped it into several jagged pieces.

Candace came out wearing an angry expression. "How dare you destroy someone else's property."

"Don't worry. I intend to replace it." He gave her a hard look. "With one that won't collapse and cause you to break your stubborn neck in another fall."

After glaring a dirty look at him, Candace whirled and went back inside. In the kitchen her spiteful expression dissolved into guilt and puzzlement. How could she have let Burke kiss her? Worse, how could she have kissed him back?

And she wasn't stubborn, she wasn't!

Or she never had been before now. Emotionally she was wringing her hands. What in heaven's name was happening to her?

Burke drove to the hardware store and bought the best stepladder in the place. Even so, it wasn't a costly purchase. Laying it in the back of his vehicle, he returned to the Fanon home. The whole thing hadn't taken a half hour.

Propping the ladder against the house, he went inside. Candace was in the kitchen, chopping vegetables at the counter. She barely acknowledged his presence with a brief glance over her shoulder.

"Where do you want me to put the new ladder?" Burke said to the back of her head.

"In the toolshed," she replied without turning around.

"And where will I find the toolshed?"

"It's on the opposite side of the house from the driveway."

"Is it locked?"

"The key's on the ledge over the door."

He was about to say something caustic about the ledge over a door being the first place a thief would look for a key, but Ronnie ran into the room with a big grin before he could speak.

Burke's attitude instantly softened. "Hi, pal."

"H'wo Mitter Ma . . . Ma . . ."

Burke hunkered down to be on a level with the boy. "'Mr. Mallory' is a mouthful for a young fellow like you. Can you say 'Burke'?"

Candace spun around. "I would prefer he call you Mr. Mallory, if you don't mind."

Burke ignored her. "Can you say 'Burke,' Ronnie?"

"Burke," the boy said.

"Great. That's what I want you to call me, okay?"

"Okay."

Burke smiled. "Let's shake on it." He held out his hand. "That's what men do when they've come to an agreement on something."

The boy put his tiny hand in Burke's. "Me big boy, Burke."

"You sure are, pal, a real big boy. You and I are going to be good friends."

"Is that a fact?" Candace said coolly.

Burke pulled himself up and looked at her just as hard as she was looking at him. "Are you sure you want to discuss this at this particular moment?"

Candace's gaze went to Ronnie, who was staring up at Burke with an expression she could only describe as adoring. It stunned her. Ronnie had his grandfather for a male role model; he didn't need Burke Mallory.

Furious, she again showed her back to Burke. He stood there for a minute, staring at her and not caring if she knew it. Then he looked down at Ronnie.

"I have to leave now, pal. See you later, okay?"

"Me go, too?" the boy asked eagerly.

"I don't think so. Maybe some other time."

That was too much for Candace to take silently. Bristling, she faced Burke and her son. "Ronnie, darling, why don't you go and see Grandpa? I'll bet he's lonesome for you."

The boy took off running. Candace's eyes narrowed on Burke. "You will never take my son anywhere, do you understand? Not only that, do not undermine my authority with Ronnie ever again."

"I undermined your authority by making it easier for him to address me?"

"I told you I preferred him calling you Mr. Mallory. You ignored what I said and did as you pleased. Doing whatever suits your fancy might be how you're accustomed to living, but when it comes to my son, you will abide by my wishes. Do you understand?"

This could turn into a real fight, Burke realized. After a good long stare at this small, fire-breathing woman, he turned on his heel and walked out of the house seething. Oh, yes, he understood—perfectly. Not only didn't she want to like him herself, but she didn't want her son to like him.

So how in hell had she lain in his arms after her close call with that old ladder, and then not only permitted him to kiss her but kissed him back?

Climbing into his vehicle, he drove away shaking his head.

In the kitchen Candace didn't know whether to weep or shriek. Who *was* she with Burke Mallory? Kissing him one minute, telling him off the next?

Her emotions were out of control. She recognized the problem, but had no solution for it.

And just why was Burke hanging around Rocky Ford in the first darned place? Anything of historical or geological import in the immediate area could be seen and explored in minute detail in a matter of days. Why hadn't he looked around and moved on, as would be expected of a man dedicated to exploring a vast region such as Montana?

There was something fishy about his story. Charlie had been completely taken in by Burke's charm, obviously, but she smelled a rat. Was he even a teacher at all? It wasn't out of the question that he was a clever con man, drifting around the country, charming gullible people like Charlie and then moving in and living off of them for as long as he could.

The flaws in that reasoning began stacking up in her mind. Burke wore quality clothing. He drove an expensive vehicle. He didn't appear to be without financial means, not when he'd gone and bought a new ladder just because he didn't like the old one. Would a man looking for a handout spend what money he did have on a ladder?

Okay, so it didn't add up. He might not be conning Charlie into free room and board, but there was still something very peculiar about his extended stay in Rocky Ford.

And there was also something darned peculiar about her personal reactions to Burke. She wasn't looking for a man, and yet she had let one kiss her.

Candace lifted her chin and straightened her shoulders. It was *not* going to happen again, not if he lived under this roof for the entire winter.

Immediately she wilted. He certainly wouldn't be here that long, would he?

## Chapter Six

Burke got back a few hours later, washed up, then sat in the living room with Charlie awaiting dinner. He wondered about offering to help Candace in the kitchen, then thought better of it. Candace wouldn't want him in there with her, not when she didn't want him in the house at all.

Ronnie was in and out of the room, wearing a red cowboy hat and galloping along on a hobby horse.

"He loves horses," Charlie informed Burke with a warm, indulgent grin for his grandson. "Duke took him for a ride on a real horse a couple of times. Our little cowboy here was instantly hooked."

"Duke? Oh, I know who you mean. Duke Sheridan, your niece's husband. Owns a big ranch, I believe you said."

Charlie nodded. "We'll take a drive out there one of these days so you can see the ranch and meet Duke. Real nice fellow. You'll like him. For that matter, I'm sure you'll like Trav, my daughter's husband, too. Trav's got a great sense of humor. Both of my girls made good marriages."

"So did your son," Burke said quietly.

After a moment of introspective silence, Charlie nodded again. "I know."

"I didn't say that to renew your grief, Charlie. It's just that Candace..." He shut his mouth. What had he been going to say? Something personal, no doubt, and how dare he say anything personal about Candace to her father-in-law?

Charlie's eyes narrowed shrewdly. "You like her, don't you?"

There was no point in lying or hedging; he'd given himself away. "Do you object?"

"You want to hear something funny? The first day you walked into the shop and we talked, I thought of Candace. No, I don't object."

"I appreciate your trust, Charlie."

"That works both ways, Burke. We hit it off right away, didn't we?"

"I'd say so," Burke replied. "Charlie, I've been thinking of something. Do you see any pattern to the suspect's visits to your shop? What I mean is, does he come in every two days, for instance? Every three? Is there any pattern at all, time of day, for example? Or maybe he only comes in when the sun is shining. I know I'm grasping at straws with this theory, but if there is any kind of pattern... Well, I'm sure you know where I'm coming from."

Thinking about it, Charlie rubbed his jaw. After a few moments he shook his head. "I wish I could say yes, Burke. But if there's a pattern to his visits, I haven't noticed it."

"Yes, well, like I said, it's only a theory. Besides, there was no reason for you to—" Candace suddenly appeared in the doorway, and Burke stopped talking.

Her expression cooled considerably, as though she had just caught him talking about her. Burke felt a surge of frustration. She thought the worst and he couldn't explain. And she looked so beautiful in another nice dress. Apparently it was her habit to change for dinner—a thoroughly commendable practice, in his opinion.

Her gaze finally moved to Charlie. "Dinner is ready." Gathering up her little buckeroo and his hobby horse, she left the room.

"Damn," Burke muttered. "She thinks we were talking about her, Charlie."

"Yes, I believe she does." Getting up out of his chair, he gave Burke a smile. "But I'm sure you can handle it, my friend. Maybe not tonight and maybe not next week, but eventually you'll handle it. Come on, let's go have our supper."

Candace just knew that Burke had been pumping information about her out of Charlie. Or trying to. After all, what could Charlie tell him? She lived a simple life, tending her son and the house, and wouldn't have it any other way. Considering her widowhood, that is. Charlie was a wonderful man, but he wasn't a substitute for Ron. There *was* no substitute for Ron, she thought fervently, shooting Burke an accusatory glance across the table.

In the next instant she was glad he'd been looking at Charlie and hadn't seen it. Since there was nothing she could do about Burke moving in, she should try to be civil. Especially at the dinner table. Besides, she trusted Charlie implicitly; however clever Burke might be, he would get only so much information out of Charlie, particularly about a member of the family.

The two men had been talking about the Sheridan Ranch while they ate, with Charlie finally asking, "Ever been on a really big ranch, Burke?"

Burke could barely hold back a laugh. Among the Mallorys' many assets was a thirty-thousand-acre cattle-and-horse ranch in New Mexico. It was the one asset he didn't mind checking on, and, in fact, had the ranch been in Montana instead of New Mexico, he would probably be living on it. Moving to New Mexico was out of the question. He felt obligated to remain near his mother, at least within the boundaries of Montana, and didn't feel that a strong sense of responsibility made him a mama's boy, either. Meredith loved and needed him, however much he disagreed with some of her ideas.

Even so, he let her run his life only so much. If she had her way, he would be living in the Mallory mansion with her, which he hadn't done since he'd gotten out of high school and went away to college.

As for "really big ranches," yes, he'd spent quite a lot of time on one. His answer to Charlie's question, however, was a casual "I have had that pleasure, yes."

"During your exploration of Montana?" Candace asked, surprising Burke, as she hadn't been participating in the conversation. A second surprise was the doubt he saw in her eyes when he looked at her to respond to her question. It hit him then that she doubted everything about him, especially his story of exploring Montana. Obviously she was an intelligent, perceptive woman, and something about his story didn't ring true.

He decided to be truthful in this instance. "No," he said clearly. "That particular ranch is in New Mexico."

"Oh? Then you've also explored New Mexico. Isn't it nice that you can take so much time from your teaching career to explore various states." It was an observation, not a question.

"There are also summers and holiday vacations, Candace," Burke said.

Charlie started fidgeting. Candace's comments and questions startled him. He had never seen her behave rudely to anyone, and what she was saying to Burke bordered on rudeness.

And then, out of the blue, he caught on. She was attracted to Burke and fighting it. Probably thought liking another man was disloyal to Ron's memory. That was too bad, and he would like to tell Candace that she was entitled to happiness. He couldn't do that, of course. Not at this point. But there was one thing he knew for certain: if these two great people actually fell in love, nothing would make *him* happier.

Charlie's eyes suddenly sparkled. A romance was in the making right in front of him, and he was actually helping a cop—a special agent and friend—to bring down a drug dealer.

For Charlie Fanon, at least, life was good.

Candace heard Charlie come into her son's bedroom. Bending over Ronnie's crib, she kissed his soft, smooth cheek. "Grandpa's here, little darling. Sleep well."

Smiling at Charlie, she left him alone to say his special good-night to his grandson. Sometimes, if Ronnie didn't seem inclined to go right to sleep, Charlie would read him a story. This evening ritual had been Charlie's idea, and after only a few times, Ronnie wouldn't close his eyes until he'd said good-night to Gampy.

In the hallway just outside the room, Candace stopped. Undoubtedly Burke was parked in the living room. Her plan for the evening was to look through a stack of home-decorating magazines she had recently purchased, and she wanted to do it in the chair she was accustomed to using, with Charlie and the television set for company. Burke's presence in the house changed everything. The way he looked at her was especially disturbing, as it kept her constantly aware of his maleness.

She could sit in the kitchen, of course, or in her bedroom. But she wanted to sit in her chair in the living room, under her reading lamp. In fact, the magazines were already on the small table next to her chair.

"Oh, well," she mumbled with an exasperated sigh. Burke was going to be a thorn in her side for as long as he stayed in Rocky Ford. She couldn't hide in her bedroom every evening.

With a more determined set to her shoulders, she headed for the living room. To her wide-eyed surprise, it was empty. Was Burke hiding in *his* bedroom?

But then, maybe he wasn't even in the house. Curiosity drove her to a window. Peering out into the darkness, her lips pursed; his vehicle was gone.

So, she wouldn't have to put up with him gawking at her, after all, she thought as she went to her chair, turned on the reading lamp and sat down.

But why didn't Burke's absence bring a sense of relief? Was it because she was wondering where he had gone?

Yeah, right, she thought cynically. Where does a young, virile man go at night? To a bar, of course. To find a woman, of course.

With her jaw clenched tightly and resentment in her soul, she reached for the stack of magazines and brought them to her lap. It *was* resentment she was feeling, she told herself. She most definitely was not jealous. Why on earth would she be jealous because a man she didn't even like was on the prowl?

She flipped her hair back in a disdainful gesture. Who cared what Burke Mallory did at night? Certainly not her.

But after turning only a few pages of the first magazine on her lap, she laid her head back and stared into space. Was some mystical force toying with her emotions? She didn't want to like Burke, and it seemed to be happening anyway. How could that be? She wasn't ready for another man, and yet she had let Burke kiss her. His strong arms holding her had felt... heavenly. If Ronnie hadn't awakened from his nap and come in when he did... If she and Burke had been all alone in the house...

She breathed a sigh of utter confusion just as Charlie walked in.

"Our little guy is out for the night," Charlie announced as he sat in his own special chair. He noticed the magazines on her lap. "What are those, honey?"

"Home-decorating magazines. They're full of photos and ideas for dressing up a house. Most of them are too elaborate, though. I don't want to do anything fussy. The best part of this house is its homeyness. Changing that would be a mistake. Even though I'm far from an expert on home decor, I know that much."

Charlie couldn't agree more, but he only nodded pleasantly. "I have faith in your good sense, honey."

"Yes, well, sometimes I wonder," Candace muttered. She wasn't talking about the house now. "Um, Burke went out, apparently."

"Apparently," Charlie said calmly. While Candace had been bathing her son and putting him to bed, Burke had told Charlie about how he'd been dropping in at various taverns at night with the hope of spotting Benny. He had to stick with it, even though instinct told him that his best bet was right here in Charlie's Place.

It bothered Charlie to lie to Candace. In the first place, he wasn't a liar with anyone, and in the second, now that he was pretty certain she was interested in Burke, maybe she should know the truth.

But he'd given Burke his word to remain silent about the true nature of his business in Rocky Ford, and Charlie's word was his bond.

"Want the TV on, honey?"

Candace knew Charlie had favorite programs for almost every night of the week, so she said yes. Using the remote, Charlie clicked on the set.

Before Burke's intrusion into Charlie's and her lives, Candace had truly enjoyed their quiet evenings with television and each other. Tonight she felt fragmented and edgy. How late would Burke stay out? Was he a drinker?

Oh, no, not that, she thought frantically. She had to find out. No matter how long he stayed out, she had to wait up and see his condition for herself. If he was a drinker, that was the end of it for her.

Her heart sank with that thought. Did it mean that if he *wasn't* a drinker, she was susceptible to a personal relationship with him? Oh, if only he would tire of the area and leave!

That wish dissolved into a heap of ashes when she realized it had created a painfully empty sensation in her midsection.

She suddenly couldn't sit still any longer. Getting up, she told Charlie, "I'm going to bake some cookies."

Chewing on his bottom lip, Charlie watched her leave the room. She wasn't happy over liking Burke. Probably feeling guilty and suffering over it. Things would work out—they always did—but he hated Candace having to fight her way from grief to normalcy all on her own.

And yet there was no other way. Everyone who lost a loved one had to go through it; he was doing it himself.

The cookies were baked and put away, Charlie had gone to bed, the TV was off and Candace was back in her chair, thumbing her way through the stack of magazines. It was nearing midnight, long past her usual bedtime, and she was yawning. When the pages began blurring, she laid her head back and closed her eyes. In minutes she was sleeping.

Burke let himself in with the key Charlie had given him, moving very quietly. But then, once inside, he saw the light coming from the living room. It was much brighter than the dim night-light burning in the kitchen. It was only reasonable to assume that someone was still up. Still, he tiptoed across the kitchen floor and then stopped cold at the living-room doorway. Seeing Candace asleep in her chair startled him, and he immediately wondered if he should wake her. There were magazines on her lap; obviously she'd been reading.

Frowning indecisively, he silently walked into the room and perched on the edge of a sofa cushion. In sleep she looked like a teenager. Her hair shone like spun gold in the light from her reading lamp. She touched him in a way that no other woman ever had, and he couldn't stop himself from looking at her and absorbing every tiny detail of her beautiful face and figure. Even her hands were perfectly formed, with pretty oval nails. Her wrists looked delicate, as did her ankles.

Realizing that he was getting some very serious ideas about Candace Fanon, he leaned back to ponder it all. He'd never thought about love or marriage very much; his chosen profession and life-style had always been full and rewarding. Certainly he hadn't felt that anything was missing from his life before meeting Candace. Now he wasn't so sure.

And he was deceiving her every hour of every day. Hell, he was still deceiving Charlie. Charlie thought he was a cop and that was the long and the short of it. But there was so much more that Charlie didn't know. If Charlie was familiar with Helena, the Mallory name might register. The truth was that Burke didn't like telling people about his family's wealth. It seemed like bragging to him, and since he hadn't contributed one dollar to the family coffers, he felt that he had nothing to brag about. Except for some financially shrewd and probably not altogether honest ancestors.

Well, he couldn't go to bed and just leave Candace sleeping in a chair. Rising, he went over to stand next to her. "Candace?" he said softly. She never budged.

He took a breath and tried again. "Candace?" Her slow, even breathing remained constant. Finally he knelt at the side of the chair and leaned forward. "Candace?" At this range her unique scent assailed his senses. What kind of soap or perfume did she use to attain that arousing fragrance?

"Candace," he whispered, shaken by the intensity of desire he was suddenly feeling for this special woman. He wanted to kiss her, to take her in his arms, to make her his.

His next breath nearly choked him. Candace, still asleep, had lifted her left arm and wound it around his neck. Then, with a soft, moaning sound deep in her throat, she snuggled her head into the curve of his neck and shoulder.

He knew she wasn't aware of whom she was snuggling with, but she was exactly where he'd just been dreaming of having her and he couldn't push her away. He brought his own arm up and curled it around her, bringing her even closer. His hand cautiously rose to the silken strands of her hair, and he turned his head slightly to press his lips to her forehead.

His heart was hammering in his chest. His mind was feverish with erotic images. If they were alone ... if this was their house ... if there was no dissension between them. He could see himself slowly undressing her, ardently caressing and kissing every inch of her face and body. His own body was in agony; this was utter torture, but he couldn't back away.

No, he *had* to back away, and before she woke up, too. If she suddenly awoke and found herself in his arms, she would accuse him of taking advantage of her while she slept.

With his jaw tightly clenched, he carefully and gently took her arm from his neck and laid her hand on the magazines on her lap. Then he staggered to his feet and stumbled to the doorway, where he leaned against the woodwork, giving his raging system and overfast heartbeat time to calm down.

He knew he would never forget the past few minutes. They would haunt his dreams and forever remain the most magical of his life.

Finally he returned to the kitchen, opened and closed the back door with a noticeable bang and then stomped across the hard kitchen floor to the living-room doorway.

This time Candace was stirring. She opened her eyes and saw him. "Oh! I . . . I must have dozed."

"I didn't know who was still up," Burke said. "It's past midnight."

Candace was scrambling, moving the magazines to the table, getting to her feet. Burke didn't look or sound drunk, and that simple fact unnerved her.

She spoke nervously. Heaven forbid that he should think she had waited up on his account. "I rarely stay up this late. Once in awhile, but...not usually." A fragment of a dream suddenly flitted through her mind. She'd been with a man, a gentle, loving man who had tenderly touched her hair and kissed her forehead. The thing that bothered her about the sliver of dream was that she knew without the slightest doubt that the man wasn't Ron.

"I . . . really must get to bed. Good night." As hastily as she could manage without looking silly or schoolgirlish, she headed for the door.

"Good night," Burke said quietly as she passed in front of him. After a few minutes of internal combustion—Lord, that tiny woman affected him—he turned off her reading lamp and went to his own bedroom.

Thinking of Candace in bed just across the hall kept him awake for a long time. Moving in with Charlie was sensible as far as his investigation went, but how wise was it for him personally?

After all, falling for a woman who was so openly opposed to any sort of a relationship with him was hardly smart. He could be in for some big-time heartache, and that had never happened to him before.

He didn't much care for the idea.

Burke was wrong about Candace being in bed. After checking on her son, kissing the soft baby curls at his nape and straightening his blanket, she went to her bedroom, changed into a nightgown and robe, then sat in her rocking chair instead of going to bed.

That scrap of a dream bothered her, not because she would dream of a man but because it seemed so real. The more she thought of it, the more real it became. What was most upsetting was how certain she was about her dream-lover not being Ron. Was she dreaming of another man because of Burke? Because he had kissed her—reminding her that she was a young, healthy woman living a celibate life?

A shudder passed through her body, and she wrapped her arms around herself to ward off the emotional chill. She had been a virgin when she met Ron. Falling in love with him had been wonderful, but she had started worrying about the first time they would make love. He had seemed so confident and sure of himself, and she couldn't visualize him as anything but very experienced with women.

Imagine her surprise during their first time together when he confessed in loving tones that he was almost as inexperienced as she was. It had made her love him even more. They had experimented and discovered the joys of sex together.

Candace sighed soulfully. Sex had become a major factor in their marriage. To be deprived of sexual fulfillment hadn't seemed so cruel until now; obviously there'd been other aspects of her grief that had been far more important.

But tonight she deeply, painfully felt the emptiness of living without a man. Her heartache lay in the pit of her stomach, instead of in her taut, rigid chest where it belonged. Her body malevolently throbbed with desire, angering her to the point of fixing blame. This was all Burke's fault. His kiss after the ladder had collapsed had awakened her libido, she thought resentfully. How dare he take advantage of the situation and kiss her?

At least now she knew why she had kissed him back. Any attractive man would have caused the same reaction. If Charlie knew the misery Burke was causing her, would he ask him to move out?

Candace's pulse beat faster at the thought of discussing her problem with Charlie. *He's too sexy, too handsome, and he's driving me up the wall, Charlie.* No, she couldn't embarrass them both with that sort of conversation. This was something she had to work through herself. Every problem had a solution; hers in this instance was to stay out of Burke's way.

Her shoulders slumped. She was kidding herself with that idea. There was no way she could ignore Burke, not as long as he lived in Charlie's house.

And her discomfort wasn't all Burke's fault, either, she thought in a sudden burst of honesty. Why had she worried whether he was a drinker or not? Why had she waited up to find out?

Groaning in abject misery, she covered her face with her hands. It was too soon for her to be wanting another man. What was wrong with her?

## Chapter Seven

"Candace? Lola's on the phone for you," Charlie called through the connecting door between the coffee shop and living quarters of the house.

"Thanks, Charlie." Candace picked up the kitchen extension. The phone had rung about ten minutes earlier, so he and Lola had obviously chatted. "Lola, how are you?"

"Planning a family get-together. It's about time we all saw each other under one roof, don't you agree?"

"Absolutely. So, what've you got in mind?" Candace was smiling, though slightly envious. Lola was the most upbeat person she knew, vivacious and aggressive. Candace's shyness had often been a burden, and she couldn't help wishing she could be more like Lola.

"Dinner at the ranch on Sunday. Trav's out of town, but Serena's coming. Charlie seemed excited about it. He was sure you'd come, but I wanted to ask you for myself. How does it sound?"

"Wonderful. You know I love the ranch. It'll be great fun."

"I think so. Oh, by the way, Charlie mentioned a guest in your house. Naturally I told him to bring the guy along on Sunday. Charlie said he's a college professor from Seattle and then changed the subject. Anyway, I got the impression he'd said all he was going to about it. But I have a most intriguing question, and maybe you can answer it. How did a professor make his way from a college in Seattle, Washington, to the Fanon home in Rocky Ford, Montana?"

Candace heaved a small sigh. "Who knows? He says he's been exploring Montana and became particularly fond of this area. Then he mentioned something to Charlie about getting tired of motels, and apparently that was all it took. Charlie invited him to move in."

"Yes, well, you know Charlie. Everybody's his friend. Guess that's one of the reasons we all love him so much. But you live there, too. How do you feel about having an old geezer underfoot?"

"Uh, Lola, he's not an old geezer. I mean, he might be a geezer, but he isn't old." Candace suddenly giggled. "Something just occurred to me. What's a geezer?"

"You got me. I think it has something to do with eccentricity. What's the man's name? Charlie never said."

"Burke Mallory."

"Is Burke Mallory eccentric?"

"He's different but I'm not sure I'd call him eccentric. Then again, why would he fall so hard for Rocky Ford? I mean, it's a nice little town—I like it myself—but you can see every nook and cranny of it in one day, and then explore everything around it in another two. Besides, in my opinion, he isn't doing much exploration. Right now he's in the coffee shop, reading newspapers and drinking coffee, and he's been in there all morning."

"What subject does he teach, and at what college in Seattle?"

"Sociology, and I don't think anyone's mentioned the name of the college. Not in my presence, anyway."

"Sociology?" Lola laughed. "Maybe he's studying the habits and eccentricities of the old geezers who hang around

Charlie's coffee shop. In fact, maybe he's trying to better define the universally blurred definition of exactly what an old geezer is. Research, you know?''

They laughed together. Lola was always good medicine for Candace.

''How long is he going to be staying with you and Charlie?'' Lola asked.

''Charlie said a few weeks. Both Burke and Charlie seem completely content with the arrangement. Burke has a yearlong sabbatical, so heaven only knows when he'll leave.''

''Sounds like you'd just as soon have him leave.''

''Oh. Well, I didn't mean to sound like that,'' Candace said quickly. As close as she felt to both Lola and Serena, she didn't want either of them thinking that she had any kind of personal interest in Burke Mallory. ''He can stay or leave, as far as I'm concerned,'' she added. ''It's all the same to me.''

Lola was silent a moment, then said slowly, ''Hmm, interesting.''

Candace groaned inwardly. She had spoken a little too strongly, whetting Lola's curiosity.

''Well, I'll meet him on Sunday, won't I?'' Lola said casually, intimating that she would form her own opinion on Burke Mallory.

''Did Charlie say he would bring him along?''

''Sure did. Enthusiastically, I might add.''

''Then I guess you'll meet him on Sunday,'' Candace said with a sigh she hadn't been able to suppress.

''Candy, is he bothering you?'' There was a note of concern in Lola's voice. Without waiting for an answer, she rushed on to another question. ''Have you told Charlie?''

Candace couldn't talk about Burke any longer. As cautious and tactful as she'd tried to be about Burke, Lola had read between the lines.

''Let's have this conversation after you meet him, okay?'' she said quietly. *Better yet, let's never have it.* But she knew now that Lola was going to be especially watchful on Sunday, and if Lola didn't alert Serena to the situation so that she, too, would be analyzing Burke's every word, Candace would forever be amazed. The prospect of Sunday dinner at the ranch was suddenly more burden than pleasure. Couldn't she even talk about the man without giving away the inner turmoil he was causing her?

"Yes, of course," Lola agreed, also speaking quietly. Her voice brightened then. "How's the baby?"

"Ronnie's fine."

"Bring warm clothes for him on Sunday. I know Duke will want to take him for a horseback ride. He adores your son, as we all do. Have you heard the weather forecast? We could have some snow this weekend."

"Yes, I heard it on the news this morning. I'll bring Ronnie's snowsuit and boots."

"Great. I have to hang up now, Candy. The store's full of customers. See you on Sunday."

"Bye, Lola. See you then."

Candace put down the phone with a frown. Burke was even horning in on family affairs now. Darn that man! Why didn't he get his fanny out of Rocky Ford?

Burke had so much coffee in him he couldn't face another cup. Seated at one of the tables, he had also read every newspaper Charlie carried, eyeing the customers as they came and went. No Benny. He felt as disappointed as Charlie looked, but that was the investigation process for you. Surveillance was usually boring enough to put a man to sleep, but it was a necessary evil and not to be avoided.

However, it did give a person time to think.

Finally there was no one in the shop except him and Charlie. Burke got up, stretched his back and moved to the counter.

"He's not going to show today," he told Charlie.

"Doesn't look like it," Charlie said glumly.

"So he only reads the newspapers once in a while? I don't think so, Charlie. Benny's too sharp to let anything in the papers pass him by. On the days he doesn't come in himself, I think someone else is picking up the newspapers for him.''

Charlie blinked. ''But there aren't any other strangers coming in.''

''Exactly. Which means that Benny has befriended someone. I believe it's one of your usual customers. First, let me ask you this. When the man we think is Benny appears in person, which papers does he buy?''

''A copy of everything I carry.''

''Who else does that?'' He'd seen only a few people buying every paper Charlie sold. Everyone else had picked up only one or two newspapers.

Charlie was getting the picture. ''You're a darned good cop, aren't you? Let me get a pad and pencil.'' Seating himself behind the counter, he started making a list, stopping to think every so often.

Then, suddenly, he looked at Burke. ''I know who's buying Benny's papers. Until a few weeks ago, Virgil Hathaway only came in for coffee and gossip. I didn't think anything of it at the time, but about two or three weeks ago he started buying a copy of every paper on the stand. When he comes in, that is. Burke, when Virgil doesn't come in, Benny does! That's it! I'll be damned. And guess where Virgil lives.''

''In one of those apartment houses?''

''Bingo! The gray one with the white trim. He moved in when that apartment house was first built, about three years ago. His wife passed away and he sold their house. Said it was too big for one person.''

''Was Virgil in here this morning?''

''Sure was. He was wearing a red stocking cap and a black-and-white-plaid jacket.''

Burke nodded. ''I remember him.'' He got off the stool with a grin a yard wide. ''This is great. You did it, Charlie.''

''*I* did it? No way, Burke. I never would have put it all together the way you did.'' But there was self-pride all over Charlie's face. He might not have done it all but he had helped, and that was enough for him. "So, what comes next?"

"Well, I can't go bursting into apartments in that gray-and-white building. It's still a waiting game, Charlie, only now we've got more to go on. A lot more." He paused. "How well do you know Virgil Hathaway? What kind of man is he?"

"Seems nice enough. Losing his wife was an awful blow, and he was pretty forlorn for a long time. I think he's coming out of it, though."

"Does he have kids in the area?"

"No, he doesn't. Both of his sons moved to Denver. They started some kind of business there, small-equipment rental, if I remember right."

"Then he's probably lonely and eager for companion-ship. Benny's smart enough to play up to an old man's loneliness to get him to help him out. Okay, what about this? How come Virgil doesn't come in every day?"

"He has arthritis in his hips and knees. Probably some days he just can't get around very well."

"And on those days, Benny takes the chance and comes in himself."

Charlie looked thoughtful. "Do you think you should talk to Virgil?"

"I don't know. If he considers Benny a good friend, he's apt to tell him I'm looking for him." Burke looked Charlie in the eye. "What's your opinion?"

After a moment Charlie spoke reflectively. "You know, that's a tough one, Burke. I never saw much of Virgil until he started coming into the shop after he moved into that apartment. He seems to be a decent sort, but we've never become what you'd call chummy so there could be a lot of things about him I *don't* know. If he's pals with Benny, for instance..." Charlie frowned. "Maybe you shouldn't risk it. Not when you're this close to nailing Slocum."

"Assuming the man really is Slocum, Charlie."

"I'm pretty sure about that, Burke." After a moment he added, "But I guess you're going to have to see him for yourself, aren't you?"

"I think so," Burke said gently, not wanting to hurt Charlie's feelings.

Candace walked in with a plate of sandwiches and a pitcher of lemonade. "Here's your lunch, Charlie." She set the plate on the counter without looking at Burke, although there was enough food for his lunch, too.

"Thanks, honey."

As was beginning to happen every time he and Candace were in the same room, Burke's system went haywire. Everything fled his mind but her, how pretty she was, how she smelled, how she had felt in his arms and how she had kissed him back.

He couldn't go on like this, acting mealymouthed and with no more gumption than a schoolboy just because she kept trying to pretend he wasn't visible. It was best to get their feelings out in the open, even if he might not like Candace's.

"Candace," he said calmly. "How about taking a drive with me this afternoon?"

Her head jerked around in blatant surprise. "I beg your pardon?"

Burke noticed the amused little twinkle that had appeared in Charlie's eyes. "Ronnie, too, of course," Burke added. "It's a nice day for a drive. The boy might enjoy it, and I know I would."

Candace was regaining her composure. Burke's invitation had all but floored her. Right in front of Charlie, too. Did the man have no tact?

"Ronnie naps right after lunch," she said coolly. "I like to keep him on schedule."

"Heck, honey," Charlie put in. "Why not put Ronnie down for his nap and then go with Burke? I'll be here when he wakes up, and it would do you a world of good to get out of the house for a few hours."

Candace gaped at her father-in-law, just barely believing her own ears. But his face told her she hadn't heard wrong, or misinterpreted his meaning; he was actually encouraging her to socialize with Burke. Would he be so supportive of a drive together if he knew that Burke had already kissed her and had more in mind than a kiss? Oh, yes, she knew exactly what Burke Mallory had in mind. It was in his eyes every time he looked at her; how could she not know?

"Thank you," she said, trying very hard to sound calm and unruffled for Charlie's sake. He didn't know the whole story, and she couldn't doubt that his encouragement was innocently sincere. "But I have things to do this afternoon that shouldn't be put off. If you'll excuse me now, I left Ronnie in his high chair." She all but ran from the coffee shop.

Burke and Charlie looked at each other. "Strikeout," Burke stated flatly.

"Totally," Charlie agreed. "I think she was really surprised that I said she should go."

"She was."

"She's probably been thinking that I wouldn't want her doing any dating. But heck, Burke, she's been living my life, which is fine for a man my age but not very healthy for a young woman. She *needs* to get out and kick up her heels a little. Mind you, I wouldn't be playing matchmaker if some worthless yokel was on her heels." Charlie grinned impishly. "But I sure do hate seeing her let a man of your intelligence and ambition get away."

Burke couldn't help laughing. "Think I'm a good catch, huh?" His smile faded, and he said in a serious vein, "Obviously Candace doesn't agree with you."

They started eating, both silent, both thoughtful. Finally Charlie said, "Know what I think? I think she's got it in her mind that it's too soon for her to be attracted to another man. She's that kind of person, Burke, loyal and decent. And from what I know of her and Ron's marriage, they were happy together. I'm sure that's what's stopping her from responding to you."

Burke took a breath. She had responded to him. Only physically and only once, the day he'd kissed her, but she had definitely responded. Oh, yes, she had also responded to his touch when he'd found her asleep in her chair, which counted for him even if she remembered nothing of the incident.

The memories raised his blood pressure. He wanted to feel her lips against his. He wanted to hold her. But would an opportunity to do so ever present itself again?

Some people came into the shop. Charlie got up to greet them, and they started talking about the possibly incoming snowfall for the weekend.

Burke finished his sandwich, then got to his feet. Nodding at Charlie, he left the shop and walked into the living quarters of the house. Taking that drive was no longer interesting. He'd had only a few hours' sleep last night and decided to go to his room and catch a nap.

Ronnie was down, apparently, and as he passed the laundry room he heard Candace filling the washer. He kept going, went into his bedroom, drew the blinds to dim the room, took off his boots and stretched out on the bed.

But even though it felt good to be lying down, he started thinking about Benny. Everything pointed to him living in that gray-and-white apartment house. But there was still that sprig of uncertainty to deal with. Charlie seemed positive now that the man in the photo and the one who periodically came in for newspapers were one and the same. Deep down Burke knew that he had to get a look at the guy and decide for himself. His investigation was too crucial to rely on someone else's judgment, even Charlie's.

He was drowsy but still thinking when the door of his room opened and Candace came in carrying an armload of clean, folded towels. To his startled amazement she didn't even glance toward the bed. Like a person with a mission and a lot on her mind, she went directly into his bathroom, and from sound alone he followed her movements. She opened the linen cupboard and put away some of the towels. The others she hung on the shower and sink rods. He heard water running and knew she was rinsing out the sink and wiping down the tiled counter.

His expression tautened. His bathroom did not need cleaning. He made damned sure that everything was spick-and-span in there every time he shaved, showered or just washed his hands. He also made his bed in the morning and kept his clothes in the closet. He had no intention of causing her any extra work, and still she was in there cleaning things that didn't need cleaning.

Getting off the bed, he walked over to the door leading to the hall and leaned against it. She might not have seen him coming in, but she sure as hell was going to see him on her way out.

Candace took one step out of the bathroom, saw Burke and froze. A flash of heat pinkened her cheeks. In her arms was a bunch of used towels. She hugged them to her chest while her gaze darted to his stocking feet, then to his boots next to the bed. It didn't take a genius to figure out that he'd been on the bed when she came in. How could she not have noticed?

Her legs went weak. He was blocking the door, and if that wasn't a challenging expression on his face, then she'd never seen one.

"I . . . should have knocked. I thought you were with Charlie," she said as evenly as she could manage. "Or gone," she added, referring to that drive he'd mentioned.

"As you can see, I'm not with Charlie and I'm not gone."

She cleared her throat. "Yes . . . well, um, I brought you some clean towels." Her gaze floated around the room, touching on everything but him.

"And washed out the sink and wiped down the counter, neither of which needed doing." After a beat he added, "Why do you talk to me without looking at me? Let's get to the bottom of this, Candace. Do you think I'm ugly?"

She blinked in genuine surprise. "I'm sure you know you're not ugly."

"I'm not talking about my opinion or anyone else's but yours. Am I ugly to you?"

She didn't like this conversation, particularly since it was happening in his bedroom. "That is ridiculous," she said sharply. "But if it will bring this inane discussion to an end, no, I do not find you ugly."

Burke folded his arms across his chest. "How about stupid or dense?"

"What?" Candace took a few steps toward him, toward the door behind him, actually. She was feeling almost claustrophobic with him staring at her so intently. Somehow she had to get out of this room.

"I'm speaking clearly and there's nothing wrong with your hearing. You know what I said."

"All right! No, I don't think you're stupid or dense." Her voice had risen and carried a cutting edge. "I have things to do. Are you going to let me leave?"

"You can leave in a few minutes. I want to know why you're so diligent about not looking directly at me. If you don't think I'm ugly, stupid or dense, what's the reason?" He paused. "Are you afraid of me?"

She scoffed, deliberately showing him her courageous side. Just because she was a small woman and didn't screech and make scenes, some people thought she was a mouse. Well, she wasn't a mouse, which Burke was going to discover if he kept pressing her, even if he was Charlie's friend and guest. "Why would I be afraid of you?"

"My point exactly." Advancing, aware that she was most definitely looking at him now, he put his hands on her shoulders. "There isn't a reason in the world for you to be afraid of me," he said softly.

She backed up a step, shaking off his hands. "Don't. I've not given you permission or an invitation to touch me."

His eyes darkened. "I think you did. When I kissed you, you kissed back."

Her face flushed. "You're making far too much of a trivial incident that never should have happened."

"But it did happen, didn't it? And it wasn't trivial. That's what has you so jumpy. You could like me a lot and you know it. It's why you keep your guard up, the reason you won't look at me unless it can't be avoided.''

In a defiant gesture, she lifted her chin. ''You have a vivid imagination. I'm looking at you now, and I'm not one bit jumpy.''

''The hell you're not.'' Burke's eyes dropped to the ball of towels she was clutching so tightly to her chest, as though it were some kind of shield. His gaze moved up to her face again. ''Talk to me, Candace,'' he said quietly. ''That's all I want from you.''

Her eyes began glittering, a surefire sign of the anger developing within her. ''A man and a woman can have three relationships—friendship, an affair or marriage. You eliminated friendship by kissing me, so you're either thinking of marriage or an affair. I doubt very much if marriage is on your mind, so that leaves an affair. Do you actually have the brass to presume that I'm going to have an affair with you while you're in Montana?''

That was the longest speech Burke had heard from Candace since he met her, and its content startled him.

''I wouldn't rule out any of those three options if I were you,'' he said.

''Do you expect me to believe you're working up to a marriage proposal?'' she asked sarcastically. ''And if all you want is friendship, it wouldn't even have occurred to you to kiss me. Don't take me for a fool, Burke. I'm not the most experienced woman in the world, but neither am I a complete fool. I know exactly what you want from me, and you're not going to get it!''

She started around him, heading for the door. He grabbed her by the arm, stopped her flight and glared at her. ''Under all that sweetness and light are some mighty sharp teeth, aren't there? Well, let me set you straight, honey. I won't deny that I'm attracted to you and was from the first time I saw you. But the word *affair* never once entered my mind. Try to remember that you're the one thinking and talking about it, not me.''

Candace could hardly breathe. He was so close, holding on to her arm with his face mere inches from hers. His macho maleness was on full throttle. What she had been fearing so much was happening: he was making her want him.

She dampened her dry lips with the tip of her tongue. "Please let go of me." The plea came out of her mouth in a husky whisper.

Burke studied her feverish face for a moment, then mumbled hoarsely, "I think you'd rather have me kiss you."

## Chapter Eight

Burke lowered his head and pressed his lips to Candace's. "No," she whispered, but that was her only attempt at protest. And a feeble protest it was. Instead of physically pushing him away or getting angry and verbally cutting him to ribbons, she dropped the bundle of towels, moaned deep in her throat and wrapped her arms around his waist.

The degree of passion Burke felt from her was stunning; the passion he felt within himself was stunning. Dazed and amazed, he put his arms around her and brought her up against his body. Nothing in his life had ever felt better. His second kiss was hot and hungry. So was hers. Their tongues met and they tried to wriggle closer to each other. That was when he knew there were no stoppers in this encounter. Unless they were interrupted in some unforeseen manner, they were going to make love. He picked her up and carried her to the bed.

"The door," she said raggedly. "Lock the door."

Unbuttoning his shirt as he went, he did as she asked. Turning from the door, he saw that she had shed her shoes and blouse, and was shimmying out of her jeans.

He thought he might explode from the glorious picture she made on that bed. Her skin appeared luminous in the dim light of the room. Her pale pink bra and bikini panties were lacy and feminine. She was utterly and completely female, the kind of woman that invaded men's dreams and had them waking up in a sweat.

He tore at his clothes, getting rid of them as fast as was possible. Down to his briefs, he lay beside her, leaning on one elbow to drink in the sight of her.

"You are the most beautiful woman I've ever seen," he said in a voice so thick and emotional he barely recognized it as his own. But he was so overwhelmed by what was happening, by Candace, that it was a wonder he could speak at all.

She closed her eyes and bit down on her lower lip. Knowing she shouldn't be doing this wasn't enough to prevent it. Her own body was betraying her, demanding a surcease from the misery of celibacy. Fate had intervened in her behalf, apparently, and right at the moment she wasn't in a mood to question it.

Her mood, in fact, was as feverish as her skin felt. Her heart was pounding, her pulse racing. The aching desire in her body was almost unbearable.

But...she didn't want to hear how beautiful Burke thought she was. Nor any other pretty words. This was merely a physical thing between them, and that was how it was going to remain. He was a here-today-gone-tomorrow guy, which was fine with her, as she wasn't looking for a hearts-and-flowers romance.

But she wasn't immune to biological urges. The driving, overpowering need in her body had nothing to do with romance, she told herself. Opening her eyes, she pulled Burke's head down. Her kiss was purely sexual, conveying neither tender feelings nor even affection. But it was hot as Hades, and Burke was swept into the inferno.

Her hands were all over him, which he accepted with intense satisfaction. Ever since they'd met, he'd been hoping to break through her wall of reserve, and obviously he'd succeeded astonishingly well.

In all honesty, however, he could not have placed her in this particular scenario. Never could he have foreseen the hunger of her kisses and caresses, or the breathless haste with which she bestowed them.

Breathing in audible gasps, she took off her bra and panties and immediately slid down his briefs. He would have preferred going slower, to spend long, delicious minutes touching her perfect little body, kissing her beautiful breasts and every other arousing inch of her smooth, silky skin.

But she was stroking his manhood, and her kisses were wild and exciting and leading them to the final pleasure. "Use a condom," she whispered.

He left her to lean over the edge of the bed and dig his wallet out of his jeans. His male pride swelled over bringing her to this point so quickly. At the same time, he thought of some of the things he wanted to tell her—how special she was, how important she had become to him in such a short span of time—and he also wanted to hear her thoughts. When had she started liking him? What, precisely, had he done to knock down that wall?

Protection took only seconds. When he turned back to her, her arms and legs were open to him. He stopped thinking then. She wanted him now, and what man could resist such an exciting invitation?

He positioned himself on top of her, slid into her velvety heat and groaned out loud. He wanted to just lie there and bask in the intense pleasure of their initial union, but she wouldn't let him. Moaning deep in her throat, she brought her hips up, demanding immediate action.

He looked into her glazed eyes, searching for answers, but as usual she denied him that luxury, this time by closing her eyes and shutting him out. A small warning bell went off in his head, but he himself was too far gone to wonder about it.

Then everything vanished from his mind but the pleasure of making love as he began moving within her. "You're perfect," he mumbled thickly. "Small and hot and perfect."

She didn't answer, although she could have returned the compliment by telling him that he was big and hot and perfect. But she would share no secret thoughts with him, not now, not later. Sex wouldn't unite their souls, but talking might.

Besides, her uppermost thought was how badly she had needed a man, which she couldn't possibly tell him. She met his every thrust with one of her own. Her body was slick with perspiration, and so was his. The roof could have caved in, and she wouldn't have allowed him to stop.

She ran her hands up and down his dewy back, absorbing the muscular contours of his torso. So beautiful, she thought, so very beautiful. She should have known from the way his clothes fit that his body would be like this.

And then the spasms of release began, and all else fled her mind. Her moans and whimpers, and the way her head moved back and forth on the pillow, told Burke she was reaching the pinnacle. He burrowed his hands beneath her hips and lifted her higher for the final ride.

They cried out together, and collapsed together. Burke's first lucid thought was about love and permanency. He had found the woman he wanted to share the rest of his life with, and he had no reason to think Candace felt any differently. Women didn't make love like this with men for whom they didn't have very special feelings. To think they had climaxed at exactly the same moment was incredible. He was experienced enough to know that didn't happen every day, especially the first time a man and woman made love.

His whole system felt glowing and alive with tender, loving feelings, and he raised his head to smile at Candace. She had one hand over her eyes, and he gently tugged it away.

"Hi, beautiful," he said softly, with all of the emotion he was feeling.

She had been dreading this moment. From the second the lovemaking was over, she had started worrying about it. He had satisfied the craving in her body, which was at peace for the first time in a long while. He had performed beautifully, and he was beautiful to look at.

But she didn't want to talk about what had occurred on his bed and he did; she could see it in his eyes.

She said the first thing that popped into her mind. "I think I hear Ronnie."

Burke lifted his head to listen. "I don't hear anything."

"Yes, but you're not a mother. Please let me up."

Burke's eyes narrowed. There wasn't one tiny sound in the bedroom wing, and he suddenly understood what had happened. He wasn't special to her; she had simply needed a man.

Shaken to his soul, he moved to the bed. Candace jumped up, grabbed her clothes and fled to his bathroom. Burke's thoughts, each and every one of them, were like blows to the belly. She had used him. No wonder she'd been in such a hurry. She'd felt nothing but sexual need, and now it was over and she was back to her normal distant self. He hadn't broken through her guard at all. What a damned fool he was, thinking with his ego instead of his brain.

Sitting up, he yanked on his jeans. He would take a shower later, after Candace had gone.

Nothing in his life had ever hurt more than this. And he'd been thinking about love and a future together? What kind of idiot was he? Thank God he hadn't bared his soul while they were in the throes of passion.

His lip curled. How could he have bared anything when she'd kept him so busy? She'd known exactly what she was doing. Very clever lady, very clever indeed. And she fooled everyone with a phony facade of shy reserve. Well, there wasn't a shy bone in her body in bed. Who would the next fall guy be? How many had there been before him?

Candace couldn't control the trembling of her hands enough to get dressed. In Burke's bathroom she leaned against the wall, suffered a painfully fast heartbeat and thought of what she had just done. Even breathing was difficult. Her chest felt as though a tight band were constricting it. How could she walk out of this room and face Burke? What must he be thinking of her now?

Yes, her body had demanded sex, and yes, she'd known what she was doing. But she hadn't expected any emotional involvement or ties with Burke, and at the end she had all but drowned in emotion. She was still feeling the aftermath of the most earthshaking experience of her life, and there was no way to ignore Burke's role in it. After all, she hadn't rolled around on that bed by herself. Nor could she pretend that her partner was faceless and unimportant. While taking her to the stars, Burke had stolen a piece of her heart.

''Oh, no,'' she moaned, feeling the sting of tears in her eyes and nose. She wasn't ready to fall in love again, especially with a man whose home was so far away from her own. The thing was, she had sensed an urgency in Burke's feelings. If she had lingered and listened, no telling what he would have said to her.

There was one positive factor in this fiasco: whatever feelings each of them had undergone on that bed were just barely developed. Without nurturing, they would die a natural death. She must make it clear to Burke that today meant nothing to her, and she must believe it herself. She would, in time. Who knew better than she that time dulled emotions and events?

Feeling a bit calmer, she struggled into her clothes. Not wanting to disturb Burke's things, she finger-combed her hair in front of the mirror. Then she received a shock: the woman looking back at her seemed like a stranger. It was her face, her hair, her eyes she was seeing, but they weren't the same. Would anyone else looking at her see the difference? Would Charlie? Serena? Lola?

Tension suddenly gripped her. And guilt. A terrible guilt that tore and clawed at her insides. Weak-kneed, she sank to the commode and wrapped her arms around herself. The prospect of any of the Fanons learning of her conduct today was abhorrent and frightening. They thought so much of her now, held her in such high esteem. She couldn't bear losing their respect. They must never know.

She got to her feet. Facing Burke was no longer her worst fear. She had to talk to him, and she must do it quickly so she could get out of his room before Charlie decided he needed her for something and came looking for her.

Opening the bathroom door, she stepped into the bedroom. Wearing only his jeans, Burke was sitting on the edge of the bed, his forearms on his knees, his head down.

Hearing her come in, he slowly turned his head to look at her. He'd been crushed by the weight of painful thoughts, and battling frustration, resentment and anger. But the sight of her instantly took the sharp edges off his emotions. Candace couldn't do what he'd been thinking. Not her.

He got up from the bed and forced himself to smile. "Hi."

Candace's heart sank. Just as she'd feared, he expected her to smile and maybe even act a little giddy over their lovemaking. Maybe he felt giddy about it. Certainly, from the expression on his face, he wasn't at all unhappy about it.

Stealing a quick, nervous breath, she spoke briskly. "We need to talk."

A foreboding hit him, but he nodded, praying his instinct was wrong. "I'm listening."

She wished he had on more clothes; his bare chest was unnerving.

But she didn't have to look at it, did she, even though she had the strongest desire to stare? A silent groan preceded a discomfiting thought: why did he have to be so handsome?

Dropping her gaze to her own hands, which were clutched together at her waist, she spoke as calmly and tonelessly as she could manage. "I'm hoping you won't mention this . . . this unfortunate incident to anyone. Can I rely on your discretion?"

"Unfortunate incident? Is that really all it was to you?" he snarled. He'd been right all along, and being right in this instance hurt like hell.

Startled at his tone, Candace lifted her gaze to look at him. "Are you angry with me?" She could see that he was, and it surprised her. It also put her on the defensive. "You have no right to anger. Didn't you get what you wanted? Or maybe I disappointed you." Her last remark was spoken sarcastically.

He stared at her for a long time, finally growling, "Yeah, you disappointed me." Nothing in his life had ever disappointed him more. And he knew they were talking about two different things. She was referring to the sex; he was thinking of her attitude. He didn't enlighten her, however. He was angry enough to let her think what she wanted.

Her face flamed and her own anger ignited. "In that case, I guess I can be honest. Apparently we were both disappointed. At least we've established one thing. It won't happen again."

Holding her head high, she picked up the ball of towels from the floor and walked to the door with every intention of leaving without another word. She hadn't anticipated an insult-trading session, nor was she thick-skinned enough to participate in one without painful repercussions. Obviously he hadn't shown his true colors until now, but how could he be so cruel as to tell her flat out that she had disappointed him in bed? Her flinging the same thing—an out-and-out lie—back at him didn't make her feel one bit better, either.

"Candace!"

She stopped with her hand on the knob and her back to him. "What?"

"Look at me. Please." He had never felt more miserable. Letting her think his disappointment had to do with their lovemaking was abominable. He couldn't let her leave with that awful untruth between them.

She didn't turn around. "No, I don't think so." Turning the knob, she opened the door and walked out. She quietly closed the door behind her.

Groaning, Burke fell onto the bed. After mumbling a string of curses, he stared at the ceiling. He'd had his chance with Candace and he'd muffed it.

But how? It wasn't that "disappointment" business; it had happened before that.

Then he remembered what she'd said about both of them being disappointed. Was that it? His pulse began racing in alarm. He'd been so positive that she had reached fulfillment at the same moment he had, but what if he was wrong about that? What if she really had been disappointed?

"Aw, hell," he muttered. Why was this happening to him? Why was he falling for a woman he couldn't satisfy in bed, let alone out of it?

He had to find that piece of slime, Benny Slocum, and get the hell out of Rocky Ford before he *really* fell in love with Candace. His lips set into a thin, tense line. He was already too close to the real thing for comfort. From now on he would concentrate solely on his job.

With that disturbing decision in mind, he got off the bed and went to take a shower.

Candace had spread paint chips and fabric swatches all over the kitchen table. Moving them around rather lackadaisically to try various combinations, she realized with an audible sigh that she was in no frame of mind to be deciding on a color scheme for the living room, which was the room she'd been planning to start with in her redecorating project.

After leaving Burke, she had taken a shower, then stayed in her bedroom until Ronnie had awakened from his nap. It might have been cowardly to avoid seeing Burke, but she truly wished that she never had to see him again. Her son now played on the floor near the table, she'd heard nor seen nothing of Burke and her system had calmed down a little.

But thinking of anything other than what had taken place in his room was all but impossible, and the swatches kept swimming before her eyes.

Charlie walked in. "Hi, honey." Looking at the array on the table, he asked, "Figuring it out?"

"Trying to." There were limitations on her choices. Charlie's favorite chair was covered in an excellent pastel blue leather and had to be factored into her overall plan for the room. The fireplace was constructed of a striking gray rock and rose to the ceiling, and the carpet was also gray, though there was nothing striking about *it*. If it wasn't in such good condition, she would gladly toss it out and buy new carpet.

At any rate, she felt she was pretty much stuck with shades of blue and gray, which was fine, but she did want the best combination of the myriad tones of each color.

The sofa and several other chairs needed new upholstery, which accounted for the fabric swatches mingled with the paint chips. Also she still hadn't decided what to do with the windows. The dark old drapes had to go, but what should she replace them with? Actually she wasn't particularly fond of drapes, in any case, but the windows were large, facing the driveway and had to be covered with something.

She sat back and looked at Charlie. "I'm not making much headway, am I?"

"There's no reason to rush that I know of," he said with an encouraging smile. "Take your time and don't worry about it. The reason I came in was to tell you that Burke won't be here for supper."

Candace swallowed the sudden lump of agony in her throat. Just hearing Burke's name chafed her painfully raw nerves; how was she going to act as though everything was fine and dandy when they were face-to-face again and Charlie was looking on?

He was looking at her now, she realized, expecting some comment on his news. "He . . . he went exploring?" she stammered, merely to say something.

"Guess so. He said he'll probably be back late." Burke hadn't explained where he was going or what he'd be doing, but Charlie suspected his outing had to do with Benny.

Candace was beginning to notice a very peculiar sensation within herself. Instead of relief because she wouldn't have to see Burke again today, she was feeling as though something important was missing from the household. How could she wish never to have to see his face again one minute, then suffer disappointment over his absence the next? Obviously she was very confused about Burke, which was not comforting knowledge.

With unsteady hands she pushed some paint chips and fabric swatches together. Lifting her eyes, she asked Charlie, "What do you think of these?"

He tried to look serious because she did, but what he knew about colors and fabrics wouldn't cover the head of a pin. "They're pretty," he finally said.

"Can you picture them in the living room?"

He couldn't. "Sure can."

Candace touched one of the fabric swatches. "This for the sofa." She touched another swatch. "This for the occasional chairs. Other than your leather one, of course."

"And the paint chips?"

"Well, I'm undecided about those. Should the walls be painted the pale gray or the pale blue? As you can see, there's barely any color in either one, more like a hint of color. But I don't want to darken the room with deep color on the walls."

"It all sounds great, honey. I think either color would work just fine."

"I suppose," Candace said with a sigh.

Charlie frowned. She looked and sounded despondent, and she'd been doing so well in her journey from grief to normalcy. She didn't even seem excited about redecorating the house anymore. In fact, she portrayed a person with a chore she would prefer not doing.

"Honey, you don't have to do anything to the house, you know," he said gently. "I mean, if you've changed your mind about redecorating..."

"No, no," she said quickly. "I haven't changed my mind, Charlie, not at all. It's something I really want to do."

Charlie's frown deepened. There was something wrong here. Pulling out a chair, he sat down. "Candace, I hope you know you can talk to me about anything."

Candace nodded. "I know, Charlie," she said, praying that his kindness wouldn't uncap the tears that seemed to be pressing into the backs of her eyes.

"All of my kids brought their problems to me, as youngsters and as adults." He reached across the table and took her hand. "You're one of my kids, too, Candy. You became a beloved member of this family when you married Ron, and your unhappiness is my unhappiness. I can tell something is very wrong right now. Please tell me what it is. I might not have a brilliant solution to offer you, but problems and troubles have a way of losing impact once they're in the open."

She sat there for a long moment, then pulled her hand from his and covered her face. "Oh, Charlie," she whispered tearily.

"There is a problem, isn't there? Honey, is it anything I did?"

"No...no." Gathering her courage, she moved her hands to wipe the moisture from beneath her eyes. She couldn't tell him the truth; she just couldn't. Burke was his friend and guest. Her tasteless conduct was not Charlie's fault or burden. Besides, she wouldn't be able to bear the disappointment, and maybe even disgust, he would most certainly feel if he knew what she'd done.

She wasn't good at lying, but if ever a convincing lie was needed, it was now.

"I'm just having a bad day, Charlie," she said. "It's bound to happen every so often, don't you agree?"

Charlie studied her pretty face; she'd been thinking of Ron, missing him. Charlie sighed inwardly. There were times when despondency overcame him, as well. He knew exactly what she was feeling.

"I understand," he said gently. "Tell you what. Let's go out for supper tonight. It'll be a nice change for you. You don't get out enough, and I've so enjoyed your cooking I've been remiss about seeing that you do.''

"Charlie, I'm not your responsibility.'' She felt so guilty about lying to him, and even more guilty because she had such a monumental reason *for* lying to him.

"And I'm not yours, but we pull together in this family, honey. What d'ya say? A nice meal in a nice restaurant? It'll be good for all of us, and you know something else? How can our little fellow here learn proper behavior in restaurants and other public places if we never take him anywhere?'' Charlie smiled. "Say yes, Candy. I'm already looking forward to it.''

She smiled wanly. "All right.''

"Great.'' Charlie got to his feet. "I'd better get back to work. See you later.''

Candace watched him leave, then slumped in her chair. She was making a terrible mess of things, sleeping with a man she barely knew, lying to Charlie.

What other deviant behavior was she capable of that she'd known nothing about?

She rarely swore, but she whispered a very impassioned, guilt-ridden "Damn.''

## Chapter Nine

Burke stopped his four-wheeler at the curb near the gray-and-white apartment building—identified by an unobtrusive sign as Highland Village—and studied the setup. Actually there were two buildings, one on the left perimeter of the property and the other on the right. Between them was a long, open-sided, roofed structure for resident parking. A strip of grass—dry and tan at this time of year—fronted each building, there were a few trees in no apparent pattern and there were sidewalks from the asphalt to the lower apartments and to the stairs leading to the second-floor units. No toys were strewn around, no dogs or cats were in sight. Although the place wasn't fancy, it was neat and tidy.

Along with the extended carport in the middle of the modest complex, there was some uncovered parking. Spaces marked with painted stripes were situated closer to Foxworth than the carports. About half of the total parking area was void of vehicles, although Burke could clearly read a sign on the right building that stated No Vacancy next to one that read Manager, Apartment 1.

A bank of mailboxes interested him. It was right near the street, and he counted twenty little doors. Obviously the postman had a master key to deliver the mail, and renters had individual keys to pick up their mail. Twenty mailboxes indicated twenty apartment units. Which one did Virgil Hathaway live in? It seemed reasonable to assume that Slocum's unit was near Virgil's, maybe right next door on one side or the other.

Burke could see tiny cards on each mailbox, but he couldn't make out what was written on them. Did they bear names and unit numbers?

He had to find out, and doing it in daylight was less suspicious than sneaking around after dark. Turning off the ignition, he got out and sauntered over to the mailboxes as though he had every right to inspect them. Bold was best in some situations; this was one of them.

A gleam of satisfaction entered his eyes. The mailboxes were correlated to the apartment units. On the doors of the apartments were numbers, starting with 1, and the mailboxes were exactly the same. Not only that, each little card bore a name.

It took only a few seconds to locate Virgil's name and unit number. He was on the lower floor, in apartment 12. None of the other nineteen names bore the slightest resemblance to "Benny" or "Ben Slocum," but Burke hadn't expected Benny to be that careless.

He glanced at the cars parked here and there, all with Montana license plates, wondered if one of them belonged to Benny, then returned to his own vehicle and got in.

He wasn't doubting Charlie's ID of Benny from that photo anymore, he suddenly realized. In fact, a sixth sense felt like the purest form of reality; Benny was in one of those apartments right now. He came out to buy newspapers when Virgil wasn't able to make the walk to Charlie's Place, which probably meant that Benny lived alone. But coming out for newspapers could indicate that he came out for other things, as well. Groceries, for example.

And there were no grocery stores in the neighborhood. One of those cars *did* belong to Benny, by damn. Burke would bet his eyeteeth on it. In fact, there was no telling where Benny went after dark, or what he did. For certain he was doing more than hiding out in Rocky Ford.

The final thing that caught Burke's eye was what appeared to be an alley behind the complex. He couldn't be positive from where he was parked, so he started the engine, drove to the corner of the block and made a right turn. Sure enough, the block was split in two by an alley. Not all of Rocky Ford's city blocks bore alleys—Charlie's didn't. But Charlie's immediate neighborhood was much older than this one, though only a short distance away.

Burke drove down the alley to about the middle of the block and stopped to view Highland Village from its back side. There was a wood fence between the alley and the complex, but his four-wheeler was high enough that he could see over it. Checking further, he was pleased to see no alley lights, such as erratically appeared on the streets of Rocky Ford. As in many small towns where growth was spotty and usually one step ahead of the town government, some neighborhoods were flooded with light at night and some weren't. This alley just might be an excellent place in which to conduct some after-dark surveillance.

Stepping on the gas pedal, Burke slowly traversed the rest of the alley; he would check it further tonight.

Since he was determined to avoid Candace for the remainder of the day, he drove to a restaurant on the edge of town, went in and ordered a sandwich and a glass of milk. It was a totally informal, seat-yourself place, and he'd chosen one of the booths under the front windows. There was a smattering of customers in the restaurant, and he could see everyone coming in or going out.

He was almost finished with his sandwich when a blue sedan pulled up and parked almost directly in front of his particular window. Instantly his system went on full alert. Every blue sedan he saw was suspect. One of them in Rocky Ford had been parked across the street from Charlie's Place at an unreasonable time of night, and he still wanted to know why.

But instead of a seedy-looking character getting out of the car—someone Burke could picture as sneaking around and watching people's homes at night—a very pretty young woman appeared. She was dressed nicely in tan slacks and jacket, and her long hair was a striking dark auburn.

Burke relaxed but his gaze still followed the woman, albeit rather disinterestedly. Just habit, apparently, or maybe he wished deep down that he could rip Candace Fanon's image from his brain and find himself drawn to another woman. That lady, for instance, was about as attractive as a woman got. Why weren't his damned hormones responding to her? Why was everything male in him focused on one tiny woman who kept proving that she would prefer he disappear?

The woman came in, went to a table in the far corner of the room and sat down. Burke put her out of his mind, finished off his sandwich and milk, dropped a couple of dollars next to his empty plate and slid out of the booth to go to the counter to pay his tab.

He walked out, got in his rig and drove away. He had no immediate destination, but he wasn't going back to Charlie's until late tonight. And if Candace was asleep in her chair in the living room again, she could stay there until morning.

Even though it hurt like hell, their personal relationship had come to a screeching halt. He was all through making a fool of himself over a woman who made love with no more emotional involvement than a rock.

His own feelings had gone crazy, and that's what hurt so much.

The clincher was that he was apt to be hurting for a very long time; he wasn't going to get over Candace just by deeming it so.

His lips set grimly. Maybe he deserved everything she'd dished out today. After all, he'd known from the first that she wasn't interested.

* * *

*Andrea noticed the tall man paying his check and leaving the restaurant. He was a noticeable man for any normal woman, and she considered herself completely normal as far as the opposite sex went.*

*But then he got into a black four-wheel-drive vehicle, and her heart nearly stopped. Could he be the man who had followed her that night? Oh, my Lord, what if he was?*

*After he'd driven away, she looked at the menu, but her appetite had greatly diminished and she ordered only a bowl of soup from the waitress.*

*Her system began to calm as logic kicked in. If he was the man in that frightening experience, he must not have seen her or her car well enough to identify either.*

*Or was it possible that he had identified her and was parked somewhere, lying in wait until she left the restaurant?*

*Her hands began trembling, and she hid them in her lap. Resorting to logic again, she told herself that she had seen several dark vehicles like his in town, and that this particular man did not look like a burglar. Or worse, a man who preyed on lone women.*

*But someone in Rocky Ford did. Some man driving a dark four-wheeler had attempted to follow her that night. She could only guess at his motivation for doing so, but it couldn't be anything good. If only she'd gotten a better look at the driver of that sinister vehicle, or had been able to identify its make and model. So many of those units looked alike to her.*

*But if she had gotten a better look at him, he might have seen her with more clarity, as well.*

*Staring unseeingly out the window, she thought of why she was in Rocky Ford. Not for the first time, she wondered if she should forget it all and just leave. As always happened when such thoughts occurred, however, she saw Charlie Fanon's face in her mind's eye. She should leave this restaurant, drive directly to his house and get the whole thing over with.*

*Her stomach churned sickishly. Why couldn't she do it? Fears she'd never even dreamed of possessing before arriving in Rocky Ford were keeping her practically immobile. Charlie's family had a lot to do with her dread. Before coming here, she hadn't known about his family. Now she knew too much and not enough. Who was Serena and Ron's mother? Where was she?*

*The waitress delivered her soup, and Andrea picked up her spoon. The unanswered questions gnawing at her were the real reason she couldn't yet confront Charlie, she told herself.*

*It was a weak excuse for procrastinating, but it was the best she could do. Deep down she prayed the emotional strength she needed so badly to attain her goal would one day come to her. If it didn't...? She shuddered at the thought.*

*In the meantime she had that awful man in that dark vehicle to worry about. If he was the one who had just left the restaurant, had he recognized her and parked somewhere nearby, waiting for her to leave?*

*Noticing that it was starting to get dark outside, she laid down her spoon, left a tip on the table, took her purse and check and went to the counter.*

*If that man was waiting for her, she could deal with whatever he had in mind much better in daylight than darkness.*

*With intense relief she made it home without seeing a dark four-wheeler.*

*She must have been wrong about the man in the restaurant being the one who had followed her that night.*

*Inside her house she all but collapsed into a chair. Her heart was beating like a tom-tom. This was terrible. All of it. How much longer could she bear it?*

Candace knew Charlie was worried about her, and she hated that she'd given him reason to worry. As they ate dinner in a pleasant little restaurant, she did her best to dispel his concern by telling corny jokes and laughing at them herself. Gradually Charlie relaxed, and by the time they were through eating, he seemed more like his usual self.

Without Burke in the house, Candace felt her and Charlie's evening routine went much smoother. Upon returning home, they tucked Ronnie in for the night, then went to the living room. Charlie heaved a sigh as he sat in his leather chair.

"Are you tired tonight?" Candace asked while seating herself.

"A little."

"I'm sorry."

"It's not your fault, honey. I'm just getting old," Charlie said with a short laugh. Picking up the remote control, he switched on the TV set.

He wasn't that old, Candace thought with a brand-new uneasiness. Was she beginning to be a burden to Charlie? Moods as she had conveyed today plainly troubled him, and she didn't want to trouble Charlie. Would he be happier if she and Ronnie lived elsewhere?

She cleared her throat. "Charlie, I've been thinking."

He turned his head to look at her. "About what, honey?"

"If I asked you something, would you be a hundred percent honest with your answer?"

"I'd sure try, Candy. Why? What's on your mind?"

It wasn't easy to say, and it took her a minute to get up the nerve. "Charlie, would you be happier if Ronnie and I lived in a home of our own?"

The shocked look on his face made her wish she had never brought up the subject. He turned off the television set, and got up and took another chair that was facing hers.

"This is a hundred percent honest answer, Candy. No, I would not be happier if you and Ronnie left this house. Where in the world did you get such an idea? Are you thinking that *you'd* be happier living alone?"

She felt like bawling. "No, never. But I caused you some distress today, and..."

"Listen to me, Candace," he said with more sternness than she'd ever heard from him. "There's going to come a time when I'll have to live alone. One of these days you'll meet someone and marry again, and there aren't any more kids to move in and keep me company. Don't look so doubtful, honey. It's only natural that you marry again.''

"You didn't," she said quietly after a hesitant pause. "Why not, Charlie? You're a nice-looking man and everyone likes you. And yet you left California after your wife's death, moved to Montana, raised your children and never remarried. Why would you think it's going to happen to me when your own life took such an opposite direction?''

He looked down at the floor. "Our circumstances—yours and mine—were never anything alike, Candace. And I might have remarried if the right woman had come along. She didn't and that's that. But in your case . . .''

"No, Charlie. There is no 'but' in my case. I think some people love only once in their life. I think you're one of them, and maybe I am, too." Burke's face appeared behind her eyes. But she quickly eradicated the image. She was not in love with Burke and never again was she going to succumb to sexual frustration, not with any man. As far as she could tell, Charlie lived a totally celibate life. She sincerely believed that he had lived that way since his wife's death. His self-control was to be admired. Hers was pathetic and she was deeply, abidingly ashamed of her behavior in Burke's bedroom today.

"Your theory is possible," Charlie said with an expression of sadness on his face. "But I pray you're wrong. Candace, living alone is bad for anyone. Why do you think I was so darned glad when Lola came home? She was the first to return, you know. Then Serena and now you. If you and Ronnie moved out because of something I did . . .'' He stopped talking and wiped his eyes.

Alarmed, Candace got out of her chair and went to hug him. "Charlie, you've done nothing wrong. You're the best there is. Any problem I feel is within myself. I have these up-and-down mood swings, and today I worried you. I was only thinking of you when I suggested getting a place of my own." She, too, was crying, and her little speech ended on a sob.

They hugged each other, Charlie in the chair, Candace standing next to him. He finally let go and dug his handkerchief out his pocket to blow his nose. Candace returned to her chair and wiped her eyes.

"I treasure each and every day that you and little Ron are with me," he told her. "You must never think I'd be better off without the two of you. At the same time, you have to keep an open mind. Let go of the past, honey. We all miss Ron and probably always will. But life goes on, and you can't let yourself wither up and die on the vine out of a sense of loyalty. Take Burke, for instance. He's a great young man, Candy, just great. I'm not saying you should attempt to force feelings for him that you don't have. But why not give him a chance? You might like him a lot if you spent some time with him."

She could hardly believe her own ears. One second Charlie was telling her that he treasured every day with her and Ronnie living with him, and the next he was praising Burke and encouraging her to...to what? Date Burke?

But didn't she already know that Charlie approved of Burke? Hadn't he tried to persuade her to take a drive with Burke when she'd delivered their lunch? What a strange situation this was. Her deceased husband's father was actually attempting to convince her that she should be seeing other men!

No, not other men. One man—Burke Mallory.

Candace wished she could read Charlie's mind, although she'd never had any trouble understanding him before this. Tonight she didn't understand him at all, and she suspected that further conversation would only confuse her more.

She faked a convincing yawn. "Guess I'm tired, too, Charlie. I think I'll go to bed." She got to her feet. "Good night. Thanks for talking to me."

Charlie slowly rose. There was a frown between his eyes. "Well, I'm not sure I accomplished much, but you're welcome."

She was almost to the door when he spoke again. "Candy, you've forgotten that idea about moving out, haven't you?"

Turning slightly, she sent him a smile. "It's forgotten, Charlie. Good night."

"G'night, honey. Sleep well."

Away from the living room, Candace sped to her bedroom. She knew she wouldn't go to sleep for a long time, and she also knew she wouldn't be able to read with so much on her mind. A most peculiar and upsetting question seemed set in concrete in her brain: would Charlie stop worrying about her if she went out with Burke?

She didn't like the question, wished it had never entered her mind and couldn't begin to think of an answer for it. Hastily, as though chased by demons, she threw off her clothes and rushed into a nightgown. Snapping off the lights, she crawled into bed. To her dismay, the question returned with even more force than the first time. *Would Charlie stop worrying about her if she went out with Burke?*

"Oh, damn," she moaned, burying her face in the pillow. The last thing she wanted was to worry Charlie. No one had ever been kinder and more loving to her, not even Ron, and God knew that she had believed Ron to be the kindest, most loving person in the world.

But that was before she knew his father. Charlie was wise, too, and as decent and respectable as anyone could be. If he thought she should be showing some interest in the opposite sex again, then she probably should be.

She was, of course, but it wasn't the kind of interest she could explain to Charlie or anyone else. And she had vowed all afternoon that it wasn't going to happen again.

Besides, if Burke was as great as Charlie proclaimed, why wasn't he home—watching TV, reading or just chatting with Charlie—rather than chasing around doing God knew what?

He was *not* Mr. Wonderful, however Charlie viewed him. There was something fishy about him and his "exploring Montana" story, and no one, not even Charlie, would convince her of anything else.

Even so, in spite of Charlie's premature good opinion and her own unspecific suspicions, Burke was on her mind far too often. Almost all of the time, in fact. Candace grimaced in the dark. It might stop Charlie from worrying about her if she went out with Burke, but what would it do to her?

Unhappily she lay there and went over everything that was happening, again and again. Charlie might be worrying, but he wasn't the only one, she thought wryly.

Two hours later she finally fell into a troubled, restless sleep. Nothing had been resolved, not one wretched thing.

Burke drove down the alley and parked close to the fence behind the Highland Village apartment complex. Turning off the engine, he rolled down his window to listen. After a few minutes of hearing nothing out of the ordinary, he rolled the window up again, quietly opened the door and stepped to the ground. He was going to take a silent and hopefully unnoticed stroll past the apartments, make a circle around the carports. Maybe he'd spot something of interest, maybe not. But he had to keep trying.

Along the fence was a row of metal trash cans. Carefully avoiding them, Burke opened the gate and winced when it squeaked. But the people living here were probably accustomed to hearing that particular sound, he reasoned, and went on through the opening. There were several fairly bright lights on the roof of the carport, and he stopped for a moment to see just how effective they were. They were aimed at the sidewalks fronting the apartment buildings, which left the carport itself in almost total darkness. He concluded that he could skirt the lighted areas without too much trouble.

He started walking.

Something awakened Candace, a sound in the house. After listening for a moment, she decided it was Burke coming in. She checked the time: 1:35 a.m. Her lips pursed. What did a man do until one-thirty in the morning?

Need she ask herself such an inane question? she thought with sudden, stinging anger.

The anger startled her. Why would she care what Burke did at night? It seemed that some out-of-control portion of herself *did* care, as she hadn't been happy the first time he stayed out late, either.

And she shouldn't even notice.

It appeared that pressure to like Burke was coming at her from all directions, even from within herself.

She still didn't understand Charlie's attitude about her and Burke, but it was far worse not to understand her own.

A bright autumn moonbeam found its way through a gap in the drapes at her window, and she stared at the small piece of nature's glory as tears began seeping down her cheeks. She hadn't cried at night for quite a while, but the self-pity and anger in her system were too painful to contain.

"Why did you have to die, Ron?" she whispered raggedly. "Why did you put yourself in danger by voluntarily doing something you couldn't even talk about?" She would never know exactly how Ron had died, other than that he'd been shot, or what covert activity he'd been involved in when the tragedy occurred.

Her bitter words, whispery and thick with tears, shocked her. This was the first time she had blamed Ron for his own death, the first time she felt angry at him because he had died unnecessarily and left her and their son alone.

There was some anger for herself, as well. Why hadn't she thrown a fit when Ron joined that secret special-forces unit? Why had she blandly accepted his career choices, and never once questioned his right to make them without considering the possible consequences? Without considering her and Ronnie?

She vowed that she would never be so stupidly naive again. If she ever did remarry, it would not be to a man who thrived on danger.

That was one point in Burke's favor, she thought unhappily. A college professor's job was relatively danger free.

Of course, she wasn't sure she believed that story, was she?

In all honesty, did she believe *anything* Burke said?

She moaned in utter agony then. How, how, *how* could she have had sex with a man she didn't trust?

A final question taunted her: what kind of woman was she becoming?

Sleep was a long time coming.

## *Chapter Ten*

Candace got up the following morning with the same raw, chafing feelings that had kept her awake for much of the night. She didn't vary her usual routine with her son and breakfast, but she really felt as though she'd been hit by a sledgehammer around 2:00 a.m. and was still reeling from the blow.

What she needed, she decided, was to talk to someone. Not Charlie. She couldn't even hint that Ron had been anything but perfect to Charlie. But how about Serena?

Standing at the kitchen window, Candace sighed. She probably wouldn't be able to speak of her middle-of-the-night anger to Serena, either. After all, Serena was Ron's sister and not apt to take kindly to hearing that Candace had suddenly turned bitter and was blaming her brother for his own death.

Anyway, she would see both Serena and Lola tomorrow at the ranch, and maybe an opportunity for a serious talk would come up.

Candace's eyes became sad. This, too, would pass, wouldn't it? Even if she never talked to anyone about last night's emotional upheaval, its impact would gradually dissipate. Everything did, it seemed. The pain she'd suffered over losing Ron was no longer acute and unbearable, and in time last night's incident would be merely another memory.

In the meantime life had to go on. *She* had to go on. She had dawdled much too long on decisions about colors and fabrics for the living room. And wasn't she blaming Burke for that particular procrastination? It seemed that she was looking for someone to blame for a good many things these days.

As far as her redecorating project was concerned, her equivocation was over. Determinedly she left the window, got out her paint chips and swatches, made her choices without second-guessing herself even once, then put the rest away.

After bundling up Ronnie in warm clothes and his new boots, she put on her own jacket, took her son out to the car and strapped him into his car seat.

"Go bye-bye, Mama?" he said with a happy smile.

"Yes, darling. We're going bye-bye." Candace climbed into the driver's seat. Backing up past Burke's vehicle created tension in her system, and she couldn't dispel the sensation no matter how hard she tried.

She had peeked into the coffee shop this morning before making Ronnie's breakfast, and Burke had been seated at a table with a stack of newspapers and a large cup of coffee. Obviously he had risen very early; obviously he had gotten precious little sleep last night. Last but not least, obviously he had nothing important to do.

So why get up before dawn?

Shaking her head, admitting irritably that she would never understand Burke Mallory and his peculiar habits and personality, Candace pointed her car toward the hardware store.

*      *      *

Burke noticed Candace's car leaving, and he couldn't stop himself from heaving a discouraged sigh. He would never forget her. When he finally wrapped up this case and returned to Helena, he'd be leaving a part of himself in Rocky Ford. Or taking something of the town with him. Memories, certainly. Heartache, probably.

And she just wouldn't give a damn, he thought dourly. There was something warriorlike in her attitude toward him, which he'd sensed from the first and been too sure of his ability to deal with stubborn women to take it seriously. He grimly stared at the newspaper in his hands as a seemingly irredeemable fact struck him: his ego had taken a hell of a beating since meeting Candace. And still he wanted her. Didn't that speak of a weakness of character he'd known nothing about before this?

"Aw, hell," he muttered behind his newspaper, disgusted that he would waste so much time in trying to analyze Candace and, yes, himself. He'd never done that before. There'd never been any reason to do that before. Candace had him going in circles, and he didn't like the feeling.

*Enough,* he thought with some bitterness. *So she had sex with you. Emotionally she's an iceberg. Forget her, for God's sake, forget her!*

If only he could.

Folding the newspaper in his hands and laying it aside, he took a swallow of coffee and checked the time. With Candace gone, he could use the house phone instead of going to a pay phone as he'd planned.

He was about to get up when the little bell above the door jingled. A flutter of excitement began in the pit of his stomach. Outwardly he maintained a calm, unconcerned demeanor. Casually he picked up another newspaper. There were six other people in the coffee shop. Some of them glanced at the newcomer, some didn't.

Charlie greeted him. "Hello. Cold out there this morning."

The man grunted something unintelligible and began picking up newspapers from the rack.

Over the edge of his paper, Burke studied the unfriendly stranger. He wouldn't let himself look at Charlie for fear the older man would give something away. But this guy, dressed in black pants, jacket and gloves, wearing dark glasses though the sun was pale and barely visible, and disguised as much as possible with his dyed hair and false mustache, was definitely Benny Slocum.

Burke could hardly believe he was actually looking at him, sitting calmly at a table and looking right at him. It was all he could do to keep the elation zinging through his system from showing on his face. It was all he could do to sit still and act as though this morning was like every other morning.

He could arrest Slocum right now, but he didn't want anyone getting hurt and Benny wasn't apt to give up meekly.

Benny walked to the counter and ordered a large coffee to go from Charlie. Burke still avoided meeting Charlie's eyes, and he sat in a deceptively casual slouch, appearing to be totally focused on the news of the day, and waited. Slocum paid for his coffee and newspapers, and walked out.

Then and only then did Burke look at Charlie. Burke gave a small nod of his head, and Charlie got the message: the guy in black was Benny Slocum. A smug little grin broke out on Charlie's face, conveying pride in his part of Burke's investigation.

Burke laid down his paper and got to his feet. Ambling over to the large front windows, he saw Benny walking in the direction of Highland Village. If Foxworth was a busy street with lots of pedestrians, he could follow Benny and see which apartment he went into. But there weren't a handful of people in sight. Benny would know someone was behind him in ten seconds. Burke couldn't risk it.

It was time to make that call. It didn't surprise him at all when Charlie followed him from the coffee shop to the kitchen.

"It's really him?" Charlie asked, excitement dancing in his eyes.

"It's really him," Burke confirmed. "I need to call Helena. I was going to call in this morning anyway, but I was going to do it from a pay phone. Since Candace is gone, is it all right to use the phone in here? It'll be a credit-card call."

"Darned right you can use the phone in here. You saw Candace leave? I didn't know she was going anywhere this morning."

"About a half hour ago."

"Burke, I feel like a kid in a candy store. When are you gonna arrest him? I thought any second there you'd be jumping up and putting the cuffs on Slocum."

Burke laughed. "Charlie, I'm not carrying handcuffs. A gun, either."

"But you've got some of that stuff with you, don't you?"

"Yes, I've got some of that stuff with me." He had stored all that "stuff," including his badge, on the top shelf in the closet of his bedroom. "But college professors don't walk around with handcuffs and weapons on their person, Charlie."

Charlie grinned a little. "Guess they don't. Well, go ahead and make your call. I'll go back to the shop. Damn, this is something. Imagine a real live criminal buying his newspapers from me." He left Burke alone in the kitchen.

Burke wiped his mouth with the back of his hand. His heart was knocking against his rib cage. He'd done it. The snitch who'd called had been right on the money, and Slocum's hiding place was no longer safe and secure. Burke was as excited as Charlie, only this wasn't a first experience for him as it was for Charlie, and he was able to take it more in stride.

Moving to the phone, Burke dialed Hal's office number. Because of his credit card, the call would never show up on the Fanon phone bill. If by some chance their billing arrived before this whole thing was over, Candace would never know he'd called Helena. It was important that Candace not know anything about the true nature of his business here. With her attitude toward him . . .

No, she would never deliberately give him away. She might not like him personally, but she was a law-abiding citizen, just as Charlie was.

Waiting through several rings, Burke wondered if Candace would like him better if she knew he was a cop. Maybe his persona of professor seemed stodgy to her. And there was always the chance that she didn't want to get too involved with a man who lived so far from Rocky Ford, too. If she knew the truth . . . well, some women really went for cops. The smell of danger apparently did something for them. Ordinary people equated police work to the shows on TV, after all, and there was definitely danger, violence and sex in most of those shows.

"Morrison," Hal said in his ear.

"It's Burke, Hal. I found him."

"You found Slocum?"

"I saw him with my own eyes, not fifteen minutes ago."

"And you let him walk away? Why didn't you arrest him on the spot and drag his butt back to Helena?"

"Several reasons. First, it happened in the coffee shop I told you about, and there were half a dozen older folks in the place. I didn't want to risk anyone getting hurt. Don't worry, I know where he lives. My other reason for letting him walk is this—last night I made a list of the license plates of the vehicles parked in his apartment complex. I want a rundown on those plates. Benny's driving something, and I want to know what it is."

"Why?" Hal barked.

"Because he isn't just hiding in Rocky Ford. This is the place he's chosen for his final drug deal. It's going to be big, Hal, I feel it in my gut, and if we pick up Benny now, someone else will put those drugs on the street. I want to nail him and his *compadres* with the goods."

"Hmm" was Hal's response. A silence ensued, which Burke patiently waited through. "Okay, give me the license numbers," Hal finally growled.

Burke pulled the list out of his pocket and read from it. It took about five minutes, as almost every parking space had been used last night and there were about thirty numbers. There was one he felt was especially urgent. Yesterday he'd noticed a dark green van in the uncovered parking area, and it hadn't been there last night. This morning, just as dawn was breaking, he'd gone to Highland Village and saw the van again.

"Check this one carefully," he told Hal before reciting the plate number, make and model of the van.

"Another gut feeling?"

"Something like that," Burke said, ignoring the hint of amused sarcasm in Hal's voice.

"I'll get back to you with the info," Hal said. "Or would you rather call me?"

"I'd better call you. What do you think, an hour, two hours?"

"Make it two," Hal said. "Okay, let's talk about Slocum for a minute. What're you going to do, stake out his apartment?"

"Only at night, Hal. The neighborhood is quiet at night. I can make periodic runs during daylight hours, but to just park somewhere and watch the complex would draw too much attention. Besides, from what I've figured out so far, Slocum sticks close to home during the day."

"And yet he walked into that coffee shop."

"Which he's been doing every so often for several weeks now. I'll put the whole story in my report, Hal."

"Maybe you need another agent to help out. What do you think? Should I send someone down there?"

"Hal, I've got everything under control. Another agent would only muddy the waters."

"But one man can't watch a slippery bum like Slocum twenty-four hours a day."

"He doesn't need watching twenty-four hours a day. He's waiting for something, Hal. I'll know when it happens."

"Oh, you will, even if it happens at high noon and you're nowhere around. Listen, Burke, I applaud your success thus far, but if that slimeball slips away again, your butt is on the line, understand?''

It was times like this that Burke wondered why he'd chosen law enforcement for a career. Superior officers came down hard if you screwed up and slapped you on the back if you made a good bust. The perks hardly compensated for the agonies of failure. And every officer failed on occasion.

He couldn't fail with Benny. He wasn't *going* to fail with Benny. Every cell in his body told him he was on the right track. He was getting that feeling of connection with Benny, which only happened when everything was going well in an investigation.

''I understand,'' he said into the phone. ''Call you again in about two hours.'' He hung up.

Turning from the phone, he felt his stomach drop. Candace, carrying Ronnie, was standing there looking at him with a very suspicious expression. How long had she been listening?

He tried to smile. ''I didn't hear you come in.''

''I just now walked in,'' she said coolly, letting Ronnie slide to the floor. She wanted to know what it was that he understood, and to whom he'd said it, but she couldn't ask. Bending over, she unzipped Ronnie's jacket and slipped it from his arms. Taking off his hat, she left the kitchen to put away his things and her own jacket.

Ronnie was looking at Burke, all bright eyes and sweet baby charm. ''Hi, Burke.''

Burke grinned and hunkered down in front of the little boy. ''Hi, pal. Did you go somewhere with Mommy?''

''Bye-bye.''

Burke laughed. ''That's what I thought.'' He fondly ruffled the boy's blond curls, then Ronnie bounded away.

''Go see Gampy,'' he called.

Burke stood up just as Candace returned. ''Exploring the kitchen?'' she asked dryly.

"Using the phone, which you well know," he shot back. "You don't like the idea of my exploring Montana, do you?"

She sniffed. "I don't believe it."

"What am I doing here, then?"

"I haven't the foggiest." Candace went to the sink and rinsed her hands. Drying them on a paper towel, she turned to give Burke an icy look. "But if you're exploring Montana, I'm the queen of England."

Her disdain stung. Then and there, the truth nearly came bursting out of his mouth. The words were on the tip of his tongue, and he had to physically force himself to keep silent. The fewer people who knew why he was in Rocky Ford, the better his chance of success. Right now his personal life should be on hold.

But why did she have to be so pretty? And why couldn't he stop thinking of those minutes on his bed when she'd writhed beneath him?

He was getting mighty tired of Candace's low opinion of him and suddenly wanted to ruffle her feathers. "By the way, I think you got the wrong impression yesterday."

"Oh? About what?"

"About my being disappointed with your performance in bed," he said calmly. "I wasn't one bit disappointed. Neither were you, regardless of what you said." Her face flamed. "That embarrasses you, doesn't it? I wonder why. We made love. It doesn't embarrass me to talk about it, why should it embarrass you?"

Maybe it shouldn't embarrass her, but it did. And he knew it and was deliberately baiting her. Anger wouldn't stop him, but perhaps a derogatory comment on his own behavior might.

"Mr. Mallory, sir, it could be because you're so accustomed to sleeping around, one more woman doesn't matter," she drawled in her thickest Southern accent.

"Oh, you matter, sweetheart," he said softly. "If you believe nothing else about me, believe that."

Candace wasn't going to fall for that line of hooey. She might not be the most experienced woman in the world, but she hadn't been born yesterday, either. Her phony sweetness vanished.

"If I do matter to you, which I doubt, it's only going to last for as long as you're in Rocky Ford," she retorted. "And don't call me sweetheart. I am not now nor ever will be your sweetheart."

He kept looking at her, although his eyes had narrowed significantly. "The question arises again. Why won't you let yourself like me? I know there's something between us, or you never would've made love with me. At least I hope that's the case. I really would prefer thinking you don't fall into bed with any available man. Of course, it can't be easy for a decent woman with a normal sex drive, who suddenly finds herself in bed alone every night."

Candace's face paled before his eyes. "You bastard," she said in a low, tense voice, no longer concerned about anger. "You're the only man since my husband. How dare you imply—"

Burke stepped closer to her and cut into her tirade. "I'm the only one? Doesn't that tell you something? Candace, my feelings for you aren't going to disappear when I leave town. If only I could tell you—"

"Tell me nothing!" she snapped. "You've already said quite enough, thank you very much. As for your feelings, don't you think I know they're strictly below your belt? I might have been easy, but I'm not a total moron."

He was getting angry over this absurd disagreement. Taking another step forward, he put his hands on her shoulders. She tried to shake them off, but he held on and stared into her eyes. "You're not a moron, nor do I think of you as easy. Would you stop beating yourself up over being human? Do you enjoy hating yourself because you're attracted to me? What's so terrible about liking me? Or would an attraction to any man upset you in the same way? What do you intend to do, live in someone else's home and play the bereaved widow for the rest of your life? Candace, it's not natural.''

Her eyes were snapping with unmitigated fury. ''And I suppose sleeping with you was?''

''Damned right it was. Natural and normal.''

She was thinking of some of the other awful things he'd just said to her. ''And I'm not playing at bereavement. How dare you belittle the death of my husband?''

''I wasn't belittling Ron's death. Why do you distort everything I say? All I was trying to get across was that your feeling something for another man is not a crime.''

''As long as he's you,'' she said bitterly.

''That's not true. If I thought there was someone else, I'd back off. But you just told me I was the only man since your husband.'' He softened his voice. ''Candace, I've known a lot of women. I'll never lie to you about that. But there've been none like you. Can't you accept that you're special to me? Can't you drop your guard enough to let the truth of your own feelings come through? There *is* something between us. There was from the moment we met.''

She stood there with her lower lip trembling. It was true; there had been something between them from the first. It had taken many forms—animosity, resentment, lust and anger. But Burke wasn't just any man. She didn't trust him or believe his silly story of exploring Montana. But her hormones didn't care if he was a liar, a clever con man or anything else.

''Admit it,'' Burke said in a quiet plea. She was close enough to kiss. He felt the warmth of her body on the palms of his hands. Touching her made him want her, even though all he was touching was her shoulders.

He could see the turmoil of her thoughts in her eyes. He supposed that she was thinking that admitting special feelings for him would make her vulnerable. Maybe she was worried about how Charlie and the rest of the Fanon family would take her liking another man.

''Candace, you have every right to a life of your own,'' he said in the same quiet tone.

She resorted to her old trick of breaking eye contact. Her voice was tremulous and wispy when she spoke. "You have to stop pressuring me. I can't deal with pressure, Burke."

There was something very different in her voice, an acceptance of sorts, a hint of resignation. Maybe she couldn't say it in precise terms, but she *did* like him and wasn't fighting it as hard as she'd been doing. His heart started pounding. He wanted to pull her into his arms and hold her. The need to do so was so strong and powerful, he had to grit his teeth to deny it.

But she was already feeling pressured, and he didn't want to destroy the gains he'd just made in breaking through her self-protective armor.

"I won't pressure you anymore," he said huskily, proving he meant it by letting go of her shoulders and moving back a little to give her freedom and space. "And you don't have to say anything. I know what's in your mind now."

From a foot away her gaze locked with his. "It doesn't make me happy."

"I know that, too. You still have some hurdles to get past, Candace, but it will happen. At least now we can talk to each other without anger or sarcasm, right?"

"I . . . I guess so." She dampened her lips with the tip of her tongue. Apparently their personal war was over, but they weren't the only players in this most unusual of relationships. "Are you going to Lola and Duke's tomorrow?" Wouldn't everyone sense what was happening between her and Burke if they saw them together? None of the Fanons was the least bit dense. She prayed that Burke had other plans.

"Charlie wants me to, and I'd like to go." Yes, he'd like to go, but dare he? Hadn't he been thinking only a few minutes ago that his personal life should be put on hold until this case was over? But he wanted to meet the rest of the Fanon family in the worst way. They were Candace's people and extremely important to her. How far would their relationship go without friendship between him and her family?

He would take the risk of leaving Benny in town alone, he decided. He would also take his own vehicle and stay at the Sheridan ranch only an hour or so. Tomorrow was Sunday. The odds were against Benny's drug deal coming down in broad daylight on a Sunday, when most people were at leisure and more apt to spot something suspicious.

"Yes," he said then. "I'll be going to the ranch tomorrow."

Candace heaved a sigh, which Burke didn't miss. They had made headway, all right, but it still wasn't a hundred percent between them.

But it would be. In time.

"Well, guess I'll take a walk," he said. He wanted to check out that green van again, to make sure it was still parked where it had been early this morning. When he got back he would drive to a pay phone and make that call to Hal.

Candace looked startled over his announcement, and he laughed. "I like to walk, Candace."

"You haven't done any walking that I know of."

"Then it's time I did, don't you think?" He patted his flat belly. "Gotta get *some* exercise. I've been sitting around a lot lately, and usually I'm pretty active. I'll get my jacket."

Candace stared after him with a perplexed expression. Although her mind was addled, one thing was perfectly clear: no one she'd ever known had the power to confuse her like Burke could. Now he was going to start walking for exercise?

He was as changeable as the weather, and with just about as much warning.

Were they friends now, or what? Sighing again, she went to the window and stared outside. Speaking of weather, she thought wryly, it had started snowing. Only it wasn't pleasant dry snow coming down; it was wet, sleety mush. No one in their right mind would take an unnecessary walk in that mess.

But then, was Burke *in* his right mind?

More painful to contemplate, was she?

## Chapter Eleven

When Burke returned to the kitchen, Candace was gone. He felt a strange relief. When she was around, he couldn't think of anything else, and thinking clearly was of the utmost importance right now. Things were coming to a head with Benny, and Burke didn't want to make any mistakes.

Going to the door to leave, he frowned at the sleet coming down. Okay, he thought, cancel walking. Instead, he went outside, yanked up the collar of his jacket and headed for his four-wheeler.

Candace felt just a tad smug when she saw him. Apparently he'd changed his mind about that walk. She was on the sturdy new ladder, in the process of taking down the living-room drapes. Not only had she bought the paint for the walls this morning, but she had stopped at the upholstery shop and made arrangements to have the sofa and chairs picked up for re-covering. If all went according to plan, this room would have a whole new look within two weeks.

Watching Burke backing up to the street, however, her smugness vanished. It was only sensible to reverse himself on that walk, but where was he going? In fact, how did a man without a reason to do more than breathe, eat and sleep find so many places to go in a town the size of Rocky Ford? Especially in sleety, cold, miserable weather? One would think he'd be content to stay indoors.

Charlie came in, with Ronnie on his heels. "Looks like business is over for the day. Everyone in the place went home before the weather got any worse. It'll probably freeze tonight, and the roads'll be solid ice in the morning." He was watching Candace. "Taking down the drapes, honey?"

"Can't paint with them up, Charlie. Besides, I'm going to replace them with something else."

"Oh. Well, that's fine. Can you believe those drapes came with the house? Lasted a real long time."

Candace had no trouble at all in believing the drapes had come with the house. They were worn, dusty in the pleats and folds and just plain ugly. In her opinion, they couldn't possibly have been attractive when brand-new.

But apparently Charlie had liked them, so she kept her opinion to herself.

"Burke left," she said, dropping one of the drapery panels to the floor. She noticed her son. "Ronnie, darling, don't play with the ladder. Go stand by Grandpa." The little boy obediently went to Charlie and put his hand in his grandfather's.

"Did he?" Charlie said casually, smiling down at his grandson. He had no idea where Burke might have gone, but he would bet anything it had something to do with Benny.

"Funny he would drive around in this weather," Candace said, adding a bit sarcastically, "it's hardly a day to do any exploring."

Charlie was all but bursting at the seams. He would love to tell Candace what Burke was really doing in Rocky Ford. And Charlie knew she would never repeat a word of it to a soul.

But he had promised Burke to say nothing to anyone, and that included Candace. It was kind of sad, though, that her attitude toward Burke was founded in lies. The two of them would never get together when Candace's doubt and mistrust was apparent even to Charlie.

He heaved a sigh. There was nothing he could do to help the situation, not without breaking his promise to Burke.

"Well, guess I'll do some cleaning up in the shop. See you later, honey. Come on, champ. You can help Gampy sweep the floor."

"Okay," Ronnie said happily.

Candace sighed, not so happily.

The green van was still there, now bearing an inch-thick coat of slush, Burke saw as he slowly drove past Highland Village. There was no evidential reason for him to connect the van to Benny, again nothing more than instinct. Regardless, Burke was anxious to hear the legal particulars about the vehicle.

But it was too soon to find that pay phone and call Hal again. Nor did he want to return to the house to do his waiting. Candace was there, and he needed to think without distraction. Had he overlooked anything where Benny was concerned? Why would he be in Rocky Ford alone? And if there really was a big drug deal in the making, when and where would it take place?

Driving was hazardous today, but everyone braving the weather was taking it very easy. Burke drove aimlessly for a while, then realized that he was on the very outskirts of town, in the vicinity of the new airstrip. Deciding to take another look at it, he made a right turn.

There were no fences, and he was able to drive right up to the partially completed terminal building. Today it was deserted; he couldn't see a soul. The building was coming along nicely, he thought. Should be completed in another few weeks, from the look of it. Having air service would probably be a real plus for the town.

His gaze moved to the airstrip itself, which was already completed. A plane could land there right now. Well, maybe not right now, he thought wryly. Not in this weather. But in clear weather, yes.

And then it struck him. This airstrip could be the reason Benny had picked Rocky Ford over hundreds of other small Montana towns in which to hide and do his dirty work. An airstrip that wasn't yet in use? My Lord, this was it!

Which meant that Benny's big drug deal was going to happen before the terminal building was completed.

Excitement coursed through Burke's veins. What a stroke of luck that he'd driven out here today. It was suddenly all so clear. All along he hadn't been able to come up with a solid reason for Benny choosing Rocky Ford. And here it was in plain sight, this small, unfinished airport. A plane could land any time the carpenters weren't working and never be noticed.

A deep frown suddenly creased Burke's forehead. He didn't dare leave town tomorrow and go to the Sheridan ranch, not even for a few hours.

In fact, Benny should be watched every minute of every day. Hal was right. One man couldn't watch someone twenty-four hours a day.

Still frowning, Burke put the four-wheeler in Drive and pulled away from the building. This revelation called for a whole new plan of action. He couldn't park anywhere near Benny's apartment complex every day and every night. Not in Rocky Ford, he couldn't. As sure as grass was green, someone would notice and call the police. And Benny wasn't stupid. He would catch on that he was being watched if a police car suddenly showed up.

"Damn," Burke muttered. Someone *had* to watch those apartments. But who? How? From where?

Checking his watch for the time, he shook his head impatiently. Still too soon to call Hal.

He'd stop somewhere for a cup of coffee. Kill a half hour or so. By then Hal should have the information on those license numbers.

\* \* \*

It was cold even in the phone booth. The dreariness of the day was depressing, but bothering Burke a whole lot more was that in the space of two hours his investigation seemed to have ground down to a standstill. Truth was, he couldn't come up with a feasible method of keeping a close eye on Benny, and now he knew that he had to. Benny was damned smart. He hadn't moved into some little place out of town, where a dozen police officers or agents could lurk unseen in the countryside. No, he'd chosen an apartment in a quiet neighborhood, where anyone hanging around, on foot or in a vehicle, would stand out like a sore thumb. Burke had been watching the apartment complex from the alley at night, but he'd been aware every minute of every hour that he was risking the success of the operation by doing so. One police car with flashing red lights would have put Benny on guard.

The thing was, he'd talked so positively to Hal only two hours ago. Now he had to backtrack and admit that not only couldn't he handle the case by himself any longer, but he had no alternative suggestions.

Reluctantly he dialed Helena. Hal's voice was in his ear in seconds.

"Morrison."

"It's Burke, Hal."

"Figured it was. I got the data on those plates, but I think only one of 'em is going to get your blood pumping. It's the van you mentioned. It's registered to a Peter Strausmeyer. The address on the registration is apartment 14 in a complex called Highland Village on Foxworth Street in Rocky Ford. Burke, Strausmeyer was Benny's mother's maiden name."

Burke was stunned. This was something he should have known. After all his digging and worrying about which of those apartments Benny lived in, the answer had been as simple as checking the residents' license plates. Benny had slipped up big time.

"Do you still want the info on the other plates?" Hal asked.

"Not necessary."

"What I'm wondering," Hal said, "is why he went to the trouble of registering that van in Rocky Ford."

"Because he was so damned sure no one knew where he was, Hal. He's acting out the persona of an ordinary citizen, and should the police ever stop him for any reason, he's got that registration card proving he has a local address. He's clever, but this time he outsmarted himself. Until now I didn't know which apartment was his. And that hunch about the green van was only that, a hunch. Now we've got solid facts to work with."

"Burke, I think you should bring in the local police and bust Slocum. Get the whole damned thing over with."

"We'd have Slocum, but what about the major drug deal he's waiting for?"

"Hell, if he's got a stash of drugs to sell, they're probably in his apartment."

"Could be, but what if they're not? All we'd have on Benny is unlawful flight to avoid prosecution and the same petty charges we had before. Hal, we could've arrested Benny a dozen times in Helena, but we stalled to get enough evidence to put him away for a long time. What's different now? Why tip our hand for some paltry charges that won't keep him off the street more than a few months?"

Hal didn't answer immediately, and Burke knew he was thinking. Finally he heard, "You're right. But you're only one man. Are you sure you don't want some help?"

Burke took an uneasy breath. He wasn't sure of anything at this point, other than the information Hal had just given him. But there had to be a way to nail Benny with the goods, and he was determined to find it.

His reply gave none of his uncertainty away. "I might, Hal. I'm piecing everything together right now, and if I decide another agent is needed, I'll let you know."

"Okay. Stay in touch, in any case."

"Will do." Hanging up, Burke breathed a relieved sigh. Hal hadn't pinned him down on anything. He hadn't had to admit to not having a definite plan anymore.

Now all he had to do was figure one out.

Tall order. *Very* tall order.

With a frown of intense concentration, he departed the booth and climbed into his four-wheeler. He had left the engine and heater running, and the warmth felt good.

In this weather no one—particularly Candace, who already doubted his story—would believe he would be doing any exploring or sight-seeing. He might as well do his thinking in his room at Charlie's.

Putting the shift lever in gear, he drove away.

Candace spent the afternoon masking off woodwork and wondering what Burke was doing in his room for so long. Around four-thirty she stopped working in the living room to make dinner. When it was almost ready, she asked Charlie to let Burke know.

Charlie rapped on Burke's door. "Burke?"

"Come on in, Charlie."

Charlie opened the door and went in. "Supper'll be on the table in about ten minutes." Burke was lying on the bed with his boots off. He looked drawn, not at all his normal self. "Don't you feel well?"

Burke sat up and started pulling on his boots. "I'm not ill, Charlie, but if ever a man felt stalled from a problem, it's me. Close the door for a minute, would you?"

"Sure." Charlie quietly shut the door. "What's wrong? Does it have something to do with Benny?"

"It has everything to do with Benny. Let me fill you in. Have we got time to talk a few minutes?"

Charlie nodded. "Go ahead."

Burke got up. "Okay, here's the scoop. I learned through Helena that Benny assumed the name of Peter Strausmeyer, is driving a green van that I've been noticing is almost always parked at Highland Village and last but far from least, he's living in apartment 14. I also have a gut feeling that his big drug deal is going to take place at the new airport, *before* the terminal is finished and the place opens for business, which means within a few weeks.

"Charlie, he's got to be watched, and I can't figure out how to do it without him catching on. The neighborhood—"

Charlie interrupted. "Wait a second. You said he's living in apartment 14?"

"That's right. Why?"

"Number fourteen is right next door to Virgil Hathaway's unit. Remember? The first floor uses even numbers, the second level uses odd. Twelve is next to number fourteen."

Slightly stunned, Burke fell silent while he digested information he should have put together himself. True, he had initially refused to consider bringing Virgil into his investigation, fearing that the old man and Benny had become friends and Virgil might say something he shouldn't. But Burke was feeling a little desperate now, which altered his outlook significantly.

With his eyes narrowed in deep thought, he rubbed the back of his neck and walked around the room.

Charlie's gaze never left him. "Maybe you could move in with Virgil. His apartment's small and you'd have to sleep on the sofa bed, but you'd sure be on top of things."

Burke stopped pacing while giving attention to Charlie's suggestion. But then he shook his head. "I couldn't risk that, Charlie. I'm sure Benny noticed me in the coffee shop this morning."

"Benny didn't seem to notice anybody. Hardly acknowledged me, even when he paid for his newspapers and coffee."

"Those dark glasses he wears aren't being used to protect his eyes from the sun, Charlie. You can bet he saw every person in there this morning."

Charlie looked stymied. "Well, heck, Burke, what'cha gonna do?"

A germ of an idea had sprouted in the back of Burke's mind. "Maybe we need to talk a little more about Virgil. *I* couldn't move in with him, but maybe someone else could." He paused briefly. "But I've got to know a lot more about him. You understand."

Charlie nodded. "Yep, I do. Okay, we'll talk after dinner. Let's go eat now, before Candace wonders what we're doing and comes looking for us."

On the way out Burke slapped Charlie on the back. "You're a heck of a guy, Charlie."

Charlie grinned. "I'll take that as a compliment, young fellow."

"Do that," Burke said. "It's how I meant it."

The second Burke walked into the kitchen and saw Candace, the whole damned mess regarding Virgil, Benny and Hal fled his mind. She was wearing a rosy pink sweater with a V-neckline and a gored skirt of the same striking color. Her hair shone as gold would under the ceiling lights, and there was makeup on her beautiful face. He loved her routine of looking nice for dinner; it made her very special in his eyes.

She gave him a small half smile as they sat down. "You stayed in your room so long I was beginning to think something was wrong. Are you feeling all right?"

Her unexpected concern all but melted Burke's bones, but he couldn't completely forget his goal in Rocky Ford and the fact that she knew nothing about it.

He managed to come up with a feasible lie. "I was reading." He must remember to leave a book on the bed stand, just in case she brought in fresh towels again and should look for it. Out of simple curiosity, of course. Maybe just to check his taste in reading material. What a satisfying picture that made, he thought, her wondering what he liked to read. Was she also curious about the kind of music he enjoyed? The type of movies? She seemed much less doubtful about him this evening. A result of their little encounter this morning? Perhaps because when she'd said she couldn't deal with pressure, he had backed off. She was a changeable, unpredictable woman, but weren't most people?

Charlie cleared his throat. "Let's bow our heads for a moment." He said grace, then smiled at Candace. "Supper looks delicious, as usual, honey."

"Thank you. I hope you enjoy it." She was speaking to Charlie but looking at Burke.

Then she turned away to tend to her son's dinner. For some reason, maybe because Burke had stayed home all afternoon, she felt better about him. Maybe she had been judging him too harshly, anyway. Whatever the cause, she was more relaxed in his presence this evening than she'd been since he'd moved in.

They filled their plates. "Well," Candace said convivially, "tomorrow should be fun. I know I'm looking forward to a day with Lola and Duke. And Serena, of course. It's too bad that Trav's out of town." She looked at Burke. "But you'll get to meet him another time, I'm sure."

Burke's stomach sank. Candace was treating him as he'd wished her to do from their first meeting, talking to him as though he was a welcome guest rather than an intruder. And he had to disappoint her; he had no choice. He dare not leave town, even if he couldn't watch Benny every minute.

But how he hated telling her that he wasn't going to the Sheridan ranch with her and Charlie tomorrow. In fact, he hated it so much he couldn't get the words out of his mouth.

Charlie saved the day. Only momentarily, of course. Sometime between this meal and tomorrow's departure for the ranch, Candace would have to be told.

"Guess what?" Charlie said. "I think it's only raining out now." Getting up from the table, he went to the door and peered outside. "Yep, that's what it's doing. Must have warmed up some."

"That's great," Candace exclaimed. "Maybe the roads won't be icy tomorrow."

"Unless the temperature drops again." Charlie resumed his chair. "We'll keep our fingers crossed."

And that was essentially how dinner went, with everyone trying to make conversation and not succeeding very well. Before it was over, Candace was feeling uneasy again. There was something in the air, something that Charlie and Burke were aware of that she wasn't. She couldn't get a handle on it, but it hurt her that Charlie would team up with anyone and keep a secret from her. That was what it felt like, a secret sitting at the table with them.

She tried to be brave about it, but she felt herself withdrawing from Burke again. Before his arrival in Rocky Ford, Charlie had never once made her feel this way, as though she was on the outside of something important. She was glad when dinner was over and they all got up from the table.

"I'll clean up," she said quietly to Charlie. "I'm sure you and Burke have something to do."

Charlie looked pained at her perception. "Honey, it has nothing to do with you. Please don't take it personally. And I'm going to help clean up. Some things just don't change for any reason, Candace. Do you think I would go somewhere without saying good-night to Ronnie?"

Burke discreetly left the kitchen and went into the living room. But he heard Candace asking, "You're going somewhere with Burke tonight?"

"I don't know, honey. We don't have any definite plans."

"But there's something going on that I'm not aware of, isn't there?"

"It's Burke's business, Candace, not mine."

She saw how miserable he looked, and believed again that he would never deliberately hurt her. Whatever was happening was Burke's doing. How could she have relaxed her guard with him for even a short time? He was drawing Charlie into some secretive, furtive venture that might not even be lawful. Was money involved? Charlie wasn't rich, by any means, but he had always been practical with money, and Candace knew he had savings and investment accounts, along with his retirement income.

Still, it wasn't her place to deliver any warnings or chide Charlie for being taken in by Burke. Besides, who was she to resent anyone being taken in by Burke? Wasn't she fighting that very battle herself?

She busied herself with the cleaning up. Charlie, moving much faster than normal, dived in to help. The kitchen was tidy in minutes, and Charlie quickly rinsed and dried his hands.

"Call me when Ronnie's ready for his good-night, honey," he said, hustling off to the living room.

Candace felt like weeping. Her hands were tied and frustration caused the emotional surge.

But then her spirit perked up a little. Tomorrow everyone in the Fanon family, with the exception of Trav, would meet Burke. Serena was a lawyer and as brilliant as she was beautiful. Lola had a sharp mind and eye. Duke well, she still didn't know Duke very well . . . but he certainly seemed like an honest, upstanding citizen. If any of them saw anything suspicious in Burke's behavior, they would say so. Particularly if they thought Charlie was being conned.

Sighing, she walked over to where Ronnie was playing on the floor. "Come, son, it's time for bed."

In the living room Charlie peeked around the door into the kitchen. "She's gone." He settled himself on the sofa next to Burke. "We can talk now."

Burke looked downcast. "I'm making Candace very unhappy, Charlie."

"Right now so am I," Charlie said with a forlorn expression. "But the only way to rectify the situation is to tell her the truth."

"I don't want her involved."

"I know, son, I know." Charlie heaved a sigh. "It won't go on much longer. Guess we gotta look at it that way."

Burke nodded. "Guess we do. Charlie, you said that Virgil has two sons living in Denver. Do they come to visit him?"

Charlie looked disgusted. "No, they don't, the selfish, damned louts. Neither one of them has come home since their mother's funeral. That's three years, Burke. I can hardly believe their lack of consideration for poor old Virgil. None of my kids would treat me that way, I can tell you."

"I'm sure they wouldn't, but then you've always been close to your kids, Charlie. Maybe Virgil wasn't. There are all kinds of fathers, Charlie. Anyway, we're straying from the subject. I was thinking while you were in the kitchen. We'd have to talk to Virgil about it, of course, but what if I put an agent in his apartment who pretended to be one of his sons?"

Charlie's eyes lit up. "That could be the answer, Burke."

"Yes, but would Virgil go for it?"

Charlie thought a moment, then shook his head. "I honestly don't know."

"The dangerous part of that idea is talking to Virgil to find out. His reaction will depend on the relationship he's formed with Benny. From what you've told me, Virgil's a lonely man. He would probably welcome friendship from anyone. If Benny's been playing good-neighbor, then it's a question of Virgil's loyalty to a friend."

"There's only one way to find out if he feels any loyalty to Benny, Burke."

"By talking to him." Burke looked away, thinking it over again. His eyes finally returned to Charlie. "Do you think he would take a ride with you?"

"Tonight?"

"Yes, tonight."

"I could call him, Burke. If he says yes, what then?"

"You would pick him up, then come back here and get me. I can't risk going anywhere near Benny's apartment at this time."

Charlie got to his feet. "Come on. We'll use the phone in the coffee shop."

Burke rose. "What will you say to him, Charlie?"

"I'll tell him I have to talk to him about something real important. Don't worry, I'll get him to take that ride."

## Chapter Twelve

Candace went to the living room to tell Charlie that Ronnie was in bed and awaiting his good-night. To her surprise, no one was there.

Perplexed, she strode to the undraped windows and peered out into the dark, drizzly night. Charlie's pickup was in the driveway and so was Burke's rig. So where were they?

Well, they couldn't be far, she thought logically. The coffee shop, probably, although what they would be doing in there at night escaped her.

She approached the doorway between the shop and living quarters. Charlie was on the phone. Only the low-wattage night-lights burned, but she could see Charlie sitting on his stool behind the counter and Burke standing in front of it. Actually he was leaning on it with his forearms, intently focused on Charlie.

Candace frowned. What was going on now? Silently she stepped back behind the doorframe to listen. Her heart was suddenly in her throat. Eavesdropping was not common for her, but she was thinking of Charlie, worrying about Char-

lie. Other than Ronnie, he was the most important member
of her family, and she would do just about anything for him.
At the same time, she would do almost anything to protect
him. Burke had put him up to something, and she wanted
to know what it was.

Charlie's phone call was just winding down, however, and
Candace didn't hear enough to piece anything concrete to-
gether.

"Well, fine, Virgil," Charlie said. "I really appreciate it.
I'll be there in about twenty minutes. See you then."

Charlie put down the phone and said to Burke, sounding
satisfied, "It's all set. You heard."

"You did great, Charlie, just great," Burke said. "I doubt
that I would have gotten anywhere with Virgil on my own."

Candace's eyes narrowed with a sudden, fierce onslaught
of anger. As she had feared, Burke had put Charlie up to
something. And who was Virgil? Surely they weren't talk-
ing about that nice old man, Virgil Hathaway! Why was
Charlie going to pick him up? What scheme had Burke
cooked up that involved Charlie *and* Virgil?

The longer she stood there, the angrier she became.
Without fanfare, she walked into the shop. "Ronnie's ready
for your good-night, Charlie."

Charlie started. "Uh, fine, honey. I'll go right now."

Burke had tensed the moment he heard Candace's voice.
And it surprised him that she didn't leave when Charlie did.

Instead, she came closer. He knew why in the next heart-
beat.

"I want to know what kind of mess you're dragging
Charlie and Virgil Hathaway into," she said with fury in
every syllable.

Burke studied her in the dim lighting. She was angry
enough to physically attack him, and still he wanted her.
This wasn't merely a case of ordinary attraction for a
woman; he was in love.

What a time for that revelation, Burke thought wryly.
Candace was in no mood to hear anything romantic, and if
the truth be told, he felt just about the same way. He was

worried about talking to Virgil, about how best to express himself. Before he told Virgil anything, he had to learn exactly how close the old man and Benny were. Virgil was apt to think it was none of his business and tell him so.

The topper was Candace overhearing just enough of Charlie's conversation to think the worst, and standing there now with attitude and a militant fury all but steaming out of her ears.

It was either tell her the truth or take the defensive.

"It really is none of your affair," he told her mildly.

"Charlie is none of my affair? You...you jerk, how dare you come into our home and take over?" Her anger was so intense she was trembling.

"Don't call me names, Candace," he said softly.

"Or what? Are you threatening me?"

"No, though you would probably prefer I was. You're enraged, and people as angry as you are right now can't see beyond the end of their nose."

His calm assessment of her state of mind was a final straw. Shrieking, Candace launched herself at him with every intention of slapping his smug face. He caught her flailing arms and spun her around so fast, it took a second for her to comprehend what had happened. Her back and hips were tightly wedged against him, and his hard arms were wrapped around her so effectively that she couldn't move.

"Let me tell you about anger, Candace," Burke said quietly. "It's a human emotion and we all feel it at times. But some people can't control theirs. Do you realize that if you would have had a weapon in your hands a few seconds ago, you would have used it on me?"

She was in no mood for a lecture. "What do you know about weapons?" she sneered. "I've never even touched one, have you?"

"Yes, I've touched a weapon."

Her heart fluttered in sudden dread. "And used one?"

"Let's not get into that."

His evasiveness sounded like proof that he knew all about weapons. It was a frightful moment, with her imagining all sorts of horrible things.

But she couldn't just stand there and shake in her shoes. *Calm down,* she told herself. *Stop your wild imagination. Try to remember that you know nothing for sure.* It was only the truth; her suspicions were based on bits and pieces of fragmented information.

Besides, her first order of business was to remove herself from this debasing clinch.

She could feel his breath on her hair and tried to ignore it. Being held in a viselike grip, especially with him all but curled around her, was maddening.

"Let go of me," she demanded, attempting to free herself by squirming. But all she succeeded in doing was rubbing her backside against the front of his jeans.

"Maybe you should stand still," Burke said with a suggestive clearing of his throat. Holding her like this was getting to him. "And maybe you should also think twice before trying to slap a man's face."

That was the comment that drained the anger from her system. Never in her life had she slapped anyone—man, woman or child. To think she had resorted to violence was a humiliating put-down, dropping her self-respect to an all-time low.

"I . . . I'm sorry," she mumbled. She *was* sorry, but apologizing to this man for any reason was hard to do. "Now will you let go of me?"

"In a minute, honey. In a minute. Just take it easy."

She didn't like the low, masculine timbre of his voice. It bespoke much too clearly of sexual feelings, and one mistake of that nature was all she was going to make with Burke.

But her mouth was inordinately dry, and her heart had started to beat rapidly. A silent groan welled in her throat. How could she feel anything even remotely physical for a man of Burke's caliber? No decent man trapped a woman in his arms in this fashion, even to prevent receiving a slap.

He'd moved so quickly. Where had he learned this type of self-defense?

Did it matter? Better that she question her own actions and reactions than waste time on Burke's. She was getting that languid, sensual feeling in the pit of her stomach, and if he didn't let her go very soon, he was apt to catch on.

Burke had already caught on. He could tell she was feeling warm and sexy, just as he was, only she was fighting it with everything she had. Fighting himself *or* her was the last thing he wanted to do right now.

He nuzzled his mouth against the side of her neck, then whispered into her ear, "Let honesty reign for once. You don't really want me to let you go, do you?"

His breath on her ear raised goose bumps on her skin. Candace's defenses dropped another notch. "Yes," she said, striving to speak strongly and firmly. She failed, because that one little word sounded like a lie, even to her.

"That's what I thought." Chuckling softly, Burke loosened his hold on her and slid his hands down her arms to twine with hers. Then he turned her around again and brought her up against himself. In the same fluid movement, he pressed his mouth to hers.

Candace's mind started spinning. She was being thoroughly, possessively, passionately kissed, and her list of reasons to doubt and mistrust this man was disintegrating within her own response. One second she thought, *No, no, this can't be happening,* and the next, *Yes, oh, yes!*

Her heart was beating in double time. Every cell in her body yearned and ached. There was barely a moment to steal a breath between his kisses. Her defenses were in shambles, and she didn't care. Moaning deep in her throat, she began giving as much passion as she was getting, kissing him, nipping at his lips, wrapping her arms tightly around his waist.

He lifted her then, clean off the floor, and set her on the counter. Wedging his hips between her legs, he rubbed his arousal against her. Her skirt was bunched around her hips, and his hands caressed her naked thighs. All the while he never stopped kissing her.

They both heard Charlie coming back at the same time. Candace pushed against Burke's chest at the exact moment he broke away from her and reeled backward. They were each breathing hard and struggling with that telltale condition.

Candace jumped down from the counter and frantically smoothed her skirt and hair.

"This isn't over," Burke told her just before Charlie came walking in.

She was afraid he was right. Dashing past Charlie, who looked startled at her haste, she made her escape.

"Everything all right?" Charlie asked with a puzzled expression.

Burke cleared his throat. "About normal," he said, attempting to *sound* normal. He was facing the counter again and willing his body to relax. His arousal felt like a permanent condition, however, and wishing it away wasn't working all that well.

Charlie decided to let it go, but it was obvious Candace and Burke hadn't been just talking while he'd been reading a short story about a chipmunk and a mouse and saying good-night to his grandson. The whole idea of Burke and Candace coming together pleased him so much, he couldn't help grinning. Maybe they would fall in love and get married. He couldn't think of anyone he would rather have take Ron's place in his and Candace's life than Burke. His kind of man didn't come along every day. Charlie hoped Candace was beginning to realize that.

He was already wearing his jacket. "I'm ready to go, Burke. Shouldn't take more than ten, fifteen minutes to pick up Virgil. Depends on how fast he moves. Anyhow, I won't be long."

"I'll be waiting."

The second Charlie was out the back door of the house, Burke ran to find Candace. Her bedroom door was locked. He rapped on it. "Candace?"

"Go away."

"Open the door. I only want to talk."

"For pete's sake, do you think I want Charlie knowing what a fool I am? Get away from my door!"

"Charlie's gone. He'll be back in about fifteen minutes. Unlock the door. I promise not to touch you."

"I'll believe that when hell freezes over." Candace was pacing with her arms wrapped around herself. She felt feverish and unfulfilled. The racking desire that had come to life in the coffee shop was still torturing her.

But she was not going to open that door.

After a few more minutes of pleading, Burke finally believed it. Going to his room for his jacket, he stopped again at her door. "I don't know how late we'll be." She didn't answer. "Candace, did you hear me?"

"I heard. So go. What do you want me to do, whistle a happy tune?" She went to her side of the door. "Just remember one thing. If you get Charlie into any kind of trouble with your scheming, I will loathe you forever. And if there is any way to make you pay for it, I'll see that it's done."

Heaving a sigh, Burke wearily shook his head. "Charlie is not going to get into trouble. You have my word on that."

"Thanks loads," she said sarcastically. "I feel so much better now."

Burke stood there for another few moments, pondering her attitude. She was not going to trust him until she knew the truth, and maybe he couldn't blame her. Maybe it was enough for now that she wasn't able to destroy her physical attraction for him.

Whether it was or not, it was all he had.

"Good night, Candace," he said quietly. She said nothing. Giving up on her for the time being, he strode away.

Outside, the cold, wet air cleared his head. He had a crucial job to do tonight, and it was time to put Candace out of his mind and concentrate on what was ahead.

He got into his vehicle to wait for Charlie and Virgil.

* * *

Candace sensed when the house was empty. She left her bedroom, looked in on her sleeping son, then walked through the kitchen and into the coffee shop with panic creating an acrid taste in her mouth.

She felt terribly alone and wished for someone to talk to. But if she called Serena or Lola, what would she say? *I suspect Burke Mallory of involving Charlie in something illegal.* They would want more information, and she had none to give. It was also possible they would be affronted by even the suggestion that Charlie would do something illegal, however influencing and persuasive Burke might be.

Deep down she felt the same way. Charlie never even ran a Stop sign. He would never knowingly do something illegal.

But wasn't that the very thing that was driving her crazy? Whatever was happening was Burke's doing. Charlie was being taken in, gradually being drawn into some scheme of Burke's. And now so was Virgil Hathaway.

Candace couldn't be still. She wandered the house and worried herself sick. Along with Charlie and Virgil, she worried about herself. After all, she, too, was being drawn into Burke's web of charm. It seemed that all he had to do was touch her to make her lose all traces of self-control. How could that be? How could she make love with a man she mistrusted to the point of misery?

Her misery wasn't totally focused on the mistrust firmly entrenched in her system, however. As traitorous as it was to her personal ethics and morals, she wanted Burke. Her body ached for him; her heart pounded because of him. If Charlie had delayed his return to the coffee shop long enough, they would have made full and complete love on his counter.

Thinking of it made her pulse race and increased the yearning ache in her body. She hated Burke; she loved Burke.

"Oh, my God," she whispered in utter agony. She wasn't falling in love with him—she wasn't!

Rushing to her bedroom as though it was sanctuary, she tore off her clothes, turned off the light and crawled into bed.

It was much too early for sleep, but it was a good place to quiver, weep and battle demons.

Burke got into Charlie's pickup, which put Virgil in the middle. "Hello, Virgil." He offered his hand. "I'm Burke Mallory."

Virgil shook his hand. "Charlie said we were picking you up. Nice meeting you. I think I've seen you in the coffee shop a few times."

"Burke is renting one of my extra bedrooms," Charlie said as he drove. Rain was pelting the pickup, but the wipers were keeping the windshield dry enough to see clearly.

"Are we going anywhere special?" Virgil asked Charlie. "I haven't been out at night in a long time. This is kind of nice."

"Nowhere special," Charlie replied. "Burke wanted to meet some of my friends, so here we are."

"Glad you thought of me," Virgil said. "When Helen was alive, we were always doing something. She was a pistol, wasn't she, Charlie?"

"Yes, she sure was," Charlie replied. In truth, he'd barely known Helen Hathaway. She and Virgil had lived on the other side of town, and until her death and Virgil's move into Highland Village, he hadn't even known Virgil very well. For that matter, he still didn't. But Helen had seemed like a lively woman, and if Virgil remembered her as a "pistol," it was fine with Charlie.

"You must miss her very much," Burke said quietly.

Virgil sighed. "Every minute of every day, Burke. Are you married?"

"No, sir, I'm not."

"Helen and me were married for almost fifty years."

"Charlie said you had two sons."

"Yes," Virgil said.

"I imagine they bring you a great deal of comfort."

Virgil seemed to stiffen. "They would if they ever came to see me. Always got one excuse or another for not coming. They both live in Denver. Got a good business going. Guess it keeps 'em too busy to get away."

"But you have friends, Virgil," Burke said, leading this pleasant old guy in the direction he had to know about. "Neighbors?"

"Burke, when you suddenly find yourself alone at my age, that's pretty much how it stays. I go down to the senior center once in a while, and there are a few old friends who drop in now and again, but mostly I'm on my own."

"Aren't the folks living in Highland Village friendly?" Burke asked.

"There's one widow lady that talks to me, but her kids live in town and they're always hauling her someplace. She's pretty busy."

"But what about your immediate neighbors, the ones living right next door to you? They say hello, don't they?"

"Oh, sure, but they're really not friends, Burke. Too much younger than me, I guess."

Burke felt a quiet satisfaction; Virgil didn't think of Benny, alias Peter Strausmeyer, as a friend.

"Charlie told me that you help one of your neighbors out by picking up his newspapers. I think his name is Peter Strausmeyer."

"Peter? Oh, sure, I do what I can for him. He's got something wrong with his heart. It's sad for someone his age. Can't be more than thirty, thirty-two. I've got arthritis pretty bad, and sometimes I can hardly get around. But on good days I'm always looking for something to do. Peter, though, is the strangest fellow. He stays in his apartment and keeps to himself so much, I worry about him. I've asked him over for supper a few times ... or I did when he first moved in. Coming next door wouldn't strain his heart, would you think? He always refused."

"Did he ask you to pick up his newspapers for him?"

"Yeah, he did. Sometimes when I go to the grocery store, I do a little shopping for him, too. It doesn't seem to matter what I do for him, though, he just isn't the friendly type. Not like Charlie, here. Charlie's friends with everyone, ain't that so, Charlie?''

''I like people, Virgil.''

''So do I, Charlie. It was real nice of you to ask me out tonight, real nice.''

Burke had heard enough. There was a café up ahead and only a few cars parked around it. They could do their serious talking in there.

''Charlie, why don't you stop at that little café ahead? Maybe Virgil would like a piece of pie or something.''

As they left the café an hour later, Burke's excitement didn't show. But it was there, inside of him, raising his blood pressure and putting him on the cutting edge. Charlie, however, was almost bursting at the seams.

The talk with Virgil had gone incredibly well. The elderly man had listened, asked intelligent questions and ultimately agreed to everything Burke suggested. Virgil, too, seemed excited by the plan, although he was more like Burke was about it, keeping his feelings pretty much contained. Burke was pleased about that. If his plan was going to work, Virgil couldn't be walking around with a silly, I-know-something-you-don't grin on his face.

Charlie stopped the pickup in front of his house, and Burke got out. ''I'll be right back,'' he told Burke. ''Go ahead and make your call. Use the coffee-shop phone.'' He drove away to take Virgil home.

Burke walked around to the back of the house and quietly let himself in. There were lights burning, and he expected to see Candace. Instead, everything was silent, and she was nowhere in sight. She must have gone to bed without extinguishing the lights, which could be her routine when Charlie was out at night. Whatever, Burke was greatly relieved not to run into her. Tiptoeing across the kitchen floor, he went into the coffee shop and noiselessly closed the door connecting the shop and living quarters, recalling at that moment that he'd never seen this door closed before.

Breathing more freely, he went to the phone behind the counter and sat on Charlie's stool. He dialed Hal's home number in Helena and prayed he would answer. It was Saturday night, after all, and very possible that Hal and his wife were out.

Luck was with him. After three rings, Hal came on the line. "Hello."

"Hello, Hal."

"Burke. Hold on a minute while I get to another phone. Hon, would you hang this up in a minute? I'm going to take this call from Burke in the den."

Burke heard Nancy Morrison pick up the phone. "Hello, Burke. How are you?"

"Just fine, Nancy. And you?"

"The same. Oh, Hal's on the other phone. I'll hang up now. Come by and see us sometime, Burke."

"Thanks, Nancy, I'll do that." He heard the click of her phone as she put it down.

"Okay," Hal said. "What's up?"

"I've finally got a viable plan, Hal. Let me outline it briefly. The man living next door to Benny—Virgil Hathaway—is going to help me out. Virgil has two sons in Denver who haven't been home to see him for three years. He's agreed to an agent moving in with him and posing as one of his sons. We'll be able to watch Benny around the clock."

"So you want me to send another agent to Rocky Ford."

"Right on. And the one I'd like to come down is Joe Frazier. I've worked with Joe before, and he's a good man. Plus, he's a small man, just as Virgil is."

"Joe's on another job, but I can pull him off it and send him down. But listen, Burke, I don't like the idea of involving citizens in this kind of operation."

"It's the only way in this neighborhood, Hal. There aren't any empty apartments in his complex that we could rent and set up a surveillance site, for example. There's not one single place for someone to keep an eye on Benny during daylight hours that wouldn't draw attention. I've been risking everything by watching his place from the alley at night, but

I can't do that during the day. Joe would be right next door. He'd know if Benny so much as stuck his nose outside. He'd know if anyone came to see him. I'd move in with Virgil if Benny hadn't seen me in Charlie's coffee shop, but I saw him and I doubt if he missed seeing me.''

"Well, the plan sounds feasible. Unless some old friend of Virgil's blows the whistle about Joe not being one of his sons, and Benny gets wind of it.''

"There is that chance, yes. But Virgil doesn't think it will happen. Since his wife died three years ago, he's been living a pretty isolated life. Hal, he's eager to help out. You'd have to meet him and Charlie to understand what kind of men they are. They're ethical, honest, law-abiding citizens, and if Joe does his job and I do mine, neither of them will ever be put in any danger.''

"They'd better not be," Hal growled. "Okay, when do you want Joe?''

"Tomorrow.''

"Tomorrow! Hell, you don't want much, do you? That means I have to get hold of Joe tonight.''

"I know. If he could be driving a mud-spattered vehicle with Colorado plates, and arrive happy and eager to see his father, it would be perfect. I want Benny to see that picture from the get-go.''

"Anything else?'' Hal said with some sarcasm.

"That's about it. Except for telling him the lay of the land. Charlie's Place is about three blocks west on Foxworth Street from Highland Village. Give him Charlie's phone number—555-6623. Have him call the minute he's inside Virgil's apartment. I'll be here and waiting for that call. Joe and I will work out the details.''

"All right," Hal said with a heavy sigh. "I wish I knew for sure that you were on the right track.''

"I am, Hal. Believe me, I am.''

"Well, you sound certain. That's something, anyway.''

"I *am* certain.'' Burke saw Charlie slipping into the shop through the connecting door. "Are you certain you can still talk to Joe tonight?''

"I'll find him, don't worry. And he'll be arriving in Rocky Ford sometime tomorrow."

"Thanks, Hal. The sooner he gets here, the better. Good night." Burke put down the phone and looked at Charlie. "It's all arranged."

Charlie's grin was a yard wide. "This is the most fun I've ever had."

Burke couldn't help laughing.

But in his estimation, this operation was definitely not in the "fun" category.

## Chapter Thirteen

Sunday breakfast was a silent affair. Candace avoided looking at Burke. He seemed lost in another world and barely noticed, which, perversely, aggravated her to the point of resentment, and even Charlie, who was normally talkative during meals, said little.

When it was over, Burke and Charlie went into the coffee shop and closed the door. Candace gaped disbelievingly. Charlie never closed that door, and his doing so this morning felt like a slap in the face. Still, her animosity wasn't aimed at Charlie. It was Burke who didn't want her overhearing whatever it was they'd gone in there to discuss, not Charlie.

Fuming, she washed her son's face and hands and lifted him from his high chair. While he played nearby, she cleared the table and put the dirty dishes in the dishwasher, all the time wishing she were a fly on the wall in the coffee shop.

In that portion of the house, Burke and Charlie were speaking in hushed tones.

"You know I have to be here all day," Burke said. "Please give Lola and Duke my apologies. It was great of them to include me in their invitation, and I really wish I could go. But I can't, Charlie. If Virgil sees anything unusual, however trivial, at Benny's apartment, he's going to call me. And I have to be here when Joe Frazier arrives and calls."

"I know, Burke."

"Candace is going to wonder why I'm not going."

"I'm sure she will."

Burke wandered to the window to look out. "Then again, she might feel nothing but relief," he said, sounding as though he were talking to himself.

Looking at Burke's stance—his hands dug into his jeans pockets, his shoulders slightly hunched forward—Charlie felt saddened. Burke was putting duty before his personal life, and maybe rightly so in his line of work. But Candace was so left out, so much on the outside of things, and Charlie knew women took blows to their pride very seriously. If she got hurt badly enough, she might never forgive Burke.

Charlie took a breath. "Burke, would it really be so terrible to tell Candy the truth?"

Burke turned around. "Can't do it, Charlie. I'd like to, believe me. But the fewer people who know what's going on, the better chance we have at success. Hal is already on my back because I've involved you and Virgil in this investigation. I can't involve Candace, too."

"I guarantee that she'd never breathe a word of it to anyone," Charlie said.

"But her attitude would change, Charlie. Sometimes the smallest misstep can destroy months of work. I know what you're getting at, and I agree that she would never deliberately do or say anything to undermine our plan. But there's always the chance of a slip of the tongue. I can't risk it."

Charlie sighed. "I know you're right. It's just that this family doesn't keep secrets from one another." Abruptly he stopped talking and frowned.

Burke frowned a little, too, wondering what was going through Charlie's mind. He looked so strange, as though he had mentally left this room and gone to another place and time. Burke had never seen that particular expression on Charlie's face, and instinctively he suspected that something from Charlie's past had just risen up and bitten him. They'd been talking about secrets. Did Charlie have a secret? Had his own statement about the Fanon family not keeping secrets from one another reminded him of it?

"Secrets can be damnable things, can't they?" Burke said softly.

Charlie blinked, as though coming awake. "Well... sometimes they're necessary. Sometimes it's kinder to lie than tell the truth." He inhaled deeply. "Sorry I brought it up. You're right about not involving Candace."

"I'll tell her everything when it's over, Charlie."

Charlie nodded. In essence, he agreed with Burke; in his heart he hoped the truth wouldn't come too late.

He glanced at his watch. "Time for church. I'll tell Candace you're not going to the ranch with us on our way."

"And if she asks why not?"

"You're a big boy, Burke. You have every right to change your mind about a dinner invitation. I'll just say there's something else you have to do."

Burke gave a quick nod of his head. It wasn't a great excuse for reneging on an invitation, but it would do. "Okay."

Charlie started for the door, then stopped and turned. "I think it would be best if we went directly from church to the ranch. We'll be gone most of the day, so I'll see you late this afternoon or this evening."

"Thanks, Charlie." It was a heartfelt thanks. Burke had never experienced the rapport he felt with this man. No wonder Candace and little Ron adored him. And from all indications, so did the rest of his family. What would it be like to be a member of the Fanon clan?

With his thoughts on Candace, Burke watched as Charlie walked out. Maybe someday he'd know what Candace,

Lola and Serena did feel about being part of this loving family.

If *he* had anything to say about it, he would.

Not that he'd grown up without love. Any problems with his mother had developed with adulthood. And they really weren't problems, either. Meredith simply didn't comprehend that he hadn't reached maturity in the Mallory tradition. She still believed that she could mold him into his father's image, or his grandfather's. Any of the Mallory men who'd come before him, for that matter, and it just wasn't going to happen. His choice of careers was Meredith's bane of existence, causing her to physically shudder whenever it came up for discussion. Burke had learned to live with it and, in fact, found some humor in his mother's shuddering disapproval. Maybe because he could laugh about it, often even teasing her into laughing herself, his job never caused a serious breach between them.

Since coming to Rocky Ford, though, he had noticed a peculiar dissatisfaction with his job. He knew that if he tried really hard to get to the bottom of that aberration, he'd come up with Candace. He had never been in love before—not like this—and he hated the lies and pretense with Candace. The thing was, she knew he wasn't what he claimed to be. Blame it on women's intuition. Or the fact that she was attracted to him and didn't want to be, which resulted in a determination to doubt everything he said and did. The day he could tell her the truth would be a happy day indeed.

In the meantime, he had to grin and bear the situation. Nabbing Benny Slocum was of high priority, and Hal was relying on him. Even the dissatisfaction gnawing at him couldn't change the status quo. But when this job was over...

Well, he wasn't going to return to Helena, quit his job and make a career out of counting the Mallory money. But there were other things he could do. Since mentioning the New Mexico ranch to Charlie, he'd been thinking a lot about it.

Of course, it was out. Not only couldn't he desert his mother by moving so far away, but Candace probably wouldn't want to leave her family. But what about a ranch in Montana? Would Candace like living on a ranch? He sincerely believed that once she knew his true mission in Rocky Ford, she would let herself fall in love with him. In fact, he suspected that she might already be in love with him, just as he was with her. Circumstances being what they were, each of them had reasons to avoid mentioning the subject. That would change. Candace was definitely in his future.

But until he could speak freely and honestly, he had to live with her distrust and apprehensions.

Burke's lips suddenly thinned in aggravation. He had really wanted to see the Sheridan ranch today, to meet Duke and Charlie's niece and daughter, and the knot in his gut was pure and painful disappointment.

Heaving a sigh, he went to a table, sat down and picked up one of the old newspapers lying on it. Things would work out, he told himself. He just had to be patient.

"We'll be going to the ranch right after church, honey," Charlie said. "So let's put everything in the car we were going to put in later. And we should hurry. It's almost time for services to begin."

Candace stared blankly. Would anything surprise her any more? What possible reason could Charlie have for loading the car now? There was a cardboard box on the table containing a tin of homemade peanut-butter cookies and another of fudge-frosted chocolate cupcakes to take with them. Besides, she was wearing clothing appropriate for church and had planned to change into something casual and comfortable for a day at the ranch. Ronnie, too, was dressed up. This didn't make any sense.

But arguing with Charlie was unthinkable—he had never before given her any cause for argument—and habit and respect influenced her now. "All right," she said quietly. She did ask one question, however. "Is Burke taking his own vehicle?"

"Burke's not going, honey. There's something he has to do in town."

That information simply would not be digested as Candace hastened to her bedroom to get her jeans and heavy jacket. There were also Ronnie's things to consider, and she ended up packing a small suitcase, frowning all the while. Why wasn't Burke going with them? What was keeping him in town?

Instead of relief, she felt a biting disappointment, which didn't please her but clung tenaciously. She shouldn't care two whits what Burke did or didn't do.

But she did care, dammit, she did.

On the verge of frustrated, self-denunciating tears, she took the suitcase and her purse and returned to the kitchen.

"I'm ready," she said to Charlie, who was sitting on the floor and playing with Ronnie.

He got to his feet and took the suitcase from her hand. Noticing the box of cookies and cupcakes was gone, Candace set her purse on the table and bent down to zip Ronnie into his good jacket. At least it wasn't raining *or* sleeting today. The sun was out, weak and pale as it was. Certainly it wasn't raising the temperature a great deal. By noon, though, it should be much warmer outside than the forty-three degrees it was now.

"Go bye-bye?" Ronnie asked happily.

"Yes, darling. We're going to church, then to Uncle Duke's ranch. Won't that be fun?"

The child smiled and eagerly nodded his head. "See horsies."

"Yes, you'll get to see the horses. And the dogs and kitties." Candace retrieved her purse and took her son's tiny hand. "Come, darling. Grandpa's outside waiting for us."

She left the house thinking that Burke must still be in the coffee shop. The whole thing was extremely disturbing, and she had a hard time returning Charlie's big smile.

What disturbed her the most was that Burke had the power to send her spirits into this kind of tailspin. Ever since Lola's invitation, she had been upset over Burke going to the ranch with them. Now he wasn't going, and she was even more upset. Damn it to hell, who was she now? Certainly the woman she'd been before Burke's intrusion into her life wouldn't have been so uncertain and ambiguous about anything, especially a man.

Concealing her emotional upheaval behind an ordinary expression and what she hoped was ordinary conversation with Charlie, she drove to the church. They always took her car when all of them went out together, as Charlie's pickup didn't accommodate Ronnie's car seat nearly as well as her four-door sedan.

Church services lasted an hour, then they were off to the ranch. This time Charlie drove, as Candace wanted to give Ronnie his midmorning apple juice. She sat in the back seat with her son and, while Charlie pulled the car over for a few minutes, she changed his clothes.

Under way again, Charlie chatted about the weather and how quickly it had turned from nasty to nice. Candace made appropriate responses, but her mind was not on the weather. To be honest, it wasn't in the car at all. She couldn't stop thinking of Burke and that mysterious something he had to do today that was so urgent he hadn't come with them. Charlie knew what it was, and it hurt that he would keep it from her. It wasn't as though Burke was on some sort of secret mission, after all. Not in Rocky Ford, for pete's sake.

Candace shuddered at the mere thought of men and their secret missions. Secrecy was what had made her a widow, and as for missions, she would never again subject herself to that sort of life. Worrying every time Ron packed his bag and left for God knew where. Sleepless nights while he was gone. Loneliness for weeks on end. No, never, again, not even if she fell madly in love with another man who craved danger and excitement as other people did peace and quiet.

The sad truth, she suddenly and painfully realized, was that she and Ron had not been at all compatible. Unquestionably they had passionately loved each other, but there was more to marriage than passion. There had been a whole sector of Ron's life that she hadn't been part of. Days and weeks of their marriage that he couldn't talk about, again and again.

What *had* they talked about when he was home? Staring out the side window, Candace tried to remember Ron's homecomings as they'd really been instead of the romanticized versions she'd been living with. Her recollections were not soothing to her nerves. Always, in every conversation they'd had, had been a holding back, that vexing avoidance of anything to do with his work.

She hadn't complained. She had accepted it all, as though the only truly important thing in their lives was his career. But what about her? she thought resentfully. Had Ron *really* loved her? There was room for doubt on that score, considering the fact that he had never once asked for her opinion on his career choices. No one had coerced him into that special-forces unit. He had merely come home one day and told her about it, proudly, excitedly, expecting her to feel the same.

And she had. That was the pathetic part of it; she really had been proud of her wonderful husband's new and exciting duty. But that had been before all the secrecy began, before the training he couldn't talk about, before he'd started taking those mysterious trips he couldn't talk about.

And the secrecy had continued through his death. She would never know in what part of the world or why he had been shot. It was sealed information, and no amount of pleading on her part had moved the officers that had come to her home to deliver the awful news.

Now here she was, on the outside of another secret. It couldn't possibly rank up there with Ron's activities, but it hurt nonetheless. Charlie's silence was especially hard to bear. They had been so close before Burke appeared. That alone was a very substantial reason to despise Burke, so why didn't she?

She did, she thought angrily, knowing in the next heartbeat it was a lie. Tears suddenly stung her eyes, and she had to blink hard and fast to keep them at bay.

"Candace, are you all right?" she heard Charlie ask from the driver's seat.

She'd been silent too long. ''I'm fine,'' she said, then because she wasn't at all fine and felt angry about it, added, ''What makes you think I'm not?''

Charlie cleared his throat. ''Um, no reason. How's our little buddy doing?''

Candace smiled at her son, who was drowsily lying back in his car seat. ''I think he's getting sleepy.''

''Well, we're almost there. He'll wake up when he sees where we are.''

''Yes, I'm sure he will,'' Candace murmured. To herself, she sighed quietly. Why had life become so complicated?

Burke alternately sat at the table with the old newspapers and got up and paced the coffee shop. It was going to be a long day.

Though he called upon patience, he felt impatient. Restless. He wanted Benny behind bars and the operation over with. He had *never* wished so strongly for the wrap-up of a case before.

After a walk around the room, he slouched back into his chair and watched out the front windows. Traffic was never heavy on Foxworth Street, but it was particularly light today; there was little to see.

But he'd gone through the newspapers twice, glanced through the new magazines on the shelves and had found concentration on the written word to be impossible. He thought either of Benny or Candace. One or the other was constantly on his mind. They weren't connected and yet they were. Analyzing that concept, he realized that *he* was the connecting factor. Taking his pen from his shirt pocket, he drew a triangle, on a corner of a newspaper. He was point A, Benny was point B and Candace was point C. Eliminate Benny and his part of the triangle and there was a straight line between him and Candace. That was the way it should be, the way it was *going* to be.

Returning his pen to his pocket, he looked out the windows again. A blue sedan was driving by, a woman at the wheel. He frowned in recognition because she was looking at the house and he saw her face and red hair: the woman at the café! Was her presence on Foxworth Street mere coincidence, or was she the person who'd been parked across the street that night? If so, what was her interest in Charlie's Place? And if she had no interest, why had she been looking at the house as she went past?

Burke's imagination took wing. What if Benny was on to him and that woman was a lookout? What if he had misinterpreted her presence the night he'd tried to follow her? Maybe she had absolutely no interest in the Fanons and had been following *him!*

The phone rang. Muttering a curse because of the confusion he felt over that woman, he got up to answer it. Charlie had warned him that he might be answering calls from friends or family, so he half expected to hear, *Could I speak to Charlie?* Or *Candace?*

But it was Virgil, talking quietly. "Burke, two men just went into Benny's apartment."

Burke's heart skipped a beat. This could be what he'd been waiting for. "Tell me exactly what took place."

"Well, I was sitting in my rocker in front of the living-room window. I like looking out, you know. When I'm not doing something, that's where I sit. Anyway, these two guys walked right past my window and knocked on Benny's door. He let them in and that was that."

"Did they say anything?"

"Not one word. They knocked, Benny let them in and that was that. Thought you should know."

"Yes, thanks. What do they look like, Virgil?"

"You mean their description?"

"Right. Did you see them well enough to describe them?"

"Course I did. Told you they walked right past my window. One of them was about fifty years old and had lots of gray hair. Stocky build, kind of a square face with a big nose and wearing a black jacket. The other one was a skinny little fellow, probably around thirty. Reddish hair and a thin face. A denim jacket and jeans. Do you know 'em?"

Burke had been scribbling Virgil's descriptions on the pad by Charlie's phone. "No, but the computer in Helena might. By any chance, did you get a look at their vehicle?"

"Nope. Didn't know they were in the complex till they walked past my window."

"Okay. Can you hear anything at all from Benny's apartment? Loud voices or anything else?"

"No, nothing. They must be talking real quiet, 'cause I can't hear a thing."

"All right. One more thing, Virgil, can you keep an eye out for their departure? It would be a big help to know what they're driving."

"Sure can. I'll let you know."

"Virgil, you're doing great."

"You can count on me, Burke."

"It appears that I can. Thanks, Virgil. Talk to you later." He hung up.

Now Burke wondered if there was some connection between that blue sedan driving by and Benny's two visitors. Wasn't the timing just a tad too perfect to be accidental?

Mulling it over, he rubbed his jaw. Damn, this was getting more complicated by the minute. Dare he overlook the possibility of that red-haired woman's involvement?

But if he managed to find her and she *wasn't* involved, one more person in Rocky Ford would know he was a cop.

Besides, he couldn't leave the phone to look for her.

"Hell," he mumbled. It would sure be a relief when Joe Frazier got here.

*Andrea's heart was beating a mile a minute. She had avoided Foxworth Street ever since the driver of that dark four-wheeler had tried to follow her, and now, after working up her courage to pass by Charlie's Place, thinking it should be safe to do so in broad daylight, there was the same four-wheeler parked in the Fanon driveway.*

*What did it mean? Who was the owner of that vehicle? Who'd been driving it that night?*

*That dark vehicle gave her a sense of danger. Oh, God, was Charlie in danger?*

"No, no, no," she said out loud, slapping the steering wheel in frustration. It was time to act. She couldn't put it off any longer.

Pulling into her driveway, she turned off the engine, got out and went into the house. Before her courage could desert her, she went to the phone and dialed the number for Charlie's Place. A man answered with a curt "Hello?"

Andrea swallowed the lump of dread in her throat. "Is this Charles Fanon?"

"No, it's not. Charlie isn't here right now. Could I take a message?"

"Uh, do you know when he'll be back?"

"Yes, sometime late this afternoon or early evening. I could have him return your call. May I have your name and number?"

Panic seized Andrea. This man could be the owner of that four-wheeler!

"No," she said quickly. "I'll call back." She put down the phone before the man could say anything else, then collapsed onto the nearest chair. Putting her head back, she moaned out loud. Making that call hadn't been easy. When would she find the courage to try to make contact with Charlie again?

One thing she knew. Before another attempt, she had to find out who that frightening man was.

Maybe he wasn't frightening at all. But he certainly was a stranger and appeared to be living in Charlie's house.

What did that mean?


After hugs and kisses, the first words out of Lola's mouth were "Charlie, I thought you were bringing your friend along. Where is he?"

Charlie smiled. "Burke asked me to pass on his apologies, Lola. Something came up that he had to take care of."

"Then he's not coming?" There was disappointment in Lola's eyes. Candace related Lola's expression to her own feelings.

"No, honey, he's not." Charlie looked around. "Serena's not here yet?"

"She'll be coming along around noon. Come on, let's go in. It's cold out here."

Duke had lifted Ronnie into his arms and was talking to the little boy. Charlie had opened the trunk to get the box of sweets. Everyone was occupied, so Candace walked with Lola into the house. "Are you still feeling well?"

"Absolutely wonderful, Candy." Lola put her arm around Candace's waist. "This is going to be such a fun day. I'm so glad you're here."

Candace smiled, albeit weakly. "I'm glad, too."

Lola cast her a sideways glance. "But something's wrong, isn't it?" They entered the house, and Lola faced Candace. "I can tell by your voice that something's amiss, Candace. Is it that Mallory guy? What's the real story? Why didn't he come?"

Candace looked into her cousin-by-marriage's eyes and spoke candidly. "I wish I knew, Lola. I really wish I knew."

## Chapter Fourteen

Burke endured three hours of teeth-gritting, soul-searching, self-condemning misery before Virgil called again. Analyzing himself and every segment of his life was not the best way to pass time when impatience was also eating a hole in his gut, he had discovered. He wasn't perfect, and for some reason every character and personality flaw he possessed seemed monumental today.

But at least he knew why he had put himself under a mental microscope. He could tell himself a thousand times that when this case was finished and Candace finally knew who and what he really was, any and all doubts she harbored about him would vanish, but he had no guarantees. In fact, wasn't he hanging his hat strictly on the physical attraction between them?

In truth, he felt as though he were going crazy waiting for the phone to ring. The only call since Virgil's first was the one from a woman wanting to speak to Charlie. Burke hadn't dwelled on it. He had much more important things on his mind than a female caller who'd sounded slightly panicked because Charlie wasn't home.

At any rate, when the phone rang again, Burke leapt to answer it, praying it was either Virgil or Joe Frazier. He said a quick and rather gruff "Hello."

"They finally left, Burke," Virgil said. "Got into a black van. It was parked in that uncovered parking area near the street and too far away for me to see the license number, but it was definitely a Montana plate."

Virgil's information wasn't great, but it still offered Burke some relief from the tension he'd been suffering. He cleared his throat. "By any chance did you recognize the make of the van? Was it old? New?"

"It looked about ten years old to me, but like I said, it was pretty far away. I'm not familiar enough with vans to recognize brands unless I see them up close, Burke. Sorry."

"But they left alone. Benny—or Peter, as you know him—didn't leave with them."

"No, sir, he didn't. And none of them said anything at the door again, either. That strikes me as odd. Most everyone calls goodbye or something when they leave a friend's door, don't they? Seems to me they do."

"You wouldn't if you didn't want to be noticed, Virgil."

"Then why in heck did they show up during the day? Why not sneak in after dark?"

"It's quiet in that complex at night. Maybe they figured they'd draw less attention during the day." After a moment Burke added musingly, "Their daytime visit could also mean that whatever Benny's been waiting for is going to happen real soon." He thought about that for a few seconds, then changed directions. "Be sure and have Joe call me the minute he gets there."

"Will do. Talk to ya later." Virgil hung up.

Burke put down the phone. He felt calmer now. This could be it. If Joe was already in town, he would take a drive out to the airstrip for a look-see, making sure he wasn't seen himself, of course.

But he had to connect with Joe as soon as the agent hit town.

Damn, he thought next. Waiting around like this was nerve-racking.


The men and Ronnie were outside. Serena, Lola and Candace were tidying the kitchen after the sumptuous meal they had all consumed. It was the perfect opportunity for Serena and Lola to pick Candace's brain.

"All right, Candy," Lola said with an inarguable finality. "I want to hear every detail you know about this Mallory guy, and so does Serena."

"Yes, I do," Serena confirmed. "I should have been stopping by to see Dad these past few weeks, and I've let everything get in the way of doing so."

"I've done the same thing," Lola said with a chagrined expression. "Candy, is Mallory for real? Do you believe his story about being a college professor? Tell us everything. I'm sure you can understand that we have to know your feelings. Other than Charlie, you're the only one in the family who has met him."

Candace was wiping a counter. Casually she asked, "Why would you think he isn't for real?"

"Because *you* don't trust him," Lola shot back. "I saw distrust in your eyes when you got here and Charlie was explaining why Mallory wasn't coming."

Turning around, Candace faced the two women. "You're right, I don't trust him. But I have no concrete reason for feeling that way."

Serena folded her arms. "Sometimes intuition is the best reason in the world."

"And sometimes intuition isn't worth a hill of beans," Candace retorted. "Look, I know you're both concerned for Charlie's sake, but I have nothing specific to tell you. Charlie and Burke get along unbelievably well. It . . . it's almost as though they're closely related." She paused for a second. "I guess what's really bothering me is that they're keeping something from me."

"Deliberately?" Serena asked. "How do you know?"

"This morning after breakfast, they went into the coffee shop and closed the connecting door. Have either of you ever seen Charlie close that door?"

"No!" Lola exclaimed.

"Never," Serena said with suddenly worried eyes.

"And whatever the big secret is, they've involved Virgil Hathaway in it," Candace said.

"Who's Virgil Hathaway?" Serena asked.

"He's an old guy who lives a few blocks down the street from Charlie," Lola explained. "I met him one day in the coffee shop."

"A *nice* old guy," Candace put in. "A widower."

"Nice or not, I didn't know he and Charlie were pals," Lola said. She frowned thoughtfully. "Of course, that could have happened after I moved out. But getting back to Mallory, why would a young man take up with much older men? If Mallory's merely looking for friends while he's in Rocky Ford, one would think he'd find some closer to his own age." She looked at Serena, then Candace. "Am I wrong in that assumption?"

Candace sighed. "Don't ask me. I've wondered about Burke Mallory from so many angles, I'm totally confused."

"Dad's always made friends easily," Serena said. "And let's not forget that most people like him. *Really* like him."

"Yes, that could explain Mallory's and Charlie's close relationship. Candace, what do you mean, they've involved Virgil? In what way?" Lola said.

Another sigh came from Candace. "The only thing I know for sure is that they picked Virgil up and took him for a drive. No, that's not right. Charlie went and picked up Virgil, then came back for Burke."

"Well, for pity's sake," Serena exclaimed. "That sounds like the plot of a grade-B movie. Are you saying that Mallory stayed behind on purpose? Dad drove down the street, picked up Mr. Hathaway and then came back to get Mallory?"

"That's exactly what I'm saying," Candace said. "I know it happened precisely that way because Burke was with me while Charlie was out picking up Virgil."

Lola cocked an eyebrow. "With you? Doing what?" Candace's face colored. "Uh-oh, do I detect a personal attachment to our mysterious Mr. Mallory?" she said in a teasing vein. Candace's face got redder; her embarrassment was obvious. Lola glanced briefly at Serena and immediately apologized to Candace. "I'm sorry, Candy. Sometimes I have a very big mouth."

"No, wait a minute," Serena said quietly. "Candy, is Burke Mallory an attractive man?"

Candace swallowed. "Uh, he's not ugly." After a beat she sighed. "Yes, he's attractive. Tall, dark and handsome, as the saying goes, to be honest."

"I'm beginning to grasp the situation," Serena said with an indulgent smile.

"No one could talk Charlie into doing something illegal," Lola stated with strong conviction.

"Nothing could be truer, Lola. Candace," Serena said in a kindly tone of voice. "Whatever Dad and Burke Mallory are doing, I'm certain it's neither illegal or immoral. There could be any number of reasons why they're keeping their activities from you. Christmas isn't that far off, and don't you have a birthday coming up?"

"December 3," Candace mumbled. Surely all the secrecy wasn't because of her birthday, which was still more than six weeks off. As for Christmas, Burke wasn't going to still be in Rocky Ford for the holiday season, was he? Actually her whole system rebelled against Serena's logic.

But saying so would be like a condemnation of Charlie, which she couldn't do with these two women. Their love and trust of Charlie was solid as granite, and it wasn't her place to plant doubts. Besides, her doubts weren't aimed at Charlie, although she did suspect he was being taken in by Burke. She couldn't say that, either. Serena and Lola believed Charlie to be infallible, a tower of strength. How would they ever believe he could be taken in by anyone?

Even Candace had trouble with that concept. Charlie's daughter and niece would never accept it.

She stood there and said nothing, wishing to God that she hadn't said as much as she had. After all, where was her proof? And how could she explain fears that were nothing more than suspicions?

Serena was still smiling at her. "I think you like Burke Mallory, Candy."

Candace felt her face coloring again. But before she could deny affection for Burke, which she fully intended doing, true or not, Serena added, "Candy, you have a right to like a man. Have you been worried we might think badly of you? We never will, you know. None of us expect you to live as a widow for the rest of your life. Heavens, that's not even sensible. You're young, you're beautiful and men are going to notice. If you notice one in return, it's only natural. Now, admit it, aren't your concerns about Burke and Dad somehow tied to your personal feelings for Burke?"

"I...I'm terribly confused about Burke," Candace said, which was the only thing she could admit to with any honesty.

Lola knowingly rolled her eyes. "I went through the same thing with Duke."

Serena nodded. "And I with Trav. Candace, falling in love often catches one unprepared. I fought against it tooth and nail, and so did Lola. I think that's what's happening with you and Burke. Doesn't that seem logical, Lola?"

"It does to me," Lola agreed. "I have got to meet Burke for myself. You should, too, Serena. Until we do, we really shouldn't be giving Candace advice about him."

"You're right. In the meantime, however, I do think Candace should stop worrying about Dad and Burke being up to something."

Candace was beginning to believe her imagination had simply gone wild for a while. Serena and Lola were intelligent, sensible women, and it really was a relief to know they wouldn't censure her for liking another man. Maybe that

was what had been in the back of her mind all this time, the
primary reason why she kept backing away from Burke.

Of course, she didn't *always* back away from Burke. Her
face flamed again at the thought of their intimacies, and she
quickly turned to finish wiping the counter so Lola and
Serena wouldn't see.

"I know Ron wouldn't want you to grieve ad infini-
tum," Serena said softly, her expression conveying thoughts
of her deceased brother. "If Burke's not the right man, an-
other one will be. You have my blessing, Candace, and I'm
sure Lola feels the same. Don't you, Lola?"

"Very much so."

"And I'm sure Dad would say the same thing," Serena
added. "Be happy, Candy. It's what we all want for you."

"Well, everything's done in here," Lola announced.
"Let's get our jackets and join the men outside." She
glanced out the window. "Looks like Duke is going to take
Ronnie for a horseback ride. I'd like to watch."

"So would I," Candace said.

She got her jacket and traipsed outside with Serena and
Lola as if everything had been resolved, but in her heart she
knew their kitchen conversation was going to stick with her
for a long time.

At the very least, Serena and Lola had given her a great
deal to think about.

It was almost five when the phone rang again. This time
Burke ambled over to it almost listlessly. Today had been
one of the worst in his memory. He could have been with
Candace and Charlie at the Sheridan ranch, and instead had
sat around here and watched the clock the whole damned
day. He'd done surveillance work many times and knew how
boring it could get. But today had been ten times, a hun-
dred times worse than anything else his career had ever de-
manded of him.

What really chafed was that he was only following his
own plan. Logic told him it was a good plan, but logic had
stopped being comforting hours ago.

He picked up the phone. "Hello."

"Burke? Joe Frazier here."

Relief flooded Burke's system, perking up his leaden spirits. "You're calling from Virgil's apartment?"

"Yes. I took about ten minutes to check the place for bugs before calling. Hope that's okay."

"It wasn't necessary, but you couldn't have known that. I'm not a hundred percent certain Benny isn't on to me, but I am positive he knows nothing about Virgil's involvement. Did you put on a big show when you got there?"

"Sure did. Yelled 'Dad' a few times, Virgil came out and we hugged and pounded each other's back. Like a real father and son who hadn't seen each other for a long time would do. I doubt if anyone in the complex missed it."

"Great. Has Virgil mentioned Benny's two visitors earlier today?"

"Yes. Do you know who they are?"

"No, but I called Hal. He's going to run their descriptions through the computer and see what comes up."

"Okay, fine. Is there anything special you want me doing, Burke? You're lead agent on this case, so you'll be calling the shots."

"Your primary duty is to watch Slocum. I haven't been able to do it by myself. Between you, Virgil and me, we'll cover him around the clock. Did you bring those vibrating cell phones I asked Hal to send along?"

"Got 'em right here."

"Good. It's already dark out, but we won't chance a meeting yet. Slip out at ten tonight. I'll be parked in the alley behind the complex. Bring my phone. Until then I'll be at this number."

"See you at ten," Joe said.

"Right."

Burke hung up, thinking grimly, five more hours of waiting. And after that there could be days of waiting and watching. Patience, he told himself. Patience.

Feeling hungry, he went to the kitchen and opened the refrigerator.

\* \* \*

After a supper of sandwiches, soft drinks and snack-type foods, Charlie said it was time that he, Candace and Ronnie went home. At the front door, everyone exchanged hugs and talked about the great day they'd had together. Serena said she was going to stay with Lola and Duke a little longer, but she wouldn't be far behind.

And finally Ronnie was in his car seat, Charlie was behind the wheel and Candace in the front passenger seat. They drove away.

"It really was a great day, wasn't it?" Charlie said, sounding serenely pleased with his family.

"Yes, it was," Candace agreed. She turned to look at her son and smiled because he was already sleeping. He'd worn himself out today, running from one thing to another. How he loved Uncle Duke's ranch. Wouldn't it be wonderful for a boy to grow up on a ranch?

Sighing quietly, she faced front again.

"And you enjoyed talking with the girls?" Charlie said.

"I always enjoy being with Serena and Lola."

"Duke said there's someone interested in buying the store."

"Yes, Lola said the deal looks very promising. She's anxious to be home full-time now. She showed me the room Duke and her are fixing up for a nursery. It's going to be beautiful."

"Appears that all three of you gals are currently in the decorating business," Charlie said with a chuckle.

Candace smiled. "Appears so. The living room is ready for painting, which I'm going to start doing tomorrow morning. It should go fast. All of the woodwork is masked off, so I'll be using a roller. Incidentally did I tell you about the windows?"

"No, I don't think you did."

"Well, I've decided what to do with them. I hope you like shutters."

Charlie cleared his throat. "I love shutters."

"Oh, good. I'm going to order them varnished the same color as the woodwork. It should be quite attractive."

"I'm sure it will be."

They fell silent. Charlie's eyes were on the road, and Candace put her head back. All day Burke had lurked somewhere in her mind. At times he'd been the *only* thing on her mind; at others he'd receded enough for her to talk and enjoy the family and the day.

But he had never once been completely absent. He was important to her, she finally had to admit. If he was a liar and a phony, heaven help her, because she didn't seem to be able to help herself. Certainly she couldn't eradicate her feelings for him, and God knew she'd tried. Tried so hard that she'd been waspish and downright mean to him, ignoring him as much as possible, talking to him as little as possible.

What if she was all wrong about Burke? What if he was exactly as he'd said, an educator on a sabbatical? Teaching was a wonderful occupation, a traditionally safe career. No physical danger and only the excitement of instilling knowledge into young minds.

Maybe she had misinterpreted everything Burke had been doing in Rocky Ford. And Serena and Lola were right. Charlie would never be talked into doing anything illegal or immoral.

She had been much too quick to judge Burke, probably because she'd felt drawn to him at their very first meeting and she hadn't been ready to feel anything for any man.

Was she ready now?

Did she have a choice? Weren't her feelings rather set, and weren't those feelings much more than physical attraction?

The term *physical attraction* caused a stirring in the pit of her stomach. She closed her eyes and permitted memory to expand the sensation. She had made passionate love with Burke while trying to keep her emotions from being affected.

Obviously she had failed. Just the thought of being in his arms again, of kissing him, of making love with him, was raising her temperature. She wanted it all again, wanted it desperately.

It *must* be love, she thought feverishly. If Burke was home when they got there . . .

She couldn't complete that boldly speculative thought. In the first place, even if Burke was home, Charlie would be, too. In the second, did she have the brass to approach Burke with such a vastly different attitude?

By the time they drove into town, Candace was a bundle of nerves. She had caused it herself with memory and sexually oriented conjecture, but knowing she was her own worst enemy didn't alleviate the condition.

When Charlie pulled into the driveway, she breathed a sigh of relief; Burke's vehicle was parked in its usual spot. In fact, it looked as though it hadn't been moved at all today.

How strange.

## Chapter Fifteen

Charlie carried the suitcase into the house, and Candace carried her sleeping son. The boy was really out; he barely moved when she lifted him from his car seat and into her arms.

Inside she went directly to Ronnie's bedroom and laid him in his crib. He looked so precious lying there that she bent over and lovingly kissed his soft cheek. He tried to act so grown-up and tough around Uncle Duke and the horses, but he was hardly more than a baby. Candace's heart swelled with love for her child, and she took several moments to just look at him sleeping so soundly.

Then she began removing his clothes to maneuver him into his pajamas. Ronnie slept through the process, and when he was snuggled in for the night, Candace quietly moved around his room, putting things away. After turning on the small night-light and switching off the ceiling fixture, she tiptoed out, leaving the door slightly ajar as she always did.

As she entered her own room, she spotted her suitcase. It took only a few minutes to empty and return it to her closet. She should be as tired as Ronnie, but there was an unaccustomed adrenaline pumping through her body, fueling a persistent urgency to see Burke. He hadn't gone out tonight, which pleased her. She was a little mystified over his vehicle appearing to be in exactly the same spot as it had been this morning, but that could merely be her imagination, or her eyesight and memory playing tricks on her. After all, Burke had stayed behind for a reason, and she couldn't visualize that reason being contained within the walls of this house.

Going to her bathroom, she brushed her hair and teeth, and dabbed a little perfume behind her ears and on her wrists. A lipstick was used sparingly. With her heart pounding nervously, she studied her reflection in the mirror. Looking into her own eyes, she wondered how best to express herself with Burke. She wanted to convey a less stringent, less doubting attitude to him, but her experience with the opposite sex was more or less confined to Ron and their marriage, and she wasn't at all sure of her ability to broach Burke on a subject with so many ramifications.

And yet she felt driven to do it. Unquestionably Serena's and Lola's assurances today had influenced her; she *had* been worried how Ron's family would feel about her being interested in another man. And their common-sense approach to Burke's and Charlie's furtive activities had greatly diminished her concerns. To be acutely honest, the only definitive or substantial feelings she now possessed about Burke were all positive. She had to talk to him.

Inhaling deeply, praying for composure during the upcoming conversation, she left her bathroom and walked down the hall to the kitchen.

She stopped dead in her tracks; the door to the coffee shop was closed again!

Had it been open when they got home? She couldn't remember.

But it was closed now. Candace hurried to peek into the living room. It was dark and vacant. Hurrying back to the bedroom wing, she knocked on Charlie's bedroom door. "Charlie?"

There was no answer. Candace felt her hopes and excitement draining away. Charlie and Burke were in the coffee shop again, talking about whatever it was they didn't want her overhearing. Burke hadn't even come out to say hello when she came home, and obviously Charlie had brought her suitcase to her bedroom and gone immediately to the coffee shop.

Disheartened, perplexed and irritated, Candace returned to her bedroom. She was *not* going to stand in line to talk to Burke. As a matter of fact, she might *never* talk to him! He and Charlie shutting her out as though she were a nosy child was getting darned tiresome.

It was after nine, she noticed with an angry glance at the clock on her bed stand. To heck with Burke—she would go to bed.

The sound of a car door awakened Candace. Although the driveway was on the other side of the house from her bedroom, she could always tell when someone arrived or left. Normally the distant sound didn't wake her, of course, but apparently she'd been sleeping lightly.

She checked the clock—11:03 p.m. Her lips pursed. The only nocturnal wanderer living in this house was Burke. Unless Charlie had gone with him tonight, which she doubted. She listened intently, and, exactly as she'd thought, only one person entered by the back door and began tiptoeing through the kitchen. Next she heard Burke go into his room and quietly close the door.

She lay there with an abnormally fast pulse rate. If she still wanted that talk with Burke, wasn't this as good a time as any? The idea required some thought, of course. She would be in his bedroom, which was probably not the best location for a sensible discussion. On the other hand, just where in this house was there any real chance of privacy?

Not that Charlie would deliberately barge into a private conversation, but how would he know she was seeking privacy? Certainly he would have no clue from her public behavior toward Burke thus far.

Besides, maybe she was seeking more than a talk with Burke. A shiver rippled through her body. It was impossible to think of him getting ready for bed without visualizing him undressing. That image made her feel too warm, and she kicked back the covers to cool off.

It didn't work; her fever was internal and wouldn't be quashed by cool night air on her body.

A bath would feel good, she thought next. In her anger she had come to bed without a shower or bath. She was wide-awake, horribly restless and discontent, and the decision to go to Burke's room was not an easy one to make. Perhaps considering it while soaking in a bubble bath would smooth down the sharp edges now pricking her conscience.

Getting up, she switched on a lamp and slid open the drawer of her bureau that contained her night wear. Something fresh for after her bath, she thought while studying the drawer's contents. There was an array of neatly folded pajamas and nightgowns, something for every season of the year.

A royal blue satin nightgown caught her eye. A matching robe hung in her closet. At the moment she was wearing plaid cotton pajamas, and a sudden yearning to feel satin against her skin had her lifting the nightgown from the drawer. She brought it up to her cheek and caught the scent of the tiny perfumed packets she kept in the drawer.

Yes, she thought dreamily, tonight she needed a satin nightie.

Without stopping to wonder why satin was necessary to her present state of mind, she took the gown and robe and silently stole down the hall to her bathroom. The tub was only half-full of water and bubbles when she climbed into it.

It felt delicious, and she laid her head back against the lip of the bathtub and closed her eyes. The water level rose to her breasts, and with her toes she turned off the faucets.

For a few minutes she thought of nothing at all, just lay there and enjoyed the sensation of hot water and scented bubbles on her skin. This kind of leisurely bath was rare these days, but she decided that she really should take the time to do it more often.

But wasn't she doing it now for a reason? Her eyes popped open as the question of whether or not to go to Burke's room for that talk bolted into her mind. Logically it made sense. He came and went unpredictably. Or he was with Charlie. When, during the day, would she be able to speak to him alone?

All right, so she still didn't completely trust him. But as things stood now, wasn't that *her* problem? Charlie obviously trusted him, and she should put her own misgivings aside and rely on Charlie's good judgment.

So cancel that deterrent, she thought. Besides, wasn't there really only one reason why she was procrastinating on that decision? If she went to Burke's room at this time of night, he was apt to get the wrong idea.

But wasn't the ''wrong idea'' already embedded in her own mind? Wasn't that why she needed satin instead of cotton on her skin? Wasn't she feeling sensual, feminine and tense with unrequited passion because of Burke?

She groaned quietly. If she fell in love with him and he turned out to be the phony she had initially suspected him to be, she would have only herself to blame for the ensuing misery she would suffer. Knowing that so clearly, why didn't she just forget about him? She should get out of this tub, get back into her plaid pajamas and return to her own room.

But when she finally released the drain and stepped out of the tub, her eyes were on the satin gown. After drying off, she reached for the elegant garment, lifted it over her head and let it slide down her body.

She brushed her teeth, cleansed her face, applied moisturizer and some lipstick and brushed her hair. Taking just a moment to rinse out the tub and drop her pajamas into the hamper, she put on the satin robe, loosely tied the sash, turned out the bathroom light and stepped into the hall.

There was a peculiar calmness in her system, as though the internal ruckus she'd undergone over going to Burke's room had been utter nonsense. She'd known from the moment his homecoming had awakened her that she was going to do this, so what had all the debate been about?

Drawing a deep breath, she approached his door. Then she realized she couldn't knock—Charlie might hear and stick his head out of his room to see what was going on. She would feel very silly standing at Burke's door in her satin robe, and worse, embarrassed.

Slowly she turned the knob. Just as slowly she pushed the door open a crack. The room was dark. Burke was already in bed and probably asleep.

Frowning, she cursed her poor timing. She shouldn't have lingered in the bubble bath. She probably should have skipped the bath entirely and come directly to Burke's room when he got home. Now he was sleeping, and what kind of conversation could they have with him bleary-eyed and likely annoyed over being awakened?

Candace was wrong about Burke being asleep. He'd gone immediately to bed when he came in, but he'd been lying in the dark, at first thinking about his meeting with Joe Frazier in the alley behind the Highland Village apartment complex. Joe was a good agent, intelligent and cooperative, and Burke was glad he'd asked Hal specifically to send him to Rocky Ford to help with this case. With Joe staying right next door, Benny's every move would be known. And Burke could actually go to bed without worrying about missing something crucial to the case he was hoping to build against Benny.

Then he'd heard Candace leave her room, enter the bathroom and run water into the bathtub. That picture had taken precedence over all others, canceling thoughts of duty, plans to nail Benny and even gratitude that it was Joe Frazier helping him out.

In his mind's eye, he saw her shedding her clothes and getting into the tub. Nice, he thought with masculine appreciation. Very nice. He fantasized then, imagining himself joining her in the tub, their legs entwining, their wet, slippery bodies sliding together. A small chuckle ensued; he would gladly wash hers if she would wash his.

But his amusement vanished very quickly. Candace, love of his life, naked in a tub of scented, steamy water, was an extremely arousing mental image, and the resulting sexual aches in his body weren't funny. Groaning, he flopped onto his back and tried to think of something else.

He failed abysmally. With gluelike tenacity, the picture of Candace in that bathtub refuted elimination. A relief of enormous proportions alleviated some of his discomfort when he heard the bathroom door open and close again. Now he could go to sleep.

But the next moment brought him to full alert and caused his heart to skip a beat. In the dark he couldn't see the doorknob turning, but he could hear it. Then he could see the dim night-light in the hall through a narrow crack as the door was pushed open. Candace's face, vaguely defined but visible, appeared in the gap. He thought she was frowning, but couldn't be certain. But the fact that she was peering into his room at all was astounding.

She appeared to be floundering, about whether she should go in or leave. Burke's heart was hammering, and he was amazed that he could speak so calmly.

"Hello, Candace."

His voice from the bed nearly made Candace bolt. She steadied herself. "Could...could we talk?" she whispered.

"Absolutely. Come in." Sitting up, Burke snapped on the nightstand lamp.

Candace slipped in and, after closing the door, leaned against it to catch her breath. All she could see in the light of that lamp was bare masculine skin and brawn. Burke didn't wear pajamas to bed, but had she expected he would? Did he even have undershorts on beneath those blankets?

Burke was wondering about her apparel, as well. That long, slinky robe was gorgeous, shimmering wherever the light touched it. Was this the kind of thing she wore every night? It was an exciting and provocative thought.

"Pull that chair over here," he told her. "I'd get up and do it for you, but I'm not exactly dressed for company."

"I thought you were sleeping," she said as she uneasily crossed over to the chair. Should she do as he'd asked and move it closer to the bed? Was there any reason why they couldn't talk with her sitting in it where it was?

"I was having trouble falling asleep." Even as he spoke, Burke sensed her quandary. "I wouldn't want to wake up Charlie. If you're closer, we can speak more quietly."

It was as good an excuse as any for moving the chair, and Candace latched on to it. Of course Burke didn't want to wake Charlie, not when she was in his room. But then, neither did she want Charlie knowing she was there.

The problem began when she was finally seated—about two feet from the bed—and trying not to look at Burke's naked chest and muscular shoulders. Why was she here? What had she wanted to tell him? Her mind spun with confusion.

Burke was so thrilled with the whole thing that he didn't care what they talked about. "Did you have a pleasant day at the ranch?" he asked.

"Very pleasant," she replied, trying desperately behind the mundane answer to organize her thoughts. "Um, I'm sure you're wondering why I . . . I'm bothering you at this time of night."

"Candace, you bother me every minute of every day," he said softly. "I'm not wondering anything. I'm just drinking in the sight of you and thanking the powers that be that you're here at all. You're beautiful in that robe, but then you're beautiful in anything." He paused and added in a low-pitched voice, "Or nothing."

She felt a rush of heat. Maybe it wasn't gentlemanly of him to remind her of their first time together in this room, but her being here again was hardly ladylike. If either of them was a phony, it was her. She could have managed to catch him alone sometime tomorrow, or the next day, if conversation was all she wanted from him.

Why carry on this ridiculous charade any longer? If she couldn't be totally honest with Burke, how could she ask it of him?

She looked squarely into his eyes, a bold move for her. "You like me, don't you?"

His eyes took on a sensual gleam. "What I feel for you is much more than liking. Is that what you came in here to talk about?"

"Cutting through the disguise I gave it, I think it is."

"Why would you need to disguise anything?"

"Self-protection, I suppose." After a moment she said, "You have to know how doubtful I've been about your background story."

"Of course," Burke said quietly. "Should I assume you've accepted it now? Accepted me as I am?" He couldn't have surmised this event in a hundred years. Had something happened today to alter her opinion of him? Whatever, he felt like shouting *Hallelujah*.

"I'm not sure about complete acceptance of all you've said and done," she said slowly. "But I'm not going to dwell on the doubts anymore."

"Because you like me, too."

She took a breath. "Yes, I like you, too. I . . . didn't want to."

"Something sparked between us the day we met. That kind of spark is hard to extinguish."

Her gaze drifted from his. "I guess it is," she whispered huskily. Her heart was beating wildly, with her whole system in some kind of crazy, uncontrollable mode.

"Come over here," he said in the softest, sexiest voice she'd ever heard.

She dared to look at him again. Never had she known anyone so handsome. Every part of him was perfection, his eyes, his mouth, his hair. For a moment her breath caught in her throat; was she so shallow as to be overwhelmed by a man's good looks?

No, she thought. Her feelings for this man weren't at all shallow. Why play coy and pretend she didn't want what he did?

Rising from the chair, she untied the loose knot in the sash of her robe. Burke's eyes glittered with anticipation. When she slid the robe from her shoulders, his arousal became insistent and demanding to the point of discomfort.

He moved to the middle of the bed and pulled back the corner of his blankets in blatant invitation. He watched Candace lift her chin a little, as though she was bolstering her courage.

"Don't be afraid," he said. "I'll never knowingly hurt you, Candace."

She knew he wasn't talking about physical harm, but emotional injury was sometimes much worse and she knew he possessed the power to scar her psyche forever.

But caution for a future that was nebulous at best wasn't nearly as appealing as what awaited her in Burke's bed.

Trancelike she took the few steps between chair and bed, but instead of lying beside him, she sat down. Their gazes locked. He released his hold on the blankets.

"You're reluctant," he said quietly. "Tell me why."

She drew in a long breath. He watched her breasts rise and fall within the satin bodice of her nightgown and had to suck in a breath of his own. "Candace?" he whispered raggedly.

"I . . . I guess I am afraid."

"You weren't afraid the first time."

"But I didn't like you then."

Her candor made him laugh, albeit briefly. "I love your honesty, sweetheart."

She looked into his eyes. "I love honesty, too, Burke."

Internally he winced. "You said you weren't going to dwell on doubts any longer."

"True," she concurred, recalling her determination to put her trust in Charlie's judgment.

Burke raised the blankets again. "Lie next to me. Let me hold you."

A teasing expression in her eyes surprised him. "And that's all you want to do, just hold me?" she said.

His smile contained a devilish quality. "Is holding you all you want me to do?"

She surprised him again, this time with a slow-burning smile and a sensually whispered "I think you know what I want." Getting to her feet, she slipped the straps of her gown from her shoulders. It glided gracefully down her body to puddle on the carpet. She stood there for a moment and let him look at her. His stunned gaze moved up and down her naked body, and she felt warm and rosy all over because of it.

"Have I shocked you?" she asked.

He swallowed. "You're the most exciting, the most beautiful, the most incredible woman I've ever known. Get into this bed before I do something totally insane."

Laughing sensuously, she crawled under his blankets. Immediately he gathered her into his arms. As she'd suspected, he slept nude, because the first thing that truly penetrated the intensity of desire directing her brain was his hard and heavy manhood pressing into her abdomen.

His mouth found hers, and his kiss was rough and demanding. Apparently the game-playing was over, she thought before losing herself in that kiss and the sensation of his hands moving on her body.

Her hands were as greedy as his. The hunger in her system made her wanton, bold and uninhibited. She bit at his lips, moaned when he kissed and sucked on her nipples and forgot that anything else existed in this wacky world but the wild and wonderful passion between them.

He caressed her back, her hips, her thighs, each lingering touch bringing her such pleasure she nearly wept. Kisses landed wherever they fell, both his and hers. The blankets were thrown back. Since they were both overheated internally, no extraneous warmth was necessary.

"Oh, Burke," she whispered emotionally.

"I know, sweetheart, I know."

She wanted him inside of her, ached from the wanting. "Make love to me," she moaned. "Do it, oh, please do it."

He didn't need to be asked twice. Quickly he took care of protection. His first thrust into her was gentle, only because he cared so much for her, but he couldn't sustain the gentleness and it evolved into a maelstrom of gyrations that had them both sweating.

They exchanged breathless kisses, but their real energy was poured into their rhythmic dance of love. Her fingertips made impressions in his back. Low, keening moans came from deep in her throat. The bed had a squeak; neither of them heard it.

The pressure mounted. "Stay with me," Burke mumbled thickly. He wasn't going to be able to hold back the final rush for very much longer.

His plea hadn't been necessary. Candace was going over the edge, crying out, clinging to him, squeezing her legs around him. He let go then, and kept himself from shouting her name through sheer effort. Waking Charlie at this moment would not be wise. Even though he knew Charlie approved of a match between him and Candace, he might not approve of her being in his bed before a public commitment.

Burke kissed her, muffling her gradually quieter moans by taking them into his own mouth. Then he whispered, "Easy, honey, easy. We're not alone in this house."

She drew a shuddering breath. Tears were dripping down her temples. She was still feeling the intensity of her climax, trembling from it.

"I love you," she whispered before thinking. Instantly she tensed. It was true; the worst had happened and she'd fallen in love, but she should not have told him her feelings. Not yet. There was still too much to learn about him.

Burke uneasily studied her teary face in the lamplight. Dare he reveal his own feelings when there were so many lies between them? What was best for their relationship? Dear Lord, what was best? He loved her madly, but did he have the right to say so until he could tell her everything?

But she looked so forlorn, so regretful that she'd blurted those three words. He'd promised to never hurt her, and would anything ever hurt her more than his silence at this moment?

"I love you, too," he said with all of the emotion in his soul. "More than life itself."

Fresh tears spilled from her eyes. Winding her arm around his neck, she brought his head down to lie on the pillow beside hers. Her heart was pounding with new fears. Their declarations of love were premature. They should not have spoken.

"Please be happy," he whispered in her ear.

"There...there's more to a serious relationship than sex." He raised his head to see her. "Much more."

Misery appeared in her eyes. "I don't know you."

"You will, Candace. Can you believe that and trust me?"

"You haven't been truthful about why you're in Rocky Ford, have you?"

"No."

"And you still can't tell me what brought you here?"

"Not yet. Soon. I promise."

"But you've told Charlie."

"Charlie knows, yes."

She turned her head. "Charlie can know but I can't. Is that fair?"

"It's the way it is, Candace. Not everything is fair. Besides, I'm not sure fairness should even be an issue between us. Try not to think about it. Just believe I love you."

He wasn't going to tell her anything. Her spirits plummeted.

"I have to get up," she said thickly.

He searched her eyes for a long moment, then nodded and moved to the bed. She scooted over and got off the bed.

Hastily she scooped up her nightgown and put it on, followed by her robe.

"Are you angry?" he asked.

"No. Good night, Burke." She walked to the door, opened it and slipped out.

Burke looked at that closed door for a long time. She might not be angry, but neither was she happy.

But she loved him. He at least had that to remember until this damnable case was in the past and he could talk freely about it.

Sighing, he got up and headed for his bathroom.

## Chapter Sixteen

The bell above the door to Charlie's Place tinkled, announcing a new arrival. Burke glanced up from his newspaper and damned near swallowed his teeth. Dropping the paper, he leapt out of his chair and dashed over to the newcomer. Taking his mother by the arm, he steered her back outside.

"Burke, for heaven's sake," Meredith protested. "What *are* you doing?"

Burke drew Meredith to the far end of the porch. "I might ask the same of you, Mother," he said dryly. She was dressed beautifully, in a navy wool coat with a red scarf, black leather boots, gloves and handbag. Her pale blond hair—tinted for many years now to maintain its youthful sheen—was perfectly arranged; her makeup was expertly applied.

"I came to see you, of course," she said calmly.

Burke folded his arms. "Who did you squeeze to get information about my exact location?" At the curb, just on the other side of the driveway, Meredith's car was parked, a luxury model—American made—and Burke could see her chauffeur behind the wheel. Meredith claimed that she never deliberately sought attention, but people in Rocky Ford did not ride around in chauffeur-driven automobiles. She would be the talk of the town. Burke's lips tensed.

Meredith smiled. "We're all entitled to a few secrets, Burke. I don't believe I'll answer that question. Please don't look so grouchy. There's nothing wrong with a mother paying her son a visit."

"In this case, there is," Burke growled. "You know I'm on undercover duty here."

"Oh, my, you really are upset."

Burke's mind was racing. What was he going to do with her? The first thing, of course, was to get her off this porch and out of sight.

"Let's talk in your car," he said, taking her arm and heading them both for the steps to the sidewalk.

"You really should be wearing a jacket, Burke. It's cold today. And please stop rushing me. I do not walk as fast as you do."

Charlie came out just as they were starting down the steps. "Burke, is everything all right?" Charlie asked. He smiled at Meredith, who smiled in return. Smiled quite congenially, in fact, Burke noticed with some surprise. Meredith was not normally friendly with strangers, even *smiling* strangers. Her aloofness usually stayed intact until new acquaintances proved they were trustworthy and not using her to better their own lot in life.

"Hello," she said, speaking pleasantly. "I'm Meredith Mallory, Burke's mother."

Charlie's smile broadened. "Well, isn't this nice? I'm very pleased to meet you, ma'am. I'm Charlie Fanon, Burke's friend."

Burke groaned silently. He could see three people inside the coffee shop peering out the windows. This little tableau had to end.

"Charlie, I'm going to escort Mother to her car," Burke said.

"Sure, Burke, whatever you say." Charlie was still smiling at Meredith.

"Good meeting you, Mr. Fanon," Meredith called as Burke hurried her down the steps and toward her car. "Goodness, you're impatient," she chided her son.

Burke motioned for the chauffeur to stay where he was and opened the back door of the automobile himself. After Meredith got in, he climbed in. "Hello, Roger. How are you?"

"Just fine, Burke," the chauffeur responded. He'd been with the Mallory family for almost thirty years, and was more friend than employee to Burke.

But he wanted to speak to his mother in private. "Roger, would you mind leaving us alone for a few minutes?"

"Not at all." Roger got out and closed the door.

"Now," Burke said firmly, turning to his mother, "is there a reason you drove so many miles to see me?"

"Do I need a reason to visit my son?" Meredith retorted.

"Mother, there are two people in Rocky Ford who know my true identity. Only two. I *have* to maintain that anonymity. My entire operation depends on it."

"There's something very wrong with a career that comes between a mother and son, Burke."

"You may be right, but I cannot change the status quo today." Burke took Meredith's hand and spoke gently. "I have to ask you to leave, Mother. I'm also asking for your understanding. I've put too much time and effort into this case to endanger its success for any reason."

"How could my presence hurt your case?" Meredith scoffed.

"It's a long story, which I'll be happy to tell you in minute detail once it's over. For now just believe that I'm doing what I must."

Meredith sighed. "I'd hoped we could at least spend the day together. I could get a room at a motel for tonight, and we could have dinner and catch up."

"I'm sorry, but that's impossible."

"So, I'm to leave town at once."

"I don't mean to sound coldhearted, but yes."

"I know you're not coldhearted, Burke. Well, I'm not pleased with this, but it does appear that I should not have acted so impulsively. I rarely do, you know."

"I know, Mother."

"Does Mr. Fanon know your true identity?"

"Yes, he's one of the people I trust with that information."

"And the other?"

"No one you know, Mother."

"Very well, Roger and I will return to Helena. Do you have any idea how much longer you'll be tied to this place?"

"I think things are coming to a head, but there are no guarantees. It could be a day or a week. Maybe more."

"May I at least call you?"

Burke couldn't help smiling. She hadn't only wrangled his location out of someone, but she also had Charlie's telephone number.

"No calls, Mother. But I'll call you when I can. Deal?"

After a moment Meredith nodded. "Since I have no choice in the matter, what can I do but agree? But do call, Burke." She laid her gloved hand on his arm. "A mother doesn't stop worrying about her child just because he's a grown man, which you will never fully appreciate until you have a child of your own."

Burke took her hand and leaned forward to kiss her cheek. "I know, Mother. I can't sit here any longer. Goodbye. And I will call, I promise." He opened the door and got out. "Roger," he said to the chauffeur, who had been leaning against the front fender of the car. "Everything's fine. You and Mother may leave now."

"Goodbye, Burke. Take care," Meredith said quietly. Roger was back behind the wheel. "We're returning to Helena, Roger."

"Yes, ma'am."

Burke stood by as the big car glided away from the curb. Breathing a sigh of relief even while wondering what damage might result from this incident, he watched his mother's automobile drive down the street.

Charlie was watching, as well, if rather furtively. He'd had questions hurled at him when he'd come back inside, primarily "Who is she, Charlie?"

He'd shrugged and joked and eluded an honest answer. Now he saw Burke heading for the porch. Once Burke was inside, Charlie said in an undertone, "Your mother is a remarkably attractive lady."

Burke had no verbal answer for that, but he managed a weak smile and a nod of agreement.

A third person in the Fanon household had also seen Meredith Mallory. But Candace's view had been restricted by distance and the many leafless shrubs and trees between the living-room windows and the street. She had started rolling paint on the walls right after breakfast, and it was completely coincidental that she'd been working near the windows when Burke walked his mother to her car. All Candace really saw was a strikingly dressed blond woman on his arm, just enough of a view to make her sick at heart. Last night he had told her he loved her; today a very attractive woman had come to see him.

"And they're not strangers," she mumbled as she forced herself back to work. "Not strangers at all."

How could she trust Burke, as he'd asked her to do last night, when unusual incidents kept occurring? She would bet anything that this was something else he wouldn't talk about.

Burke's instinct about things coming to a head in the Slocum case was getting stronger—persistent enough to keep him awake and on edge. That night around midnight, even though Joe Frazier was a sharp-minded agent and right next door to Benny, Burke got out of bed, dressed and went outside to his four-wheeler with the intention of driving to his special parking spot in the alley behind the apartment complex. His cell phone was hooked to his belt. If Joe should call him, the phone would vibrate rather than ring, an invaluable aid in surveillance work.

It was unusually dark outside. Wintry clouds covered the moon and stars, and the night air was stingingly cold. Burke wore a heavy jacket and gloves, and was warm enough. Climbing into his rig, he started the engine. The windshield was frosted over, so he let the engine idle a few minutes so the defroster could warm up and do its job.

Then he switched on the headlights and backed out of Charlie's driveway onto the dark and seemingly deserted street.

In her room and bed, Candace lay awake, tense as a coiled spring. She had heard Burke leave his room and the house. She'd listened to the engine of his vehicle, and could tell when he backed it from the driveway.

She heaved a bereft sigh and fought tears. She was in love with a man who snuck around like a thief in the night.

Heaven help her.

Burke slowly traversed Foxworth Street to the corner just beyond Highland Village and made a right turn. Another right had him in the alley. He braked to a stop in his usual spot and turned off the lights and ignition. He had a clear view of the front doors of Virgil's and Benny's apartments; both units were dark.

Something continued to gnaw at him. Maybe it was nothing more than his own nerves, he thought. He didn't like having had to send his mother away today, nor did he like lying to Candace. In fact, he ardently wished that whatever Benny was planning would happen this very minute so he could arrest that troublemaking jerk and start telling people the truth about himself.

After about thirty minutes of staring at those darkened apartments, he shook his head in self-disgust. What in hell was he doing out here at this time of night, other than freezing his butt off?

Wearing a glowering, dissatisfied frown, he started the engine and continued on down the alley to the first cross street, without turning on the headlights. His eyes had become accustomed to the black night, and he wanted to play it as safely as possible. A right turn took him back to Foxworth Street, where he made a left to return to Charlie's house.

He was reaching for the switch for the headlights when up ahead he noticed a car parked across the street from Charlie's Place, exactly where that blue sedan had been parked the first time he'd seen it.

"It couldn't be the same car," he muttered. But he had to check it out anyway. Leaving the headlights off, he cruised slowly onto Foxworth Street and parked at the curb. After shutting down the engine, he got out and closed the door as noiselessly as possible.

The car was at least a block away, and Burke walked quickly but cautiously toward it. This time he was going to see who was so interested in the Fanon home.

He could walk very quietly when necessary, and his boot steps were practically soundless. He heard the idling engine of the car long before he reached it, although the hike from his own vehicle took only a few minutes.

It was definitely the same car, he thought grimly as he got close enough to see it more distinctly. Now to get a look at its driver. Approaching the sedan from its back end, he stooped down low to move around the trunk to the driver's side. If that door wasn't locked, he was going to yank the person out into the street and hope he broke his damned neck.

All but on his knees, he reached for the door handle and pressed the latch. It opened. The interior lights came on. A woman yelped. But before Burke realized it *was* a woman behind the wheel, he had her by the shoulders and was pulling her out of the car.

It was the red-haired woman from the café! Peering down at her, he growled, "Who are you, and why have you been watching the Fanon home?"

Andrea felt certain that death, or, at the very least, serious injury, was imminent. She was so frightened her teeth were chattering. This was the man who drove that black four-wheeler. Since it hadn't been parked in the driveway, as it usually was, she'd thought it safe to stop for a few minutes.

"Oh, please," she moaned. "Let me go. I wasn't doing anything wrong."

Burke hung on to her shoulders. "Window-peeking is a crime, lady, whether you think so or not. What's your name?"

"I . . . I don't want to tell you."

Burke spied her purse on the seat of the car. Holding her with one hand, he reached in and picked up the purse with the other.

"Are . . . are you going to rob me?" she said in a scared, cracking voice. "I don't have much money with me."

"Don't be absurd," Burke snapped. "I'm not a thief." He handed her the purse. "Take out your wallet and give it to me."

Though her hands were trembling, she dug out her wallet and passed it to him. He flipped it open and found her driver's license. It was a California license, which surprised him.

"Andrea Charlotte Dillon," he read out loud. "Well, Ms. Dillon, seems as though you're a long way from home."

Her nerves were beginning to settle down, and she had a few questions of her own. "I've seen your vehicle parked in the Fanon driveway. Are you related to Charles Fanon?"

"Yeah," Burke said with some sarcasm. "I'm Charlie's long-lost son."

Andrea's heart skipped a beat. Another son? But why wasn't he mentioned in the newspaper articles she'd saved that recited Charlie's family? Something didn't add up. And he was still holding her by a strong grasp of her shoulder, treating her as though she were a criminal. Who was he, really?

Burke was thinking. He had scared this woman spitless—she was still shaking—and maybe she had all kinds of ulterior motives for being here. But he hadn't followed police procedure for accosting a suspect and was putting his career on the line by skipping the legalities.

He couldn't flash his badge at her, but he could treat her with a little more respect.

He spoke without gruffness. "Are you going to tell me why you've been watching the Fanon home?"

His kinder voice calmed Andrea's fearfully racing heart a little. If he really was one of Charlie's offspring—even though she had run across no evidence of Charlie having another son—he had every right to question her curiosity.

"I know it looks bad," she said tremulously. "But it's not. Please believe me."

"Good or bad, you have a reason for being here. I want to know what it is."

"I . . . can't tell you," she whispered.

"Do you have a police record, Ms. Dillon?"

"Good heavens, no!"

Her shock was so genuine, Burke found himself believing her. But she could be a great little actress, feigning all that trembling, big-eyed fear. It was only smart to learn her history for himself.

"Get in your car," he told her, steering her toward the door.

Gladly she got behind the wheel. Was it over? Was he going to let her leave now?

She bit down on her bottom lip when she realized what he was doing—copying the information from her driver's license and social-security card into a small notebook.

He handed back her wallet. "I'll know all about you in a day or so, Ms. Dillon."

"You won't unless you're a cop," she retorted, tucking her wallet into her purse.

His eyes narrowed slightly. She wasn't stupid, was she?

"Do you have a Rocky Ford address?" he asked, again speaking sharply.

She gathered her courage and spoke just as sharply. "My local address is none of your business. May I go now?"

"Yes, but my advice to you is not to come back. I don't know what you're up to, but I suspect it won't benefit Charlie or anyone living in his house. Stay away from here, Ms. Dillon. I don't want to see this car on Foxworth Street again."

Rather than argue that she had every right to drive her car on any street she wished, she put the car in gear and drove away.

Burke made one more notation in his notebook: the number of the license plate on her car. With the information he had, he would find out all there was to know about Andrea Charlotte Dillon in a very short span of time, even her local address.

The computer age was great, as far as police work went.

*Andrea kept gulping deep breaths of air as she drove home. What a ghastly experience that had been. Learning that Charlie had another son was exciting. Though she was perplexed and not sure if it was true.*

*Lord, he'd appeared out of nowhere. Andrea shuddered. She would be much more careful about locking her car doors after this—that was certain.*

*As always, pulling into her own driveway was relieving. Turning off the ignition, she laid her head on the steering wheel with a heavy sigh. She couldn't go on like this very much longer. Her nerves were all but shattered.*

*"Either do what you came here for or get out of Dodge,"* *she muttered in self-recrimination.*

Again Candace was awakened by Burke's homecoming. She stiffened under the covers, and became stiffer still when he stopped at her bedroom door. He wouldn't dare come in, would he?

After a moment he continued on to his own room, and the surge of disappointment she felt angered her.

Bitterly punching her pillow, she turned to her side. Why was this happening to her? Why had she fallen in love with a man of Burke's questionable nature? Normal people did not wander around in the middle of the night. What did he do when he left the house at such peculiar hours?

Would she ever know?

And who was that lovely blond woman who had come to see him?

That was probably something else she would never know.

The next morning Candace was painting when she saw Serena and Lola getting out of Lola's car. After wiping her hands on a clean rag, she hurried to the kitchen door to greet them.

They both looked beautiful, dressed for work, with their hair and makeup perfect. They came in smelling of cold, fresh air and expensive perfume.

Cheerful and bright eyed, they each hugged Candace and asked, ''Where's Ronnie?''

''In the coffee shop with Charlie,'' Candace told them.

Lola cocked an eyebrow. ''And where is the mysterious Mr. Mallory?''

Candace sighed. ''In the coffee shop with Charlie.''

''We're here to meet him,'' Serena announced. ''Does Dad have a lot of customers right now?''

''I don't know,'' Candace said. ''I've been in the living room painting for the past two hours.''

''Oh, I have to see it,'' Lola exclaimed, heading for the living room.

Serena and Candace followed. Lola stood in the center of the almost denuded room and looked around. ''I love the color, Candy. When will the upholsterer be finished with the sofa and chairs?''

''A few more days.'' She told them about the shutters she had ordered. ''I think they'll look good in here. What do you think?''

''I love the idea,'' Serena said. Lola concurred.

''Well, we don't have much time. Let's go and meet Burke,'' Serena said. ''You'll introduce us, won't you, Candace?''

"Why don't the two of you just go in and let Charlie do the honors? There are paint spatters all over me."

The cousins flitted away, leaving Candace to her paint roller and dour thoughts. *Depressed thoughts* might be a more accurate term, she decided. Or even *sad thoughts.* The truth was, she was riding a painfully emotional low. *Can you believe that and trust me?* Burke had pleaded the other night. She was trying, but it wasn't easy.

Fifteen minutes later Lola and Serena returned to the living room.

"He's gorgeous," Lola exclaimed.

"And charming," Serena said.

Candace smiled weakly. "I guess he is."

Lola kissed her cheek. "We have to run. Don't let him get away, Candy. A college professor who looks like that? Heavens, if I weren't already madly in love and married, I'd give you a run for your money."

Serena smiled consolingly at Candace. "Don't pay any attention to her teasing, Candy. I'm sure you'll do what's right for you and Ronnie." She, too, kissed Candace's cheek. "Bye, honey. Talk to you soon."

Candace followed them to the back door. "Bye," she called as they hurried down the steps and around the house to Lola's car. "Thanks for stopping in."

Closing the door, she turned around and there was Burke.

"Nice women," he said while looking directly into her eyes. "The whole Fanon family is nice." She could tell he was saying one thing and thinking another. Thinking something very personal and intimate. Candace's heartbeat went crazy.

She tried to duck around him, but he caught her by the arm. "Stay a minute," he said, still sounding like sin and seduction to Candace's ears.

"Please don't," she said to him. "I'm covered with paint and not in the best of moods."

"In other words, leave you alone right now? How about tonight? Will your mood be better tonight?"

"Will you be home tonight?" she snapped before thinking. Changing her tone, she added, "Or are you asking me for a date for tonight?" Yes, she thought. A real date would probably be the most beneficial thing that could happen to their bizarre relationship. They could talk about ordinary things, what he liked, what she liked, and really get to know each other. Was that what he was thinking, too?

"Sorry," he said quietly. "No can do."

"Oh, I see. When you said 'how about tonight,' you were suggesting I come to your room again."

"Don't be bitter, honey."

She looked at him for a long moment, then shook off his hand and walked away.

Burke almost went after her, but then changed his mind. As she'd said, she wasn't in the best of moods. This was not a good time for him to be putting on any pressure.

But he hoped she would think about tonight for the remainder of the day and come to his room as she had before.

Yes, indeed, he hoped that very much.

## Chapter Seventeen

Burke sat in his four-wheeler in the alley behind Highland Village with tension gripping every cell of his body. Joe had called earlier. *Benny has two guests this evening, Burke. Virgil said they're the same men who were here before.*

The descriptions of the two men Virgil had supplied Burke with had been run through the computer in Helena, and Hal had said there were several possibilities as far as their identities went. No positive IDs, though, which really didn't matter, Burke felt now. They were working for or with Benny Slocum, which made them criminals in his book, whatever their names.

He could see Benny's front door, but the setup kept bothering him. If Benny and his cohorts left suddenly, they could drive away before he got around the block to follow. He could lose them, a sickening thought. If they succeeded in whatever scurrilous activity they had planned, right under his and Joe's noses, neither of them would ever live it down. He'd put too much time, effort, worry and lies into this case to let that happen.

Using his cellular phone, he dialed Joe's number. "Yeah?" Joe said almost immediately.

"I'm going to get out of this alley and park on the street. I won't have the view of Slocum's apartment I have now, so call me the second something happens."

"What if nothing more happens than those two guys leaving? Still want me to call?"

"Yes, but I think this is it, Joe. When they leave, so will Benny. They're killing time right now, waiting for a specific hour."

"Possibly. All right, I'll call if I hear so much as a peep from next door."

"Talk to you later." Burke pushed the appropriate button to end the call and rehooked the phone to his belt. Starting the vehicle engine, he drove down the alley to the cross street, made two right turns and parked at the curb about a hundred feet west of Highland Village's entrance.

Tonight he was armed. A long-range rifle with an infrared scope and a sawed-off shotgun lay on the back seat. He wore a double shoulder holster under his jacket bearing two handguns.

He was also carrying his badge.

It was frustrating that he couldn't see anything of the apartment complex other than the bright lights above the carport, but he didn't dare park any closer. Joe was his eyes and ears from here on in. At least now he was in a position to follow Benny and his pals.

It was late and dark and cold. Burke huddled deeper into his jacket. There were two things on his mind these days: nabbing Benny and loving Candace. He'd asked her to come to his room tonight, and he wasn't there. She must be getting damned tired of this whole hide-and-seek routine. It was depressing for him; he could only imagine what must it be for her.

He took heart in the fact that she'd said she loved him. Maybe she regretted saying it, but it gave him hope. He drifted into a soothing fantasy. Benny and his pals were in jail where they belonged, and he and Candace were talking. He apologized for his lies, told her everything and

watched a relieved expression develop on her beautiful face.
She threw her arms around his neck. They kissed passion-
ately. She apologized for doubting him. He said it was all
right, that he understood completely. They kissed again, and
the grand finale of the fantasy, which made Burke smile in
pleasurable satisfaction, was him proposing marriage. She
said yes. They swore undying love for each other and then
made love.

Burke sighed as reality returned. His dream would hap-
pen—he was certain of it—but when? If his instinct was on
the money, tonight was the night for Benny's big deal. He
prayed it was true. He had never wanted to see the end of a
case more.

In spite of the cold, he was getting sleepy. Shaking him-
self awake, he went over his time in Rocky Ford again to
check for loose ends.

Andrea Dillon was a loose end, he thought with a frown
of perplexity, one he couldn't get any kind of handle on by
himself. He had called Hal with the data he had gathered on
Ms. Dillon and her vehicle, and requested a thorough
background check. It would take a day or so, then Hal
would get back to him. There was little point to Burke
wondering why Andrea Dillon watched the Fanon home in
the wee hours of dark nights, but he couldn't help himself.
He'd thought of mentioning her to Charlie, asking him if he
knew a woman with her name and description, but then he'd
decided against it. Why alarm Charlie with questions he
would undoubtedly have answers for after Hal's back-
ground check of Ms. Dillon?

What bothered Burke most about Andrea's behavior was
that she didn't seem abnormal. Stalkers were usually very
peculiar people. At least the few he'd run into during his
career had been.

It occurred to him then that Andrea Dillon was really a
very beautiful woman. Her hair color reminded him of Se-
rena's red-gold tresses. He had enjoyed meeting Serena and
Lola, and they had both been friendly and pleasant with
him. One day soon, he hoped, he would meet their hus-
bands. Shake hands with them under his true identity.

Andrea's hair color again returned to his mind, and then Serena's. Wait a minute, he thought. One day when they were alone in the coffee shop, Charlie had shown him a wallet snapshot of his son. Ron Fanon, too, had had red hair. Not the same shade as Serena's and Andrea's, but definitely a reddish hue.

Was there a connection in all that red hair?

He was still puzzling over it when the phone on his belt vibrated. Unhooking it from his belt, he pressed the Talk button. "Joe?"

"They're leaving Benny's apartment, Burke."

"Benny included?"

"All three of 'em. I'm watching them walk toward the two vans parked near the street. Can you see the vans?"

"Not very well. Are you ready to move?"

"I'm ready. They're each carrying a bag. Looks like the kind of bag I use for towels and such when I go to the gym."

"An athletic bag. Big or small?"

"Pretty good sized. Burke, they're getting into the black van."

"Okay. As soon as they're out of the complex, you make a beeline for the street. I'll pick you up."

"Got'cha." The line went dead.

Burke put down the phone and started the engine of his four-wheeler. As was usual with him when something big was coming down, he felt calm and controlled. It was during the waiting that his nerves got raw.

The waiting was over. Finally.

He saw the headlights of the van sweep the street as it backed from its parking space. Then, moving slowly, it lumbered onto Foxworth and drove east.

Burke slapped the shifting lever into Drive and stepped on the gas. He stopped at the complex's entrance, and Joe jumped in. Burke's eyes were glued to the receding taillights of the black van. He wasn't too worried about losing it, however, as he was positive it was heading for the airport.

Joe spoke excitedly as they drove away. "This is it, isn't it?"

"I believe it is," Burke concurred calmly.

* * *

Candace awoke to quiet little noises seemingly coming from the kitchen. Had Burke finally come home and was raiding the refrigerator?

She thought of Burke and his request that she come to his room tonight. Then he'd gone out. What in hell kind of man was he? Would she ever understand him? Her heart felt like a chunk of lead in her chest. When she'd fallen in love with Ron, her primary emotion had been happiness. The birds had sung sweeter, the sun had seemed brighter, everything had felt like magic.

Falling for Burke had her either crying or so far down in the dumps that even tears weren't enough. She couldn't go on like this.

But how did a woman fall *out* of love, just because she knew she should?

The small, indistinct noises continued. She had to see who was making them. Slipping out of bed, she donned a robe, slid her feet into a pair of slippers and left her room.

Moving quietly, she sped down the hall to the kitchen. Expecting to see Burke, Charlie standing at the stove surprised her.

He sensed her presence and turned his head to look her way. "Hope I didn't wake you, honey."

Candace stepped into the room. "Having trouble sleeping, Charlie?" Since she'd moved into this house, not once had Charlie had a problem with sleep. Something must be bothering him tonight. Burke's mysterious conduct, perhaps?

"A little," Charlie admitted. "I'm making cocoa. Would you like some?"

So that was what he was stirring at the stove, a pan of cocoa. "Yes, thanks."

Charlie poured hot cocoa into two mugs and brought them to the table. He and Candace sat down. She held her mug with both hands, feeling the heat of the cocoa on her palms.

Then she lifted it to her lips for a sip. "Where's Burke tonight?" she asked as casually as she could manage.

Charlie sipped his own cocoa. "Just out, I guess."

"Charlie, I know you know where he goes at night. Don't you think it's time I knew, as well?"

Gravely Charlie looked at her, then nodded. "Yes, I think you should know everything. But I gave Burke my word that I would say nothing to anyone, including the family. I'm sorry, but he's going to have to tell you himself."

Candace set her cup down and stared at it. "Can you tell me how much longer he's going to be living here?"

"If I knew, I could probably tell you that. But I have no idea, honey. Why?"

"Because..." She hesitated, suddenly wrestling with an idea she already knew he wouldn't like. But it made sense, perhaps the only truly sensible thought she'd had since meeting Burke. "If he's going to be here indefinitely, Charlie, I'm going to move out."

Charlie looked shocked. "Candace, if it's a question of you or Burke living here, I swear I'll ask him to leave. You're family, honey. I love you as much as I do Serena and Lola. No one comes before you and the baby, no one."

She had just placed Charlie between a rock and a hard spot, and she regretted it immensely.

"Oh, Charlie," she said sadly. "I didn't mean to put you on the spot. Burke's your friend. You would hate telling him to leave. I couldn't do that to you. I love you."

Charlie patted her hand. "I know, honey. Would it upset you if I spoke frankly?"

He wanted to talk about her and Burke's personal relationship. "No...yes," she stammered. "I don't know, Charlie. These days I hardly know which way is up." She sighed. "Say anything you wish."

"Thank you. Have you fallen in love with Burke?"

For a moment Candace couldn't answer. Her mind was suddenly addled and unable to formulate a complete sentence. Despite Charlie's reference to speaking frankly, she hadn't anticipated such a direct question.

She looked at her father-in-law with a helpless expression. He was a completely kind man and dedicated to his family. That question had not risen from personal curiosity; he was thinking of her, prepared to offer solace or advice.

"Would you rather not talk about it?" he asked gently.

"I..." Who better to talk to than Charlie? Who else knew the whole story, both Burke's side and hers? "I can talk about it," she said in a whispery voice. "With you, I can. I do love him, Charlie. It has me so confused, though. How can a woman fall in love with a man she doesn't trust?"

"You don't trust Burke?"

"How could I? Charlie, his background story doesn't ring true. He comes and goes at crazy hours, with never an explanation. Not to me, at any rate. If Rocky Ford had any international connections, I'd swear he was a spy."

Charlie laughed. "He's not a spy, honey."

"Of course he's not," she agreed rather sharply. "But neither is he a college professor. You wanted to speak frankly? Well, frankly he's driving me crazy."

"And yet you're in love with him."

"An affliction I don't seem able to correct," she said with a trace of bitterness. "I didn't want to fall in love with anyone. I wasn't ready, Charlie. I was still thinking of Ron a lot. And then Burke popped into our lives, and my emotions went haywire. There has to be something wrong with me," she finished gloomily.

Charlie shook his head. "There's nothing wrong with you, Candace. Burke's a fine man. Maybe you can't trust him, given your present knowledge, but surely you trust me."

"You know I do."

"Then believe that falling in love with Burke is nothing to be ashamed of. You're young and entitled to every happiness."

"He doesn't make me happy, Charlie."

"He will, honey. I guarantee it. Just give it some time."

"I think that's what I've been doing," she said, choking up.

Charlie saw the mist of tears in her eyes. "Let's talk about something else. Unless you're ready to go back to bed."

"Not yet," she said, wiping the telltale moisture from her eyes. "This cocoa is very good." She took a swallow, relieved that the discussion about Burke was over. "What would you like to talk about?"

"Well, let's see. How about your childhood? You said you were raised by an aunt, but I don't believe you ever talked about what happened to your parents."

Candace stalled by drinking more of her cocoa. "I don't remember them very well," she finally said in a small voice. "You see, my father killed my mother and then himself. I was six years old."

Charlie did a double take. "My God! Candace, I never would have mentioned the subject had I suspected anything of that nature."

"It's all right. It's time you knew. My mother had taken me and left my father. She filed for a divorce. Apparently he couldn't or wouldn't accept it. Aunt Willa talked about it when I was older. She was a great-aunt on my mother's side and already up there in years when it happened. Neither of my parents had any other family. She took me in out of a sense of duty. I was terribly...lost for a long time. Aunt Willa was a spinster and knew very little about children. She kept me fed and clothed, and sometimes she was kind. Mostly she lived in her own little world of books and crafts.

"Anyway, I grew up in an all but silent environment. Aunt Willa would not permit noise in the house, and she considered music—the kind of music young people liked then—to be the worst noise there was. She did have a television set, and occasionally there was something aired that she felt was appropriate for a young girl.

"She died when I was eighteen. I had just graduated high school and had acquired a limited scholarship to a local junior college. I was living in her house, working part-time and going to school when I met Ron."

Charlie's face conveyed the pain of his feelings. He had to clear his throat to speak. "I'm so sorry, honey."

"She was never mean to me, Charlie. It was as though she just didn't see me most of the time." Candace offered a tremulous smile. "I survived it. At least I had a home, and as I said, there were some good times. She bought me a beautiful dress for my senior prom, for instance. I knew she had very little money, so that dress was a sacrifice for her.

"After Ron and I were married, I sold the house. It was so old and run-down that it brought a very low price. But it helped us financially. We bought furniture and...and things," she said with a faraway look in her eyes, recalling the fun she and Ron had had picking out items for their base housing.

Charlie had to clear his throat again. "Life dealt you a pretty rotten hand, honey," he said hoarsely.

"Your hand wasn't so great, either," she said softly. "Losing your wife at such a young age. Having to raise your two babies alone. And you didn't have a Charlie Fanon to turn to, as I did. Charlie, I'm so thankful for you, Lola and Serena. You all made me feel like a part of the family right from the first. I don't know if I've ever told you that before."

"In a thousand ways, honey." Charlie finished off the last drop in his mug. "Well, what do you say? Should we call it a night?"

Candace slid her chair back from the table. "I think so."

After bringing their mugs to the sink, they walked down the hall together. At her bedroom door Candace said goodnight and went in.

Charlie continued on to his own room.

He couldn't help the tears that rolled down his cheeks; he had truly never heard a sadder story. If anyone deserved mountains of happiness, it was Candace.

Burke would erect those mountains for her. Charlie was certain of it.

"What do you see?" Joe asked.

They were in a grove of trees and brush right next door to the small airport. Burke had the rifle laying on the hood of his vehicle and was looking through the infrared scope. Joe was standing next to him.

"I don't get it," he told Joe. "Benny and his pals are parked behind the terminal building."

"Maybe that's the meeting place."

"Could be. Wait a minute, another car is coming." Raising his head, he and Joe watched a dark sedan without headlights drive onto the airstrip and stop. No one got out. Neither did anyone appear from behind the terminal building.

"Something's damned odd with this picture," Burke whispered.

"Sure is," Joe agreed.

"Why isn't Benny showing his face?"

"Good question."

They heard the distant sound of a plane at the same moment.

"Won't be long now," Joe said.

"We have to get closer. Come on."

Carrying their weapons, they crept through the trees to the very edge of the airstrip. Burke was thinking hard. If Benny, his pals and the newcomer in that car weren't accomplices, what were they? This was not an ordinary drugs-for-money exchange, where one person carried the cash and the other the stash. The black van was concealed behind the terminal building for a reason. He added up the logistics—three men in the van, an unknown number of people in the sedan and how many in the plane? Could he and Joe handle this by themselves?

But it was too late to do anything else. The plane was approaching the field. It was a small craft without lights. The sedan's headlights flashed on. A tall man got out of the car and stood next to it. On foot Benny and his friends appeared, staying in the shadow of the building.

Burke raised his rifle to look through the scope. "They're all carrying guns," he said tautly. "They're not here with money to buy drugs, they're here to take both from the other players." He had to do something, and fast. "I'm going to make a wide sweep and come up behind Benny. You move in on the drug exchange when the plane lands."

"Maybe it'll work," Joe said doubtfully.

"We have no choice." Burke took off running, staying in the trees until he reached the street. Crossing the road to the ditch he'd noticed before, he kept low and sped past the entrance to the airport. Breathing hard, he took a second to glance at the airstrip. The plane was on the ground. In the car's headlights, he could see someone climbing out of it. He or she held a bag. The tall man from the sedan reached into the car for a bag. The exchange was about to take place.

In a burst of speed and energy, Burke raced back across the street toward the terminal building. The dull popping of guns with silencers caused a roaring in his ears. He knew the scenario now; Benny and his cohorts were shooting the pilot of the plane and the driver of the sedan.

He reached the terminal building and kept running. He saw Joe on the other side of the field running just as hard. Three people were standing near the plane; two were on the ground.

"Police," Burke yelled. "Drop your weapons."

Joe shouted similar orders. Benny and the other two men whirled around, looking for the intruders. Their guns went off in all directions. Burke kept running, using a zigzag pattern. He felt something hot and stinging in his shoulder—a bullet—and fired his own gun. A man went down. Joe fired his weapon, and another man went down.

Cursing violently, Benny dropped his gun and raised his hands. Burke and Joe, both out of breath, walked up to him. Joe grabbed Benny's hands and slapped on a pair of handcuffs. Burke examined the men on the ground. Three were dead, and one was groaning. He kicked that guy's gun out of his reach.

Then he turned to Benny. "You're under arrest, Slocum. Joe, read him his rights."

Taking the phone from his belt, he dialed 911 and asked that an ambulance and the police come to the airport at once.

Before the dispatcher could reply, Burke passed out.

Hours later Burke opened his eyes. It took a minute to orient himself. He was in a bed, in a hospital room. There was an IV running clear liquid into one arm and another on the other side of the bed giving him blood. There were monitor tabs on his chest attached to a machine that made little beeping sounds.

His shoulder hurt like hell; it was a major effort to even turn his head. When he did, he saw Joe sleeping in a chair near the window.

His mouth was cotton dry; he had to have some water. Feeling around, he finally located the Call button and pushed it. A nurse appeared almost immediately.

"Mr. Mallory, how are you feeling?"

"Thirsty."

"Well, there's nothing on your orders about not having water. Here, I'll help you." After filling a glass from the pitcher on a stand nearby, she inserted a straw and held it near his mouth.

He sucked the cool water in gratefully.

"Not too much this first time," the nurse cautioned.

Joe woke up. "Hey, buddy, are you okay?" Getting up from the chair, he approached the bed.

"I'm all right. You wrapped up everything at the airport?"

"Not to worry. Slocum's behind bars. His wounded pal is in this same hospital under guard. You know, this is a pretty good hospital for a small town."

"I'm still in Rocky Ford, then?"

"Sure are."

"What time is it?"

"About 4:00 a.m."

"Did you call Charlie Fanon?"

"I called Hal, Burke. Do you want me to call Charlie?"

"Yes." Burke suddenly felt weaker, and his voice sounded pretty shaky.

"That's enough conversation for now," the nurse said briskly. "Mr. Frazier, it would be best if you left and let Mr. Mallory get some rest."

"Instead of calling, I'll go by Charlie's house," Joe said as he went over to the chair for his jacket. "Then I'm going to get my things from Virgil's apartment and head for Helena. I had to make sure you were all right before I left town."

Burke managed a feeble grin. "You did great, Joe. Couldn't have picked a better partner."

"Appreciate the praise, Burke, but it was your game all the way. Hal was darned excited when I talked to him, incidentally. Bet you get a promotion or something out of this."

"Joe, when you talk to Charlie, do it alone."

"Pardon?"

"His daughter-in-law lives with him. Let him tell her."

"Okay, no problem. See you back in Helena in a week or two."

"I'm not going to be in this hospital *that* long."

"Well, however long they keep you here, I'll see you when you get home." Joe patted Burke's foot through the covers. "Take care, partner."

"You, too."

The loud pounding on the back door woke both Candace and Charlie. Grabbing a robe, she bounded from her room, only to see Charlie beating a path to the kitchen ahead of her.

With her heart hammering in dread—people didn't pound on doors at this hour with good news—she stood back and let Charlie open the door.

A stranger stood there. "Charlie?"

"That's me."

"I'm Joe Frazier, Burke's partner. He was shot last night and . . ."

Candace didn't hear another word. She crumpled to the floor in a dead faint.

## *Chapter Eighteen*

Woozy from pain medication, Burke was having a hard time staying awake. Charlie had come to see him around 8:30 a.m. and left about an hour later. During that visit, Burke had related the details of last night's adventure, and Charlie had listened with a somber expression and few comments. It was evident to Burke that the gunplay had demolished any fun Charlie had been getting out of helping capture a criminal, which was usually the case when a citizen became involved in serious police business.

It was after Charlie had heard it all that he'd told Burke about Candace's reaction to him being shot.

"She fainted dead away, Burke. I brought her around with a cool cloth on her forehead. Scared me for a few minutes, I don't mind admitting. When she had her wits about her, she demanded the truth. Couldn't evade it any longer, Burke. Sorry. I know you wanted to tell her yourself."

"Was she relieved, Charlie?" Burke had asked.

Charlie's eyes had taken on a reflective gleam. "I wouldn't exactly describe her mood as relieved. Can't rightly say what it was, to be honest. Anyhow, you'll be finding out for yourself. She said when I got home to keep an eye on Ronnie, she would come to the hospital.''

And that was why Burke was trying so desperately to stay awake. Any minute now Candace could come walking through that door. He wanted to be alert so she would know immediately that he was all right. *A couple of days in the hospital should do it, Burke,* the doctor had told him. *We'll see how you're doing then, but barring complications, you should be home by the weekend.*

He had also talked to Hal and his mother by telephone, assuring them both that his wound was minimal. He didn't tell them that it hurt like the very devil, or that he might need some physical therapy because of possible nerve damage. He'd undergone surgery for the removal of the bullet, and the doctors weren't a hundred percent sure he would have complete mobility in his shoulder without therapy. Time would tell on that score.

He would do what had to be done and wasn't worried about it. If one could construe the foggy machinations of his drugged mind as worry at all, it was aimed at Candace. Her fainting was a major concern. She didn't seem like the fragile sort of woman who couldn't take shocks on her feet, but then, wouldn't he feel a little faint himself if he heard she had been injured?

His thoughts became more vague as the medication saturated his system. Finally it had its way, and he drifted off to sleep.

About an hour later Candace appeared in the doorway. She tensed when she saw the paraphernalia Burke was hooked up to. His skin was pale, his eyes closed.

Walking into the room, she sat in the chair next to his bed, slipped off her jacket and let it fall back against the chair.

She was dry-eyed and determined, but looking at Burke lying so still in that bed, a private portion of herself suffered the agonies of the damned.

She blamed no one but herself for the misery in her soul; even without just cause, she'd known all along that falling in love with Burke was a mistake. Charlie's tale about Burke's true identity had proved her right, an ironic consolation prize for being so perceptive.

Burke's eyes fluttered open. His heart swelled with joy when he saw Candace sitting there. She was beautiful in a white turtleneck sweater and plaid slacks. A red jacket framed her small form in the chair.

He smiled. "Hi."

"Hello," she said coolly. "How are you feeling?"

"I'm okay. How are *you* feeling? Charlie told me you fainted this morning."

She waved away that topic as trivial. "He told *me* who you really are. A cop."

A fearful premonition struck him. She had said the word *cop* as though the word tasted bad.

"I hope you understand why I couldn't tell you myself," he said.

"No, actually I don't. But it's immaterial now."

"Immaterial? Sweetheart, I couldn't involve you in the case. Involving Charlie and Virgil was bad enough."

"Did you think I would run up and down the streets of Rocky Ford telling everyone you were a cop?" She spoke derisively.

"No, I never thought that. But I couldn't risk a slip of the tongue."

"My tongue does not slip, no more than Charlie's does." Candace paused. "That's beside the point anyhow. I came here to tell you something."

He tried to make light of her serious tone by grinning teasingly. "You're a secret agent for the CIA."

She gave him a retiring look. "Get real. I'm very serious."

"Too serious, my love," he said quietly, all traces of levity gone from his voice and expression.

She took a deep breath. "That's why I'm here. I am not your love nor do I intend to be in the future. It's over between us, Burke, whatever 'it' was."

He swallowed hard. "You can't turn off love just like that, Candace. You love me, you said so, and I love you.

Don't you think I suffered over lying to you? I wanted to tell you the truth every minute of every day.''

"Console your conscience with this, Burke. Had I known you were a cop, nothing *ever* would have happened between us.''

She was ripping out his heart. ''Why, sweetheart? Tell me why?''

"Because you're another man who thrives on danger. What do you think the women of such men are doing while they're out playing cops and robbers? Or war games?'' Her voice dropped to a lethally low level. ''You're like Ron was, Burke, happiest when you're in the middle of something so secret and dangerous you can't even tell the woman you're supposedly in love with about it.''

"You're comparing my job to Ron's, comparing me to him.'' Burke sounded as sick as he felt, and it wasn't his wound causing the terrible feeling, either.

"Maybe I shouldn't be doing that, but I can't help it. Your friend Joe coming to the door and telling Charlie you'd been shot was much too reminiscent of the officers who knocked on my door in Germany with the same news about Ron.''

"But I was only wounded, Candace,'' Burke argued helplessly. How could he make her understand?

"This time, yes.'' Candace got up and reached for her jacket.

"Don't leave. Please!''

"There's nothing more to say.'' She put on her jacket. "Except for this. I would appreciate your not trying to contact me when you're released from the hospital. I do not want to see you again.''

"Candace, please don't leave like this. We need to talk about it.''

"No...we don't. Goodbye, Burke. I hope you have a speedy recovery.'' She walked out.

He was so shaken he could barely think. She didn't want to see him again. My God, my God. What was he going to do? He loved her. He'd never been in love like this before, and she didn't want to see him again. She was the only woman in the world for him, and she didn't want to see him again.

Tears filled his eyes and rolled down his temples to the pillow. There was nothing he could do today, nothing he could even try until he was on his feet again.

He didn't want to think about it anymore. Wiping his eyes, he pushed the Call button. A nurse walked in.

"I need another pain shot," he said gruffly.

She glanced at her watch. "The timing's all right. I'll get it for you, Mr. Mallory."

This time he didn't fight the drug. He was out in minutes.

Candace knew Burke was staying in touch with Charlie, but whenever Charlie mentioned Burke's name, she reacted with total indifference. Nevertheless, she learned through Charlie's unsolicited but cleverly insinuated remarks that Burke was back in Helena, and that the doctors hadn't yet permitted him to return to work.

She was not going to reverse her decision about never seeing Burke again, no matter how many restless nights she put in. During the days she worked like a Trojan. After three weeks every room in the house—other than the coffee shop—had a new coat of paint and some decorative touches. Lovely new bedspreads and curtains in the bedrooms, for example.

The living room had turned out wonderfully well. Everyone in the family praised her taste and talent, and Serena asked if she would help decorate her and Trav's new home. Candace said a quick and elated yes. If she was going to get through this awful period of distress, she had to keep busy.

Burke, too, was busy, although not in the same physical way as Candace. He went to the office one day and laid his written resignation on Hal's desk.

Hal picked it up and read it with a glower. "You really don't mean this."

"Yes, Hal, I do," Burke said.

He also talked to Meredith. "I'm through with police work, Mother."

Her eyes lit up. "You have made me a very happy woman, son."

"You might not be so happy when I tell you the rest of it, Mother."

He was right. Meredith wasn't at all thrilled with his plans.

But maybe Candace would be.

It was in the fourth week since his release from the hospital that he returned to Rocky Ford. Before he drove to the Fanon home, however, he located another address.

He pulled into the driveway and parked behind a blue sedan. For a moment he studied the house, a pretty little place with snow on the roof and smoke lazily rising from the chimney.

Getting out, he walked the shoveled path to the front door. He rang the doorbell.

The door opened a crack, and startled gray green eyes peered at him.

"Hello, Andrea."

"What do *you* want?"

"Some conversation. First, let me tell you I'm a police officer. Or I was until I resigned a few days ago. I was living in Rocky Ford to work on the Benny Slocum case—"

"You're one of *those* officers? I read the whole story in the newspaper."

"Yes, my name is Burke Mallory." He could see how hard she was thinking.

"Then you were the one who got shot. Apparently you've recovered."

"Yes." He saw no need to mention the therapy he was still undergoing to regain full use of his shoulder and arm. "Andrea, we need to talk."

"You know who I am, don't you?" she said, sounding saddened. "You were able to get the information from the data off my driver's license and social-security card."

"May I come in?"

She hesitated, then gave a resigned nod. Opening the door wider, she stood aside for him to enter. "Come into the living room," she said in a quiet voice.

They sat down. "What, exactly, do you know?" she asked.

"Quite a bit, Andrea. You were born in San Bernardino, California, to a Sandra and Harry Dillon. Moved around the state a lot. Sandra divorced and remarried several times. She died last February, and you came to Rocky Ford in the spring. You have a good education and inherited a sizable estate from your mother."

Burke paused with a steady gaze on Andrea. "When Sandra applied for the license to marry Harry Dillon, she gave her name as Sandra Fanon. You were born six months after their wedding. Inasmuch as Sandra obtained a quickie divorce from Charlie in Nevada and married Harry shortly thereafter, the question of which man is your father sort of leaps out at you. At least it did with me. You know the answer, don't you?"

"Yes," Andrea whispered. Nervously her hand rose to her throat. "Mother claimed Harry was my father, but he disappeared after their divorce. While I was growing up, it hurt terribly that my father never tried to see me. Mother wouldn't discuss it. Harry was out of her life, and it never bothered her that he was also out of mine.

"After her death, I went through her papers. The date of her and Charlie's divorce and the date of my birth struck me as important. I hired a detective agency to locate Harry. As it turned out, he wasn't hard to find. I went to see him, and he told me that what I had been suspecting was true. Mother was pregnant when they got married. Harry knew I wasn't his daughter, and since I was still an infant when he and Mother broke up, he hadn't developed a lasting bond with me.

"He's a nice man and he apologized for letting me grow up thinking I had a father who didn't care about me." Andrea looked off into space, appearing forlorn and unhappy to Burke. "It *was* the truth, though. I did have a father who didn't care about me, only he was a man I'd never even heard of before Mother's death."

She took a long, slow breath and looked at Burke again. "I wanted to confront Charles Fanon and hired the same detective agency to find him. When they gave me the information, I came to Rocky Ford.''

Burke was remembering what Charlie had told him about his wife dying young, and about his move to Montana with his two children. Why would Charlie lie about losing his wife? And considering the deep and abiding feelings he had for his family, it wasn't like him to ignore a third child. Burke could tell that Andrea believed she knew the whole story, but he knew she didn't. There was more here than met the eye, much more.

But he wasn't going to interfere, although he did have to ask one more question. "So why haven't you confronted Charlie?''

Biting down on her bottom lip, Andrea sat perfectly still in her chair for a long time. Finally she answered. "My plan was to go directly to Charlie's house the minute I drove into town. I couldn't do it. I still can't. I'll do it . . . I *have* to do it, but . . .'' Her voice trailed off.

"Andrea, Charlie is an exceptionally fine man. You shouldn't be afraid to meet him.''

"An exceptionally fine man who didn't want me.'' There was a trace of bitterness in Andrea's words. "I have a sister I never knew existed, a brother I will never know, a cousin. Perhaps *none* of them ever wanted me.''

"I wouldn't look at it like that, Andrea. You're only torturing yourself with what-ifs. Go and see Charlie. Tell him who you are.''

Andrea gave him a hard look. "Or you will?''

Burke got to his feet. "No, I will not. None of the Fanons will hear anything you and I have talked about today from me.''

Andrea looked stunned as she scrambled up from her chair. "You're not going to say anything to Charlie about me?''

"You have my word on it.'' He smiled. "The main reason I came by was to let you know you needn't worry about the man in the dark four-wheeler anymore.'' He held out his hand. After a cautious hesitation, Andrea took it. "Good luck, Andrea. I mean that.''

"Thank you. I...I really don't understand your attitude. You're a friend of Charlie's, aren't you? Why wouldn't you tell him about me?"

"Because it's none of my business. I'll be going now."

Andrea walked him to the door. "I really don't know what to say. Except to thank you again."

"You're very welcome." With another smile, Burke stepped out onto her front stoop. "Nice day, isn't it?"

Andrea looked at the cloudy sky and smiled. "A very nice day, Mr. Mallory."

"Call me Burke. Oh, and if we should happen to run into each other in front of other people, go ahead and ignore me. I promise I won't be offended."

Whistling under his breath, he followed the shoveled path to his car.


Candace was again studying fabric swatches and paint chips. The kitchen table was laden with them, as well as catalogs and home-decorating magazines. She was working on a theme for Serena and Trav's new home. They wanted country comfort and charm, and Candace was finding their request an exhilarating and challenging task.

Ronnie was napping and the house was quiet. Charlie was in the coffee shop, although from the few sounds drifting from that room, Candace could tell he had only a couple of customers.

When the back door opened abruptly, she jumped a foot. Her entire system went crazy when she saw Burke walking in as though he owned the place.

Her eyes blazed with anger as she got to her feet. "What makes you think you can come into this house without knocking?"

He never said a word, just walked over to her and pulled her into his arms. She tried to evade his kiss, but he succeeded in pressing his mouth to hers. She had been striving so hard to forget his kisses, to eradicate him from her memory, and now this. It wasn't five seconds and she was weak in the knees and kissing him back.

When he let go of her, she reeled and grabbed the back of a chair for support. As breathless as if she'd just run a mile, she gasped, "How dare you?"

"I dare because I love you. And I've got a few things to show you." He reached into his jacket pocket and pulled out some papers.

"I am not looking at your stupid papers."

"Yes, you are. Here's the first one." He held it up in front of her face. "Read it, Candace."

She turned her head. "No."

"All right, I'll read it for you. It's brief and will only take a second. 'I hereby resign my position with the Helena police department and my special assignment with the governor's task force, as of today.' It's dated three days ago and bears my signature."

Candace's head slowly came around. There was shocked confusion in her eyes. "You . . . quit your job? You're no longer a cop?"

"You catch on fast." He smiled. "Ready for the next one?"

"No, uh, I . . . why did you resign?"

"It's been coming for a long time. Here's the other document. Several pages to this one." He held it up. "Want to read it for yourself?"

What was he doing? Candace was too dazed to think clearly. He wasn't a cop now, so what was he?

Numbly she accepted the document. The word *Deed* popped off the first page at her. She looked questioningly at Burke. "Deed to what?"

"To our ranch."

"*Our* ranch? *Our,* as in who?"

"You and me. And Ronnie, of course."

She turned a chair from its position under the table so her back wouldn't be to him and sank onto it. "You bought a ranch for you and me and Ronnie." Her glassy eyes rose to focus on him. "Have you lost your mind?"

"You like ranches, don't you?"

"That's hardly the point." Candace swiveled slightly and laid the deed on the table, on top of a swatch of hunter green corduroy.

Burke folded his arms and locked his gaze with hers. "I love you. I'll *always* love you. You're the only woman I've ever loved in the way I love you. I want you for my wife. I want us to grow old together. I'd like to have children, but maybe Ronnie's enough for you. I'll leave that up to you. Whatever you decide about kids is okay with me."

He moved to lean over her chair, putting his face close to hers. "There's only one thing I would never do for you, and that's to walk away without trying everything in the book to convince you to marry me, so don't waste your breath asking for that. I know you love me, I know you're *in* love with me. You fell just as hard as I did, probably at exactly the same moment the day we met."

"You . . . you made me miserably unhappy," she said in a shaky voice.

"I know I did. It will never happen again. I'll never lie to you about anything, even if the truth hurts. There'll be no secrets between us, unless you're the one concealing something."

"I . . . wouldn't do that. I hate secrets."

"So, what d'ya say? Want to take a drive and see our ranch?"

She looked into his eyes, which were so near she could see flecks of black and silver in his brilliant blue pupils. "Is it far from here?"

"About seventy miles."

"I can't leave Ronnie. He's sleeping." She was beginning to grasp all that Burke had told her. Everything he'd done—quitting his career, buying a ranch that he probably couldn't afford and Lord only knew what else—was because of her. Guilt struck suddenly, without warning and with all the force of a battering ram.

"We'll wait until he wakes up and take him with us," Burke said. "He should see his new home, too, don't you think? Candace, he can have his own pony, and dogs and cats and anything else he wants. He's all boy. He'll love living on a ranch.''

She slid from the chair and ducked around him, putting space between them. ''You resigned because of me.'' Her tone was accusatory.

''Only partly, Candace. I was getting burned-out on the job before I even knew you.''

''I think you're only telling yourself that to make it easier to accept. You loved being a cop.''

''And how do you know that? You never knew me as a cop.''

''Well, I certainly never knew you as a sociology professor! Of course I knew you as a cop. It was the only way I *did* know you, even though the word was never mentioned and I was too naive to add one and one.''

''I just told you I would never lie to you again. Candace, you have to stop doubting everything I say.''

''It's a hard habit to break.''

Abruptly he changed directions. ''Are you going to marry me?'' She looked at him for a long time. ''Are you?'' he repeated. Still she hesitated. ''Are you even going to answer me?'' Then it occurred to him that she hadn't immediately said no. He smiled. ''You are, aren't you? You're just having trouble saying so.''

He walked over to her and gently tugged her into his arms. Cradling her head against his chest, he stroked her hair. ''You're the love of my life, Candace. Tell me you feel the same about me.''

She heaved a sigh. What chance did she have against such overwhelming tactics, especially when her own emotions were on his team?

''I feel the same,'' she whispered, at last resigned to her fate.

''And you'll marry me.''

''Yes.''

Burke tenderly kissed her forehead, then her lips. Almost immediately the kiss turned passionate. When they both needed air, he looked into her eyes and said hoarsely, ''I want you.''

Her own desire was a painful ache. "I know. But we'll have to wait. Ronnie's due to wake up any minute, and Charlie—"

"Charlie! We have to tell Charlie." Taking her hand, he pulled her from the kitchen to the coffee shop.

Charlie and two customers looked at them. Burke had a grin on his face a yard wide. "We're going to be married!" he announced before Charlie could even say hello.

He got up from his stool, walked over to them and put his arms around them both. "I couldn't be happier," he said, sounding choked.

Candace's eyes filled with tears as she hugged Charlie and Burke, the three of them huddled together as closely as three peas in a pod.

Neither could she be any happier, she told herself.

But if that was true, why was there a discomfiting pocket of worry in the back of her mind?

Charlie insisted they leave Ronnie with him for Candace's first look at the ranch Burke had purchased. "You two need some time alone," he said firmly. "Go and enjoy yourselves." As they were leaving, he called, "Is it okay if I call Serena and Lola with the news?"

Burke said an instantaneous yes, and Candace smiled a bit weakly. Things were happening so fast, maybe a little too fast.

But she couldn't tell Charlie to keep her and Burke's engagement to himself, not when he was bursting to pass it on to his daughter and niece.

They were about ten miles from town when Burke said, "I have something to tell you, Candace."

Her stomach sank. All along she'd known there was *something else*. "What is it?" she asked, praying she sounded only normally curious rather than rabid with dread.

Burke was reluctant to broach the subject on his mind. He'd never liked talking about the Mallory wealth with anyone, and springing it on Candace now seemed akin to admitting he'd been harboring another secret.

But she had to know, and he was the one to tell her. "You're not from Montana, so the Mallory name probably means nothing to you. Hell, it didn't even register with Charlie, so why would it mean anything to you?"

Candace cast him a quizzical look. "What *are* you talking about?"

He kept his eyes on the road ahead. "My family. I'm talking about my ancestors. And my mother. Myself, too, I guess."

Candace blinked in puzzlement. "Go on."

He cleared his throat. "Well, it's like this. We...my mother and I...we're very, uh, rich."

Candace stared at him for a few moments, then faced front, saying nothing.

"You heard what I said, didn't you?" he asked, sending her a worried glance.

"I heard. You and your mother are very, uh, rich."

"You don't believe me."

"You said you would never lie to me again, so yes, I believe you. But how rich is 'very' rich? I mean, you held a job for many years, didn't you?"

"Only because I wanted a job, Candace. What I didn't want, much to my mother's almost permanent dismay, was to spend my life watching the family fortune grow. In that respect, I'm a great disappointment to Mother." He chuckled softly. "She wasn't overly thrilled about my buying a ranch, either. Poor lady. First a cop, then a rancher. Maybe someday she'll accept her oddball son as he is. Don't misunderstand. Mother and I get along very well. I'm anxious for the two of you to meet. I told her about you, and she said to bring you and Ronnie back to Helena with me. We'll figure something out to get all of you together very soon."

"She's the woman who came to see you, isn't she?"

"You saw her?"

"By accident." Candace explained how she'd been painting near the living-room windows that day. "And only from a distance. I thought she was a...friend."

Burke chuckled. "Friend, my left foot. You thought she was a girlfriend. Mother would get a good laugh out of that."

"Please don't tell her. I would feel so silly."

He sent her a warm smile. "Whatever you say. Is it okay. . .I mean, are you comfortable with what I told you about my having money?"

"Burke, I was worried about your buying a ranch you couldn't afford to impress me," Candace said solemnly.

He took his eyes from the road to look at her, and they laughed together at the absurdity of her worrying about money. That led to an overpowering urge to kiss her. He began scouting the area on either side of the road for a private parking place.

Candace could hardly believe how carefree she felt because Burke hadn't gone into debt to buy his ranch. *Their* ranch, she amended, realizing that was what had been marring her happiness since saying yes to his determined marriage proposal. Now nothing marred it. She didn't care how rich he was, although it was indeed a surprise. But the idea of them starting their marriage with a load of debt had been extremely unsettling.

She laid her head back against the seat, stretched like a cat and declared, "I feel absolutely wonderful."

"You look wonderful. Beautiful. Sexy. Damn, isn't there a pullout on this road?"

She laughed. "By any chance, are you planning an unscheduled stop, my love?"

"Any objections?"

She smiled seductively. "None whatsoever, you handsome devil, none at all."

## *Epilogue*

Andrea received very little mail, so a letter with Burke Mallory's name in the return-address corner was truly a surprise. Anxiously she tore it open.

Dear Andrea,
Candace Fanon and I are going to be married. I would like to put your name on the guest list, but it would definitely raise some questions. However, should you like to attend the wedding, please feel free to do so. We've invited so many guests, one more will hardly be noticed. I've enclosed the formal announcement, naming time and place. I would be pleased to see you there.

I hope everything is going well for you. I've already told you how I feel about your going ahead with your plans to call on Charlie, so I won't repeat myself in this letter.

But just think. In a roundabout way, you and I will be related after Candace and I are married.

Sort of related, anyhow.

Your friend,
Burke Mallory

Andrea sat back in her chair. He was so nice, and to think how frightened she'd been of him.

Reading the wedding announcement, she wondered if she dared attend another Fanon event before braving that meeting with Charlie.

She should do it and get it over with, even though the mere thought of confronting Charlie for a discussion of the past gave her goose bumps.

After all, he hadn't wanted her as a child. Why would he want her now?

After Burke had mailed that letter to Andrea, he began to worry about keeping another secret from Candace. He had promised her faithfully there would be no more secrets between them, not ever, and here he was, guarding one even before they were married.

And yet he couldn't break his word to Andrea. This really wasn't his secret, he told himself. It belonged entirely to Andrea Dillon. He had merely stumbled across it.

Still, someday it was going to come out. One day—soon, he suspected—Andrea would work up her courage and knock on Charlie's door. All hell could break loose when that happened. Candace's trust in him could once again be sorely tried.

"Damn," he muttered. He wanted a good marriage, a strong, healthy marriage. No cross words between him and Candace, no resentments, old or new. Certainly he didn't want someone else's secret causing an unnecessary rift.

Two days before the wedding, he realized he had to talk to someone about it. He wished that person could be Charlie, but Charlie *was* Andrea's secret. Besides, Burke had been trying not to let too many questions about Charlie's role in her background badger his mind. Charlie had said his wife had died young; Andrea and the state of California said she'd died in February. Was it possible for a man to think his wife was dead for so many years when in fact, she was marrying and divorcing other men right and left? Stranger things had happened, Burke told himself. But what about Andrea's birth? The whole thing was a mystery, but, thank God, it wasn't *his* mystery.

Still, the urge to discuss it with someone he could trust was too strong to ignore. In desperation, he dropped in on his mother.

Meredith greeted him warmly, lifting her cheek for his kiss. "This is a pleasant surprise. I thought you were in Rocky Ford."

"I need some advice, Mother."

"And you came to me? How lovely. Let's sit in the sun room." As they traversed Meredith's large, elegant home, she asked, "Would you like some coffee or tea? Something to eat, perhaps?"

"Nothing, Mother, thank you."

Entering the room that was situated so well to catch the sun's rays, they sat in comfortable chairs.

"Now," Meredith said, "what is troubling you?"

"A secret."

"*Your* secret, Burke?"

"No, that's the problem. It's someone else's secret, and I gave her my word not to tell anyone about it. At virtually the same time, I promised Candace to never keep another secret from her. I put her through hell pretending to be a teacher while I was working undercover in Rocky Ford, and the promise came out of my mouth before I remembered telling this other person I would keep *her* secret. Hell," Burke exclaimed as a finale to his tale.

"Burke, surely you're not thinking that you and Candace are going to have a marriage without secrets."

"What's wrong with that idea?" he asked almost belligerently.

"Don't get upset. Your idea of marriage is not wrong, merely naive and unrealistic. My darling son, I know you're madly in love and planning a perfect life with your little Candace. But life is filled with intrigue, mysteries and secrets. Goodness, do you think I had no secrets from your father? Or he from me?''

"What did you keep from Father?''

"My secrets were none of his business, nor are they yours.''

"I don't remember Father as being secretive.''

Meredith laughed. "Of course you don't. You do recall that we had a wonderful marriage, don't you?''

"That's how I remember it, yes.''

"Well?''

"You're telling me to keep my word to the lady with the secret and hope for the best.''

"Burke, if you and Candace truly love each other, which I trust is the case, the best is what you'll get. You're making too much of this little problem. Believe me, after you're married and falling more in love with each other every day, someone else's secret is not going to come between you.''

Burke left the Mallory mansion feeling a little better. At least his mother thought he was doing the right thing.


"It was a beautiful wedding, wasn't it?'' Candace murmured while lying in her husband's arms on their wedding night. They were in a hotel room in Billings. Tomorrow they would be flying to Hawaii, which was where Candace wanted to spend their honeymoon. Burke had told her they could go anywhere, and she'd chosen Hawaii, a state she had always hoped to see.

"Beautiful,'' Burke agreed softly, tenderly kissing her forehead. "You were the most gorgeous bride there ever was.''

"Could you possibly be just a little bit prejudiced in my favor?'' Candace asked teasingly. After a moment she asked another question. "Burke, did you notice how well your mother and Charlie got along at the reception?''

Burke chuckled. "I've never seen Mother have a better time. She actually danced with Charlie and drank champagne with him. If I hadn't witnessed it with my own eyes, I never would have believed it. You don't know her well enough yet to be surprised about her letting her hair down like that, but it sure surprised me.''

Candace was quiet for a while. Then she blurted, ''Burke, do you think she likes me?''

''Of course she likes you, sweetheart. Everyone does.''

''That's not what I meant. I'm not expressing my. . . my concern very well. Would she have chosen me for you to marry? I mean, if it had been up to her, would she have picked me to be your bride?''

''Absolutely,'' Burke replied without hesitation. Ah, and so it begins, he thought to himself. This is what Mother meant about husbands and wives having secrets from each other, and what Charlie meant when he said that a lie was sometimes kinder than the truth. What earthly good would it do for Candace to hear that Meredith *had* chosen a bride for him, a very nice lady named Diane Prescott? ''Absolutely,'' he repeated, kissing his beautiful wife.

She sighed contentedly. ''It's all like a wonderful dream, Burke. Pinch me and see if I'm awake.''

''How about if I do this instead?'' he whispered. His hand slid down her body to the cleft between her legs.

Her breath caught. ''Oh, yes, do that instead.''

They had already made love twice in this pleasant hotel room, but her body responded to his touch as though starving for it. Hungrily she caressed his manhood. Their kisses quickly grew frenetic and demanding.

''I will never get enough of you,'' Burke said in a ragged, raspy voice.

''Nor I of you.''

It was a good half hour before they said anything coherent again. Sated and exhausted, they closed their eyes for sleep.

Candace was nearly out when her eyes suddenly opened. ''I know how I'm going to decorate the house on our ranch.''

''Did you say something?'' Burke said drowsily.

She smiled. ''No, darling. Go to sleep.'' He wouldn't be interested in fabrics and such. That was her department. His was running the ranch.

She lay there awake long after Burke was snoring lightly. Was she going to tell him about her sad and unhappy childhood? Was it something he should know? Wouldn't it only make him feel bad for her? She didn't want him feeling badly about anything, and never would she want his pity.

Maybe that was something she should keep to herself. Keep the past *in* the past. Charlie wouldn't mention it if she asked him not to.

Snuggling closer to Burke's warm body, she made her decision: there wasn't a reason in the world to bring up those old hurts. It was just a small secret, and Burke would understand why she'd said nothing about it if it ever came out.

Besides, if anyone understood the sensibility of some secrets, it was Burke.

Smiling ecstatically, simply because she was married to the most wonderful man in the universe, Candace closed her eyes.

Tomorrow was the first day of the rest of their lives. She could hardly wait for dawn.

\* \* \* \* \*

*Watch for Andrea's story in*
*MONTANA CHRISTMAS*
*coming in December 1997,*
*from Silhouette Desire®.*

# COMING NEXT MONTH

## NOBODY'S BABY  Jane Toombs

*That's My Baby!*

Karen Henderson was claiming that he, Zed Adams, was a baby's dad! He knew he wasn't, but he could tell that this gorgeous blonde with the baby spelt trouble. And trouble had never looked *so* appealing...

## ONE BIG HAPPY FAMILY  Andrea Edwards

*Great Expectations*

When Samantha Scott was six years old, an old woman had promised her love...if she found the courage to fight for it. Now gorgeous Kevin Delaney had come along...only he insisted he was too old for her. *Old!* Absolutely not—this was destiny!

## A STRANGER TO LOVE  Patricia McLinn

Emotionally wary Jessa Tarrant sparred constantly with Cully Grainger...especially over the way he was bringing up his troubled nephew. Sparks flew between them in other ways, too, and Jessa had to confront her fears and learn to trust again...

## STOP THE WEDDING!  Trisha Alexander

Revenge was on Nick Petrillo's mind when he encountered Kristin Blair, his former sweetheart. But would learning that Kristin's father was the one who had caused their break-up be enough to turn Nick from retribution to renewed passion?

## DANIELLE'S DADDY FACTOR  Sherryl Woods

*The Bridal Path*

Handsome single dad Slade Watkins had trouble taming his mischievous kids—until Danielle Wilde took them under her wing. She wanted to call the whole family her own. And once a Wilde woman put her mind to marriage...a man could kiss bachelorhood goodbye!

## BUCHANAN'S RETURN  Pamela Toth

Kirby Wilson was still reeling from the shock—she'd found out she was adopted, had two long-lost brothers, and she'd met enigmatic J.D. Reese. Now she must confront her past, and capture J.D.'s stubborn heart!

# MISSING LINKS

How would you like to win a year's supply of Silhouette® books? Well you can and they're FREE! Simply complete the competition below and send it to us by 31st March 1998. The first five correct entries picked after the closing date will each win a year's subscription to the Silhouette series of their choice. What could be easier?

| 1. APPLE | P I E | CRUST |
|---|---|---|
| 2. STRAWBERRY | _ _ _ | TARTS |
| 3. MINCED | _ _ _ _ | BALLS |
| 4. PICKLED | _ _ _ _ _ | RING |
| 5. GRAPE | _ _ _ _ _ | JUICE |
| 6. FRENCH | _ _ _ _ _ | SAUCE |
| 7. TOFFEE | _ _ _ _ _ | CRUMBLE |
| 8. PEANUT | _ _ _ _ _ _ | BEANS |
| 9. TANDOORI | _ _ _ _ _ _ _ | CURRY |
| 10. PRAWN | _ _ _ _ _ _ _ _ | SAUSAGES |

**Please turn over for details of how to enter** ⇨ C7I

# HOW TO ENTER

There are ten missing words in our list overleaf. Each of the missing words must link up with the two words on either side to make a type of food.

For example, the word *Pie* links with *Apple* and *Crust* to form *Apple Pie* and *Pie Crust*:

APPLE - PIE - CRUST

As you find each one, write it in the space provided, we've done the first one for you! When you have linked up all the words, don't forget to fill in the coupon below, pop this page in an envelope and post it today—you don't even need a stamp!

Hurry, competition ends 31st March 1998.

## Silhouette Missing Links Competition
## FREEPOST, Croydon, Surrey, CR9 3WZ

EIRE readers send competition to PO Box 4546, Dublin 24.

Please tick the series you would like to receive
if you are a winner:

Sensation™ ❏  Intrigue™ ❏  Desire™ ❏  Special Edition™ ❏

Are you a Reader Service™ Subscriber?      Yes ❏   No ❏

Ms/Mrs/Miss/Mr _____

(BLOCK CAPS PLEASE)

Address_____

_____

_____ Postcode_____

(I am over 18 years of age)                                    C7I

# COMING NEXT MONTH FROM
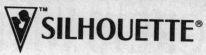
## SILHOUETTE®

## Intrigue
*Danger, deception and desire*

**SHADOW LOVER** Carly Bishop
**SUNSET PROMISES** Carla Cassidy
**MAN WITHOUT A BADGE** Dani Sinclair
**THE SILENT GROOM** Kelsey Roberts

## Desire
*Provocative, sensual love stories for the woman of today*

**HALLOWEEN HONEYMOON** Merline Lovelace
**INSTANT DAD** Raye Morgan
**TIGHT-FITTING JEANS** Mary Lynn Baxter
**PARKER AND THE GYPSY** Susan Carroll
**THE WRONG WIFE** Eileen Wilks
**CHANCY'S COWBOY** Lass Small

## Sensation
*A thrilling mix of passion, adventure and drama*

**COMPROMISING POSITIONS** Beverly Bird
**THE QUIET ONE** Alicia Scott
**DAYS GONE BY** Sally Tyler Hayes
**PRINCE JOE** Suzanne Brockmann

# DISCOVER

# THE SECRETS WITHIN

*Riveting and unforgettable -
the Australian saga of the decade!*

*For Tamara Vandelier, the final reckoning with
her mother is long overdue. Now she has
returned to the family's vineyard estate and
embarked on a destructive course that, in a
final, fatal clash, will reveal the secrets within....*

Valid only in the UK & Eire against purchases made in retail outlets
and not in conjunction with any Reader Service or other offer.

---

# 50ᵖ OFF COUPON

### VALID UNTIL 30/11/1997

## EMMA DARCY'S *THE SECRETS WITHIN*

9 904170 180504

0472 00166